JANE AUSTEN
IN SCARSDALE
or
LOVE, DEATH,
AND THE SATs

JANE AUSTEN
IN SCARSDALE

or

LOVE, DEATH,
AND THE SATs

PAULA MARANTZ COHEN

**Doubleday Large Print
Home Library Edition**

St. Martin's Press
New York

This Large Print Edition, prepared especially for Double-day Large Print Home Library, contains the complete, unabridged text of the original Publisher's Edition.

This is a work of fiction. There is a Scarsdale, of course, but no Fenimore High School, and any resemblance between characters in the novel and actual people is unintentional.

ISBN 13: 978-0-7394-6592-9
ISBN 10: 0-7394-6592-9

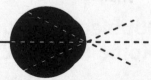

**This Large Print Book carries the
Seal of Approval of N.A.V.H.**

*In memory of my mother,
one of the great high-school teachers*

ACKNOWLEDGMENTS

I want to thank those who read and responded to earlier versions of this manuscript: Rosetta Marantz Cohen, Anne Hartman, Alan S. Penziner, Gertrude Penziner, and Gail Rosen. Additional thanks go to those who supplied anecdotes and information on college admission, guidance counseling, high-school life, Westchester geography, Manhattan real estate, and assorted other matters: Fred and Rosemary Abbate, Vicki and Simeon Amon, Marianne Beauregard, Rebecca Bowlby, Catherine Campbell-Perna, Barbara Coleman, Albert DiBartolomeo, Alice Gaines, Mark and Vivian

Greenberg, Cheryl Jones-Holaday, Barbara Kutscher, Kimberly Lewis, Susan Lipkin, Liz Margolin, Marilyn Piety, Lori Rizzi, Sam Scheer, and Patricia Tamborello. Thanks go as well to my agent, Felicia Eth, and my superb editor, Hope Dellon.

I want to thank my husband, Alan S. Penziner, my most trusted reader and critic, and my children, Sam and Kate Penziner, whose humor informs everything I write. Finally, I owe a debt of gratitude and love to my father, Murray S. Cohen, and my late mother, Ruth Marantz Cohen. They were my first and best teachers.

JANE AUSTEN
IN SCARSDALE

or

LOVE, DEATH,
AND THE SATs

PROLOGUE

"SO YOU WANT YOUR KID TO GO TO HARVARD? OR maybe it's Duke or Stanford? WELL, I'M GONNA TELL YOU HOW TO DO IT!"

The speaker, a young man in black jeans, a black turtleneck, and a ponytail, addressed the parents who sat huddled in the Fenimore High School auditorium. You could hear a pin drop. Everyone was hoping that the mystery of college admission was about to be resolved and they would finally get a good night's sleep.

The speaker paused for a few beats, then continued in a clipped, authoritative tone:

"The cornerstones of any successful college application are the two P's: 'Push' and 'Package.'

'Push' means you do what it takes to make your kid crack the books. You nag, you bully, you threaten. Enough with the 'Sweetie, wouldn't it be nice if you did your homework?' You gotta say: 'Do your homework, buster, or you're never going to get season tickets to the play-offs or own a Porsche.'

"And don't be afraid to raise your voice!" instructed the speaker sternly. "These kids can't hear the normal speaking voice. You gotta be forceful, or they'll turn you off the way they always do.

"The second P is 'Package,'" the speaker proceeded. "Here's where you make the colleges sit up and pay attention. I once took a kid who never got off the couch and got him into Haverford. Gave him a political spin and turned him into the Westchester Gandhi.

"I won't pretend that packaging is easy, especially if the kid isn't Albert Einstein or the Olsen twins. But lucky for you, there are people around who know how to do it!"

These remarks were delivered with staccato rapidity, like a machine-gun blast, so that the audience looked initially stunned. Soon, however, hands flew up.

"Isn't there such a thing as pushing too hard?" asked a normally timid woman, who had nonetheless resorted to hand-waving.

"No," pronounced the speaker firmly. "These kids are lazy; they'll never do anything if you don't push them."

"Can you talk a bit more about packaging?" asked an intense-looking woman, formerly a successful accountant, who had quit her job to devote herself full-time to getting her son into Yale.

"Sure." The speaker nodded. "I'll give you an example. Let's say your kid happens to excel at music. Let's say he's a freaking music genius. Do you think that's going to do him any good?"

He waited, so that the former accountant, who was typing her notes on a laptop, nodded tentatively.

"Well, you'd be WRONG!" pronounced the speaker exultantly. "Music geniuses are a dime a dozen. There are music geniuses growing on every tree. A music genius applies to a college and the admissions people say, 'Not another freaking music genius!' So what do you do?"

The former high-powered accountant shook her head in mystification.

"You package the kid so they say, 'This kid fits our music niche; we can't afford to pass him up!' You're probably wondering how to do that."

The hush of anticipation in the room was deafening.

"The key," declared the speaker, "is cluster assets. Take our music genius. Let's say the kid makes all-state orchestra. Fine— but every kid who doesn't have a tin ear makes all-state orchestra. You need to build on that: have him get involved with a regional wind ensemble or a rock band that opens for Springsteen or Simon; get him to tutor underprivileged children in music appreciation or write a music column for the school paper that gets picked up by *Salon* or *Slate*. You get the idea. You'd be surprised what you can dig up, even for the poor shlubs who aren't music geniuses. It just takes some imagination and legwork; it's like growing a pearl from a grain of sand."

"But I thought the colleges wanted well-rounded applicants," protested a haggard-looking woman, who appeared to have stayed up nights worrying about what the colleges wanted.

"Yes and no," said the speaker smugly. "A range of activities and courses are important, but schools like kids with purpose and direction."

Everyone pondered how to get purpose and direction out of sixteen-year-olds who mostly wanted to go to the mall and play video games.

"That's why you have to 'Push.'" The consultant returned to his former keynote. "Which would you rather have: a mentally healthy loser or a winner who's a little neurotic?"

The answer here seemed incontrovertible: neurosis was a small price to pay for the lifelong happiness guaranteed to ensue from getting into a good college.

"My daughter writes for the school paper, runs track, and volunteers at a battered women's shelter," proffered a concerned man toward the back. "We thought she had a good shot at Cornell, my alma mater. Are we being overly optimistic?"

"Being a Cornell alumnus is a plus." The speaker nodded, as though giving the father credit for helping his daughter. "But you can't put too much confidence in the legacy factor anymore. I've seen third-generation alums who donated a million to the college whose kids didn't get in. That's why I tell people: never assume; never presume; make the case bulletproof. Your daughter has some nice activities, but they sound diffuse. Do some clustering. Maybe she could write a series for the school paper on the battered women or organize a mini-marathon to raise money for the shelter—enough to win presidential recognition or at least an award on the state level. That's turning disparate assets into cluster assets that can build on the legacy factor."

"My son plays ice hockey," submitted another parent. "Is that going to help him?"

"It could," said the speaker doubtfully, "if he's really, really good. But how many schools have ice hockey? We're not in Canada. It's too late with this one, but if you have a younger kid, steer him to lacrosse—it's really hot with the top schools right now."

"You spoke about honors and awards. What if my child hasn't won any?"

"Then get on the stick and make sure he does," barked the speaker. "Do some research on the Internet. Find the contests in those literary magazines no one reads. Dig up the kid's old papers and submit them. If nothing else, you'll get a certificate of recognition that you can put down on the application. Admissions officers don't read these things too closely. If you're lucky, they'll think the kid won."

"What about test scores? Can activities compensate for weaker scores?"

"No," said the speaker, "they can't."

"And grades? What if they fell off one year?"

"A few B's during freshman year can be overlooked," conceded the speaker, "but after that, there better be a good reason: a death in the family, serious abuse, alcoholism—that sort of thing."

"How often should a student take the SATs?"

"As many times as it takes to get really high scores."

"What about APs? Do you recommend a certain number?"

"As many as possible. Have them take every one that's offered in the school. And a few more if you can find the courses at a local college. It shows initiative. And extra APs can really boost the GPA."

"What about application essays? Do they matter?"

"Absolutely. The essay tells a college: This kid may not have perfect scores or grades, but he writes like Ernest Hemingway and has one hell of a heart."

"What makes a good essay?"

"Originality without controversy. The key is to make the college feel they're getting a unique voice but not someone who will blow up the school. It's a fine line."

"Do you recommend humor?"

"No. One person's joke is another's insult."

"Political statements?"

"No, too risky."

"What sorts of topics?"

"Personal sob stories are best. A dead parent works well, or a brother or sister who's a druggie or a prostitute; those are pretty solid. If they need material, look into the new teen tours to impoverished locales. Maybe they can irrigate the desert or defuse land mines. It's best if it's on a world scale and connects with current events. 'Save the whales' isn't going to cut it anymore. Other than that, it's hard to say."

A sort of pall had settled in the Fenimore High School auditorium. Some parents appeared to be considering whether it might be worthwhile to murder a spouse in the interests of their child's college application.

"The key is to be creative," concluded the speaker. "For most people, it's over their heads. Which is why they hire me."

CHAPTER ONE

"GREAT SPEAKER LAST NIGHT, RIGHT?" VINCE Flockhart, Fenimore's principal, looked hopefully down at Anne Ehrlich, head of guidance, as she ate her grilled cheese sandwich in the faculty cafeteria. Report had it that the parents had been impressed by the speaker—though half had left in tears and the other half had been digging in the bottom of their bags for Valium.

"He was very high energy," conceded Anne.

"You didn't like him!" declared Vince, peering more closely at Anne's face. He liked to look at that face—it had a sweetness and unconventional beauty that was undeniably appealing—but he was also attuned to its judgment, which he had learned to ignore at his peril.

"My only concern," acknowledged Anne carefully, "is that he may have upset some of our more high-strung parents."

Vince swallowed queasily. The idea of Fenimore parents, jumpy under normal circumstances, whipped into a frenzy by the speaker made him reach in his pocket for an antacid.

"Don't worry," Anne reassured him, "I'm sure they'll be no worse than usual." This, admittedly, was small consolation—"usual" for Fenimore parents was very bad. "Besides, we just have to get through the next few months. It's downhill after that."

Her tone was encouraging, but she was not without her own sense of dread. If Vince as principal was the last line of defense against Fenimore parents, Anne as head of guidance was the first. Soon, anxious parents would be dropping by her office to ask whether to capitalize the S in "Secretary of the French Club" and whether to use Times Roman or Courier font on their kids' college applications. Soon, she would be witness to pitched battles between kids and their parents that went well beyond the scope of the curriculum ("Maybe if you and Dad had worked harder at staying married, I'd have worked harder at honors chem!"). Last year, three mothers had collapsed in her office from nervous exhaustion, and one of the fathers, an expert in international law, had confided that he hadn't been so tense since he drew a low draft number during Vietnam.

Applying to college was a big deal in Westchester County, as it was throughout much of the country. This was due, in part, to the prestige that certain colleges were assumed to confer—the decal on the car functioning in the manner of a designer logo and marking the kid as a high-end accessory. This was also due to the insecurity of parents, who sensed that their children were unformed artifacts at eighteen and were hoping that an excellent college would hand them a finished product. (What a finished product was supposed to look like, of course, was open to question—although the next Steven Spielberg or Bill Gates, with a burning desire to live next door to their parents in Westchester, wouldn't be so bad.)

Fortunately, as Anne reminded Vince, the

most stressful period occurred during the first few months of the school year, when the best students (often those with the pushiest parents) applied for early admission. Once that notification had been made by mid-December, things grew relatively calm until the final decisions for regular applicants arrived in April. By then, changes in the angle of light, not to mention the approach of summer vacation, moderated the tendency to hysteria.

Vince, however, did not seem comforted by the reminder that he had only three months of pure hell ahead of him. He heaved a sigh, popped the antacid into his mouth, and lumbered off.

After he left, Marcy Fineman, who taught history at Fenimore and was sitting across from Anne, looked up from scraping the mayonnaise off the top slice of her turkey sandwich.

"Was he cute?" she asked.

"Was who cute?" responded Anne, confused.

"The speaker last night. The one Vince just mentioned. Did he have potential?" Marcy had a way of lagging behind in conversation, her mind distracted by what she wasn't going to eat.

"Marcy, please, he wasn't a day over twenty-five!"

"And what's wrong with twenty-five? You're only thirty-four. You see thirty-four-year-old women marrying twenty-five-year-old men all the time in the *New York Times* wedding section."

"Really?" Anne looked unconvinced. She knew that, as a historian, Marcy felt obliged to cite evidence for her assertions, but since she often asserted what she wished to be true rather than what actually was, her evidence tended to be fabricated.

"The point is," continued Marcy, disregarding Anne's question, "age shouldn't be an issue. You know you don't look a day over twenty-five. I read in *Cosmo* that most women don't start to age until their late thirties."

Anne looked doubtful again, but Marcy continued unfazed. "All I'm saying is that you shouldn't rule people out. It's not that you don't attract men—I mean, they're always looking at you. But you don't encourage them. You can't know if you don't like someone until you give them a chance."

"I give people a chance," said Anne, "within reason."

"But your idea of reason isn't reasonable. Personally, I think you're too picky." Marcy paused here to wipe the mayonnaise off the lettuce in her sandwich with her napkin, then continued: "You've met some nice enough guys, but they're never good enough. There was Chris who had that great car and Steven who sent you flowers."

"Steven was sweet," Anne admitted.

"He cooked you dinner. He served you breakfast in bed. He fixed your computer. For God's sake, what did you want?"

"He didn't like to read," noted Anne.

"So he wasn't into books. Big deal."

"Marcy, how can you say that? You're a history teacher."

"Yes, well, I happen to like to read. But I wouldn't judge someone else for not liking to."

"We're talking marriage here," said Anne, "not jury selection. Shared interests are important."

Marcy sighed and looked momentarily despondent. "Rich and I used to have lots of shared interests. We once read through the Declaration of Independence and pretended we were the Founding Fathers. It was very romantic."

Anne was about to say she was sure they would do such romantic things again—but Marcy had already plunged ahead: "I think that you're comparing them all to that first one, what's his name—the one you let get away."

Anne was silent for a moment. "Ben Cutler," she finally said. It was odd how just saying his name could still move her. Marcy was right; she did, unconsciously, compare every man she met to Ben Cutler. "He was exceptional," she admitted in the detached tone she tried to adopt on this subject. She liked to think that she had gotten over Ben, though in moments of solitude his memory still haunted her. "I did let him get away. I was young, and my family thought he didn't have the right background or enough ambition. Even Winnie was against it."

"Your grandmother is a fabulous woman," said Marcy, "but she's a snob."

"Maybe," Anne said quietly. "But I think she's mellowed and would see things differently now. Not that it matters. Ben Cutler is rich and successful and proved us all wrong with a vengeance."

"You're in touch with him?"

"No."

"You Googled him?"

"Is there anyone we haven't Googled?"

Marcy agreed. "Yesterday I Googled some kid who picked his nose behind me in the fifth grade. He owns a chain of optical shops in New Jersey. So your guy, Cutler, what does he do now?"

"He writes those travel books, *Cutler's Guides to Culture.* Sort of a high-end version of Frommer's. They're very popular."

"No kidding," said Marcy, impressed. "Rich and I used *Cutler's Guide to Sicily* on our honeymoon. It had a great section on *Godfather* shooting sites and the best places for canneloni—not that I ate any, but it was nice to know." She drifted for a moment. "Rich and I haven't gone anywhere since that trip. They say that you can't really take time off at a top law firm until your first heart attack."

"Marcy!" exclaimed Anne, but Marcy waved her hand.

"So did you contact him? Did you write this travel mogul Ben Cutler?"

Anne shook her head. "I could never contact him now. He's probably married with kids—and it would seem like I was only interested because he's successful and I'm—well, you know—"

"And how *is* that situation?"

"The same," Anne said wearily. If anything, she thought to herself, things were worse. Her father had just bought a new cashmere sports jacket—she had found the bill for it in his desk drawer on top of a mountain of other bills. The only consolation was that if you were already over a million in debt, a thousand more or less hardly mattered.

As her mind pondered the "situation," as Marcy put it, a small line formed over Anne's forehead, giving her gentle face a touch of severity. Countless Fenimore boys, summoned to the guidance office for the conventional misdemeanor, had kept to the straight and narrow in order to avoid seeing that line form again over Anne Ehrlich's forehead.

"We're going to have to sell the Scarsdale house," she explained to Marcy now. "I hate to do it; I grew up there and Winnie's lived there for so long, but I don't see another option."

"What does your father say?"

"Not much. You know my dad . . ."

Marcy rolled her eyes to indicate that she did.

"But it's Winnie I'm worried about. I

haven't told her yet, and I really don't know what she'll do."

"Well, if you ask me, now's the time to give Harry Furman a chance," said Marcy, returning to the subject of Anne's love life. Harry Furman was a partner in Marcy's husband's law firm, who she'd been pushing Anne to go out with for weeks. "Harry's rich. He has a duplex on Park Avenue. I'm sure he'd love a weekend home in Westchester. So what if he's been married before?"

"He's been married *twice* before."

"OK, twice. *Glamour* magazine says twice-divorced men make great husbands; they don't want to strike out. So he's not perfect. I'm sure that this Cutler fellow wasn't perfect either. They're never as good as you think they are."

Anne let herself consider this. Had she idealized Ben Cutler? It was possible, given the time that had elapsed—thirteen years, after all. And even if he had been as good then, he was probably a very different person now. Perhaps her rejection had contributed to making him different: less trusting and less kind. It would be natural for such a thing to happen.

Marcy was about to expound on the advantages of Harry Furman's twice-married state and duplex on Park Avenue, when Anne interrupted. "I have to go," she said abruptly. They were over the half hour she usually took for lunch, and the mention of Ben Cutler had unnerved her, making her eager to get back to work. "I'm up to my neck in early-admissions letters, and the Hopgoods have a one-fifteen that's probably going to take up the rest of the afternoon. Mr. Hopgood asked me to prepare a full strategic plan for getting Trevor into Williams. When I told him I couldn't do that, he said they were going to hire their own Ivy packager."

"Ivy packager?"

"It's our guidance lingo for a college consultant. Like the speaker last night. He charges two hundred and fifty dollars an hour to package kids for college."

"Are you saying that parents hire people to sell their children?"

"Absolutely. They do it for toothpaste, toilet paper, and deodorant, so why not your standard-issue teenager?"

"I must have missed that one," noted Marcy, who admittedly missed a lot, since her mind, when not teaching the Louisiana

Purchase, tended to be occupied with whether to have lo-cal Italian or lo-cal French dressing on her salad that day. "But come to think of it, I did have a weird thing happen with a reference letter last week." She paused, taking a sip from her unsweetened iced tea. "Tim Dougherty, one of the seniors in my second-period American history class, asked if I was 'into letter writing.' That's how he put it. Then his mother called to ask what my 'philosophy' on reference letters was. I didn't know that I had to have a philosophy."

"They just want to know if you're trustworthy. They've all heard stories about teachers who seem supportive but then go ahead and screw the kid in the reference letter."

"How awful!" said Marcy. "Are there really teachers who do that?"

"Of course, screwing is a matter of perspective. Nowadays, saying that a student is diligent and nice can be the kiss of death for admission to a good school."

"What's wrong with 'diligent and nice'?" asked Marcy, looking worried—she had used more or less these words in her reference letter for Tim Dougherty.

"You might as well say the kid is an unassuming clod who'll add nothing to the vibrant atmosphere of the college. You have to say he's of exceptional caliber—the best you ever had, or at least the best in some particular area; it doesn't matter what. A good packager can turn 'the best at being rude and disruptive' into 'a fiercely independent spirit.'"

"Thanks for the clarification." Marcy sighed. She wondered if she should send out another reference letter saying that Tim Dougherty was the best she'd ever had in the production of flatulence during a fifty-minute period. No other exceptional quality came to mind.

"It's ridiculous how competitive things have gotten," admitted Anne, "which explains why the parents are going nuts. They want their kids to have everything for a happy, successful life, and a good college seems to be part of the equation. God knows, I'd probably be buying the prep books and hiring the tutors if I had kids of my own," she noted wistfully.

"Well, thank God, Rich and I don't," declared Marcy. She and her husband had made the decision not to have children, owing, in part, to a desire to remain in Manhattan (a relative impossibility once the financial albatross of a child entered the picture), and because the prospective weight gain associated with pregnancy had a way of making Marcy hyperventilate. "I've got the kids in my classes," she rationalized, "who I didn't have to carry for nine months and who, thank God, I don't have to see after three P.M. I suppose I'll be losing out on those lifetime events like the bar mitzvah and the wedding—but I don't think I'd be very good with the caterer anyway."

Anne said nothing. She secretly believed that Marcy would make an excellent mother—if only she could get herself to eat a doughnut.

CHAPTER TWO

AFTER LUNCH, ANNE HAD JUST STARTED WORK ON a pile of early-admission reference letters when Cindy, the guidance secretary, buzzed. "It's Jen Forsythe," Cindy announced, cracking her gum. "She says it's an emergency again."

Jen Forsythe, a small girl with a large capacity for tears, was what the counselors referred to as a "guidance groupie." She was continually appearing weepily in the office in need of bucking up. Anne took this job seriously; she suspected that there was no one to buck Jen up at home.

Today, Jen had come to the guidance office to complain about Mr. Fenster, Fenimore's misanthropic English teacher. Fenster had given her a 79 on her "Cask of Amontillado" paper.

"It's not fair," whimpered Jen, the usual tears trickling down her face. "He hates me."

The pronouncement by a student that a teacher hated him or her was familiar to Anne. Students were constantly voicing this complaint, and in many cases, it happened to be true. In the case of Stuart Fenster, it was. Fenster had a deep-seated aversion to anyone between the ages of fourteen and eighteen, so that why he had become a high-school teacher, where he was forced into daily contact with such people, was anyone's guess. Teachers like Fenster, for whom teaching was a perpetual source of anger and irritation, were scattered throughout the system and served as both the scourge of youth and a preview of what lay ahead in the form of cruel bosses, irrational colleagues, and abusive spouses. There were life lessons to be learned from the likes of Stuart Fenster, which made him, in the cosmic sense, a boon to the system. For the individual student, however, this was perhaps too large and abstract a lesson. For them, Fenster, on top of problems with bad skin, catty friends, and nagging parents, was a real bummer.

"I think he gave me the seventy-nine just to be mean," wailed Jen.

Anne did not refute this. Her experience with Fenster was that he probably did withhold the point simply to be mean. It was his way.

"He knew it would keep me from getting a B for the term," continued Jen plaintively. "I really need a B to get into Villanova next year."

Anne said she doubted that a C+ in one marking period of eleventh-grade English would make a difference—though she wasn't so sure; things sometimes did come down to the wire that way.

"How does he know it's a seventy-nine," asked Jen, "and not, say, an eighty-eight? Is he God or something? My aunt, who's in public relations, read it and said it was really good and she'd give it an A."

"I'm afraid she's not your teacher," said Anne. She was sympathetic to students' gripes about grading, especially now that so much seemed to ride on a point or two. And yet she also felt a loyalty to the authority of teachers, who were being second-guessed at every turn. "Did you speak to Mr. Fenster about it?"

"No," Jen moaned. "He's so angry all the time, he'd probably lower my grade if I did."

This was a possibility, Anne thought. Fenster's pedagogical philosophy was one of outrage at the imbecility of youth, and he could sometimes be heard screaming three corridors down, "What kind of morons are you?" when the class had shown some sign of what he took to be unconscionable ignorance (this ran the gamut from not knowing who Charlie Chaplin was to being unable to identify a gerund). Despite such outbursts, there existed a core group of students who were devoted to him, perhaps for the very reason that he scorned them so completely.

"I suggest you tell Mr. Fenster that you really want to improve," said Anne, "and ask if you could rewrite the paper. I wouldn't mention that your aunt said that you deserve an A. That's the sort of thing that teachers don't like to hear."

"OK," said Jen, who seemed to grasp this point, "I'll try. But he's really scary and he'll probably yell at me."

"That is a possibility," admitted Anne. "If he

does, put it down to his having a bad day."
She didn't want to say that Fenster's yelling
would have to be put down to his having a
bad life.

"OK," said Jen, who could see that this
reasoning applied to her father, when he
came home from work and yelled at her
mother for undercooking the potatoes.

In all likelihood Fenster would yell at her
tomorrow. And yet part of the point of high
school, as Anne saw it, was to prepare for
life, where there was bound to be plenty of
mistreatment. Life, in short, was full of Fensters, and one might as well start getting
used to having them yell at you. It was
Anne's hope that Jen would learn to steel
herself to the Fensters of the world and, perhaps eventually, learn to yell back.

"There's a really weird-looking group out here
that wants to see you about club sponsorship,"
drawled Cindy over the intercom after Jen left.
Cindy had graduated from Fenimore only a
few years earlier and had a way of lapsing into
the cruel perspective of a high-school student.

"Sorry," said Cindy, after Anne chastised
her for calling the students in the waiting
room "weird," "but they *do* look weird."

A weird-looking group paraded into the office.

"What is the club?" Anne asked with trepidation. She had been approached before to sponsor clubs of a dubious nature: the Body Piercing Club and the Slackers Club, for example—both invitations she had declined. But she had also taken on clubs that others wouldn't touch with a ten-foot pole—like the Banned Book Club, which had made it through *The Tropic of Cancer* and *Lady Chatterley's Lover* but had stalled at *Ulysses*. "We couldn't find the dirty parts," explained the club president. Anne had also sponsored the Agnostics Club, though Vince had advised against it. "Elements in the community will say it's a cover for a satanic cult," he warned. As principal, Vince had a heightened sense of what "elements in the community" might say, since these elements were continually badgering him about everything from the length of Ms. Gonzales-Stein's skirts to the fact that Mr. Simonides had referred to "that goddamn piece of junk" when one of the computers broke down. Receiving a daily barrage of such complaints necessarily skewed Vince's conception of what was genuinely controversial and what simply pushed the buttons of the nuttier parents. In the case of the Agnostics Club, Anne had held firm, and when Vince tried to avoid announcing meetings over the PA system, she had threatened to call the ACLU.

"It's a Puppeteering Club," the spokesperson for the weird-looking group now explained. She was a moon-faced girl with long braids, a dirndl skirt and middy blouse, an outfit that located her far outside the bounds of high-school cool. She looked at Anne fearfully, as though expecting an adverse reaction. When this did not occur, she seemed relieved and continued: "One teacher told us we were too old for puppets. That was painful. Puppeteering is a very dissed art form, which is one of the reasons we want to form the club. We plan to start off with a puppet production of *Much Ado About Nothing*. We think doing Shakespeare is the way to get puppets more respect."

Anne thought this was unlikely, but she didn't say anything. It had been her experience that high-school students were unpredictable. Perhaps there existed a large group of potential puppet enthusiasts with a taste for Shakespeare who would mob the puppet production of *Much Ado About Nothing*.

She had no idea how these students had developed their interest in puppeteering or, for that matter, how they had found one another and organized the club. It was again one of the great uplifting mysteries of high school that kids seemed to find their peers in eccentric tastes—whether it was an interest in low-cal snacks (the Calorie Counters Munchies Club), browsing discount outlets online (the Computer Shopping Club), folding old homework assignments into frogs and cranes (the Origami Club), or discussing whether people who ate Chinese food on Sunday nights could call themselves kosher (the Kosher Club).

In light of these clubs, a puppeteering club seemed downright conventional. Anne surmised that the failure of the group to find a sponsor was owing to fear on the part of faculty members, always wary of being lassoed into extra work, that they might have to help make the puppets.

"And you don't have to help make the puppets if that's what you think," said the dirndled spokeswoman, as if reading Anne's mind. "I think Ms. Fineman didn't believe us when we told her that. Emily is already working on the Beatrice and Benedict puppets."

She indicated a very thin girl with a waxen complexion who had perhaps spent too much time with the flour and water that were used to make puppets. "And Arthur is doing the supporting-character puppets. Casey and Fred are our writers; they're working on making Shakespeare's play puppet-friendly." The speaker indicated two young men, who blinked anxiously at being singled out. It occurred to Anne that puppets gave them something to hide behind while still managing to have a "voice."

It made sense, Anne thought. If you weren't lucky enough to find support and understanding from other people, puppets were a logical alternative. And that's what these kids were after, wasn't it? Some way to gain acknowledgment and appreciation in a world that seemed indifferent, if not outright hostile, to their existence. The need that she discerned in these kids was the basic human need for recognition and love.

The thought made her conscious of her own search for these things, and her mind swerved suddenly to Ben Cutler. She had spoken his name to Marcy at lunch, and now the image of the person, whom she had not seen in thirteen years, pressed itself into consciousness. There was the tall, somewhat slouching figure, the unruly dark hair, and the intelligent, amused eyes that had looked at her in a way that no one else ever had. Men had desired her, had loved her even, but none had looked at her like that— with such undiluted pleasure in who she was; none had listened to her with the concentrated attention that he had. She shut her eyes for a moment as the memories flooded in, making her feel almost dizzy with a sense of longing and loss.

CHAPTER THREE

ANNE'S MOTHER HAD DIED OF A VIRULENT BREAST cancer when she was four and her older sister, Allegra, six. It had fallen to her grandmother to step into the maternal role.

It helped that Winnie Mazur was a highly intelligent and practical-minded woman, and it helped even more that the Mazurs had money—lots of it. Winnie's husband had made a fortune in the garment industry before keeling over from a heart attack, a year before his own daughter's death. "Two in two," Winnie had said philosophically—she was not a sentimental woman. "He smoked like a chimney, so it was no wonder; with your mother, who knows?" Winnie, to her credit, had her granddaughters get breast exams and mammograms twice a year from the age of thirteen.

Neither of the girls had ever wanted for anything. There had been plenty of private lessons, trips to Europe, and expensive toys and clothes. Growing up, they had lived in the Mazurs' large and gracious home in Scarsdale, where their widowed father, Elihu Ehrlich, would materialize periodically for what he termed "a little R&R," when not in his own family's Manhattan apartment or at the Harmonie Club, the Princeton Club, or the Union Club. He was particularly proud of his membership in the last of these because it was still largely restricted. "You can count us on one hand," he liked to say, obviously seeing such selectivity as a point in the club's favor.

Playing golf and wandering among his various clubs took up a great deal of Elihu Ehrlich's time. He was descended from a German Jewish family that had done something once in the way of refined commerce but, for several generations, had taken the less strenuous route of marrying money.

Elihu had decided early on that Anne was

a disappointment. Unlike her older sister, Allegra, she did not look like his side of the family. In the rare instances that he deigned to notice her, it was to criticize some minor detail of her appearance. "Anne, why did you cut your hair? It looked better before." Or: "That's quite an unsightly break-out on your chin, my dear. Perhaps you should consult a dermatologist."

Anne could remember when she was ten years old and had asked her grandmother why her sister had gotten the pretty name and she the plain one. Winnie had paused to frame her answer.

"The name Allegra was your father's choice," she finally explained. "Elihu wanted something head-turning and dramatic. When you came along, it was your mother who chose your name. She was already ill, you see, and the idea of getting back to basics appealed to her. She had always liked the name Anne—Anne of Green Gables, Anne of Cleves, Anne Bancroft, her all-time favorite actress. Your father wanted to name you Ariel, but she fought for her preference and he finally gave in."

Anne had spent many afternoons sprawled on the Laura Ashley bedspread under the John Travolta poster in her bedroom, contemplating her name. She sometimes felt a surge of resentment against her dead mother for insisting on naming her Anne. As Ariel, she believed, she would have been prettier and more seductive, at least in the dramatic way that she associated with her sister. Anne, by contrast, was lacking in drama; it seemed to denote a rather drab and lackluster self—until the day she met someone who changed her mind.

It had been a few weeks before her twenty-first birthday. She had stopped off at a travel agency on upper Broadway to book the spring-break trip to Italy that her grandmother had decided would be her gift.

"I want you to go in style," Winnie had specified. "You're to stay at the Hassler in Rome and the Excelsior in Florence, and you're to meet an Italian prince out of a Henry James novel."

Anne had said she would do her best. In those days, the idea of cutting corners had not occurred to them.

Anne had been in her senior year at Columbia at the time. Both her father and sister had gone to Princeton, but Anne had preferred the more cosmopolitan atmosphere of the city, and her grandmother had backed her choice. "Much better to be mugged on the Upper West Side than buried alive in New Jersey," observed Winnie in typical acerbic fashion.

On the particular morning in question, a warm late March day, Anne had walked briskly into the travel agency not far from her dorm. She intended to book the trip quickly so she could get back to the library and study for an exam that afternoon. A quick look around the agency suggested she would not have to wait. There were no other customers, though only one person on duty, a young man who seemed unaware that she had come in.

He was engrossed in reading a book—Ruskin's *Stones of Venice*—apt, though not conventional, reading for a travel agent. The book was propped up on a desk cluttered with travel brochures and flyers. He was wearing the student uniform of jeans and a sweatshirt, and his face was scruffily handsome—he had very dark eyes and un-ruly hair, a well-shaped if prominent nose, and a trace of stubble.

Anne happened to have just finished reading *Stones of Venice* in her Victorian prose course and felt prompted to show off. "So, do you agree that glass beads are a mark of slave labor?" she asked rather flippantly, referring to a passage where Ruskin condemns glass beads as the corrupt products of an exploitative factory system.

The young man looked up from his book. He examined Anne for a moment with attention and then paused a bit longer, as if giving her question real thought. "I don't know," he finally said. "Working conditions in Ruskin's time were nothing like factory conditions today. But the general idea seems right to me: that people need fulfilling work in order to be happy."

The response was more measured and serious than Anne had expected. She noted that the young man, having delivered it, continued to look at her closely.

"And what do you plan to do in the way of fulfilling work when *you* graduate?" she said lightly, trying to counteract the not unpleasant feeling of being looked at so intently.

"I've already graduated and I'm working here."

Anne paused, embarrassed. "It's nice to travel," she finally said.

"I can't say I travel," said the young man.

"But planning other people's trips has its points. I like researching destinations, both in practical ways—and literary ones." He motioned to his book. "Not that too many people really want to know about Ruskin's impressions of St. Marks."

"So you like what you do?" She somehow felt a need to press him.

"It's a paycheck"—he shrugged—"and I suppose I like it, up to a point. I'm not suited to law or medicine, and I figure that, for now, this gives me time to imagine the world and 'find myself,' as they say. Plus, I get to work in a new part of town."

"You're not a Columbia grad?"

"No, I'm a product of the city system." He motioned to the words on his sweatshirt, which she now saw read *Queens College*.

"Well, I've come in to book a trip to Italy," Anne said, flustered by her mistake and feeling she should get down to business. "It's a birthday present from my grandmother."

"Lucky you," said the young man. There was envy but not rancor in his tone. "I'm hoping to go there eventually. If you work here a year, they spring for a vacation—airfare at least. Paris and London are first on my list. Another year earns me Florence and Rome.

That assumes two years of hard labor—not slave labor in Ruskin's terms, but a lot of hours checking airfares and registering frequent-flyer miles."

At this point, he closed his book, as though he wanted to concentrate more fully on her. "My name's Ben Cutler, by the way," he said, putting out his hand. "You should ask for me whenever you book your trips— we earn a commission."

"I will," said Anne, taking his hand. "I'm Anne Ehrlich."

"Anne's a great name," said Ben.

"I'm sure you say that to all the Tiffanys that come in."

"I don't. I happen to like the name Anne."

"And why is that?"

"It's simple and pure."

Anne looked at him skeptically, but his expression was serious.

"Anne and Ben," he mused, continuing to study her, "there's a bookend quality to our names."

"Like Dick and Jane," observed Anne.

"No—Dick and Jane are the shallow products of 1950s suburban culture."

"And Anne and Ben?"

"Anne and Ben are the profound products of spiritual history."

She laughed—and after that, never saw fit to question the absolute perfection of her name again.

CHAPTER FOUR

"MR. AND MRS. JEFFREY HOPGOOD ARE HERE," announced Cindy, after the puppeteers had shambled out—then she whispered into the phone, "That's what *he* told me to say."

When Anne came out to the guidance waiting room, Mr. and Mrs. Jeffrey Hopgood were sitting in the guidance rocking chairs. Vince had ordered the rocking chairs after reading that they could lower blood pressure ("Anything to take the parents down a notch," he rationalized)—but the chairs did not appear to be doing the Hopgoods much good. They were sitting in them stiffly, not rocking. Mrs. Hopgood looked like she wanted to go home and have a drink; Mr. Hopgood was leafing morosely through a college brochure. An avalanche of brochures (expensively produced, more-or-less-identical advertisements for "a unique educational experience") were scattered around the waiting area as though blown there by a typhoon.

"Never heard of this one," observed Mr. Hopgood sourly after Anne greeted him. He held up a brochure for St. John's College in Annapolis, Maryland, a small liberal arts college where students spent four years reading the Great Books in order to lay the foundations of knowledge. Anne had left the brochure out in a token gesture. She knew that St. John's was unlikely to appeal to Fenimore parents, who wanted prestige and the prospect of a good job when shelling out forty grand a year for their kid's college education. Laying the foundations of knowledge wasn't high on their list.

In the case of Jeffrey Hopgood, the school he wanted for his son was Williams. He had gone to this venerable institution himself, as had his father before him. It was his unshakable determination that Trevor would go there too. That Trevor did not have the academic record to get into Williams did not faze him. Mr. Hopgood was of the view, common among certain affluent parents, that he could get what he wanted if enough money and bullying were applied to the situation.

"We're thinking early action to Williams," announced Jeffrey Hopgood pugnaciously, once settled in Anne's office. "With backup applications to Wesleyan, Duke, Dartmouth, and Amherst."

Anne hesitated. She had already addressed this issue with Mr. Hopgood on the phone, but her words apparently had not penetrated. "I think you're being a tad unrealistic," she reiterated now. "Trevor barely has a 3.0 grade point average. The schools you have in mind want GPAs that are much higher."

Mr. Hopgood looked insulted, as though mention of his son's bad grades was in bad taste. "Trevor's SAT scores are excellent," he countered huffily. "We are very pleased with Trevor's SAT scores." Trevor had, in fact, scored an impressive 2250 on the SATs, shocking everyone, most of all his father, who had never before dreamed that his son had a brain in his head.

"His scores are impressive," acknowledged Anne, "but they can hardly counteract his grades."

"His grades are a reflection on the school," declared Jeffrey Hopgood, resorting to the tactic he used routinely in business of shifting into the attack mode. "The school obviously failed to teach him."

Anne refused to rise to this bait, which she knew could lead to a tangled argument about whether the school had failed to teach Trevor or Trevor had refused to be taught. "Be that as it may," she proceeded briskly, "the colleges you have in mind want sustained academic achievement. I think Trevor would do better to apply elsewhere."

"We don't think so!" declared Jeffrey Hopgood.

Anne glanced quickly at Mrs. Hopgood, wondering if the "we" bore any relationship to her. "Be that as it may," she repeated, "I wouldn't want Trevor to be disappointed. It might be very upsetting for him to get too many rejections."

Mrs. Hopgood, silent up until now, seemed to rouse herself at this. "She has a point there, dear," she proffered meekly. "We wouldn't want Trevor to be hurt."

"What the hell are you talking about?"

snapped Jeffrey Hopgood. "Since when would Trevor give a damn!"

Mrs. Hopgood retreated back into silence, but Anne felt prompted to respond: "If you talked to Trevor once in a while, you might find that he did give a damn." No sooner did she say this, however, than she felt herself relent. It occurred to her that Jeffrey Hopgood had probably been mistreated as a child by his own father; she had a sudden image of a pint-sized Hopgood in a baseball uniform being yelled at for not catching the "goddamn ball." Sports used to be the primary arena for parental abuse, at least for boys, but now parents had upped the ante, and the once-bullying baseball dad had become the bullying college dad, berating the child for not buckling down with the review books and raising that SAT score by 100 points. It all boiled down to the pressures of modern life—of being conditioned to be competitive and status conscious and having no clue about how to channel one's anxiety. Although she could not condone such behavior, she could understand and at times even sympathize with it. Jeffrey Hopgood was a boor and a bully, but at some deep level, she felt he loved his son.

"Even if Trevor chooses Williams as his 'reach' school," Anne continued in a gentler tone, "common sense dictates that you add a few safety schools that would be more within the range of his grades. I'd suggest some of these." She extracted a sheet from a file on her desk containing a list of schools that tended to accept students with erratic records, if their parents were able to pay full price.

Jeffrey Hopgood looked at the list and handed it back. "None of these schools would be up to our standards," he noted curtly.

"Perhaps you could take a look and discuss them with Trevor," said Anne, offering the list to Mrs. Hopgood. The fact that her husband had rejected it placed her in the difficult position of overriding his judgment. She paused for a moment, then slipped the list furtively into her purse.

"It's important that your son have a say in where he goes to college," Anne explained. She knew that most kids weren't likely to employ the best criteria in making their decisions; they chose schools based on the friendliness of the tour guide, the weather on the day they visited, and the kinds of snacks available in the student union. But she didn't think it really mattered how they chose, so long as they felt they had. The idea of free will was as fundamental to the development of the adolescent psyche as it was to the health of the species.

"I'll arrange to meet with Trevor tomorrow," she continued. "We'll see if we can figure out some of his preferences. Sometimes a child has tastes that a parent may be unaware of: an interest in art or drama, for example"— Jeffrey Hopgood rolled his eyes—"or a desire for more variety among his peers." Mrs. Hopgood sighed softly, as though such variety would be pleasing to her. "And sometimes they'll speak more freely with a guidance counselor, a relative stranger, than with their parents, whom, as you might expect, they don't want to disappoint."

"Trevor never gave a damn about disappointing us!" Mr. Hopgood's irritable tone was not unmixed with sadness.

"You'd be surprised at how much he may care about your opinion," noted Anne. "As I said, I'll talk to him tomorrow."

"You can talk to him all you want," snapped Jeffrey Hopgood, who had returned to his earlier pugnacity, "Curtis is going to start working with Trevor on his Williams application this weekend."

"Curtis?"

"Curtis Fink of Fink and Fisk Educational Consultants, the firm we retained to advise us on the college admissions process. He'll probably be calling in the next week to meet with you."

"I don't know if I have time in my schedule to meet with individual consultants," Anne responded doubtfully. She wondered if the school had a policy on this.

"We'll see about that," said Hopgood, as though he knew something she didn't.

Anne turned again to the cipher that was Mrs. Hopgood. "Please look over the list of additional schools," she reiterated. "My sense is that Trevor might be happier in a less competitive environment. And we could always talk another time," she added, sensing a maternal current in Mrs. Hopgood that might be tapped in the absence of her husband. "I know that Mr. Hopgood is a busy man, so that in the morning, if you're free and want to chat, I'd be glad to meet with you individually."

"I can't see how you'd have time for my wife and no time for Curtis Fink," observed Jeffrey Hopgood suspiciously.

Anne did not respond, and Hopgood, sensing a strategic maneuver meant to exclude him (which indeed was the case), rose angrily and strode from the room. Mrs. Hopgood sighed and followed her husband out the door.

CHAPTER FIVE

"DR. FLOCKHART WANTS TO SEE YOU," CINDY AN-
nounced over the guidance intercom once
the Hopgoods had decamped. "He sounded
kind of tense."

This was no surprise. Dealing with
Westchester parents would make the Dalai
Lama tense. During his days playing college
football, Vince Flockhart had never flinched
at having his bones crushed by a three-
hundred-pound defensive back, yet he
appeared genuinely alarmed when a
ninety-pound woman in a jumpsuit descended on him to complain that her daughter had been overlooked in debate class

("Just because Carly had laryngitis didn't mean she didn't have worthwhile things to say!"). At such moments, Vince wondered why he had bothered to earn his Ed.D., and whether the modest salary increase and the kowtowing of parents (when they weren't screaming at him) were worth the aggravation. Fortunately, a talk with Vivian Flockhart about the expense of clothing and nourishing the four young Flockharts, followed by an hour on the rowing machine in his basement, was usually enough to make him feel better.

As Anne approached the main office now, she caught sight of Vince monitoring the front hall, an activity that he performed on a regular basis in order to keep track, literally as well as figuratively, of the Fenimore student body. It was indeed amazing what you could see if you just stood in the hall and let the river of adolescent humanity swirl by. Vince had spent the last half hour sending girls whose cutoffs exposed much of their butt cheeks and boys whose pants were around their knees to Mr. Tortoni, the assistant principal, for dressing down (or, as it were, dressing up).

When he saw Anne, he looked relieved and ushered her into his private office, directing her to one of the large armchairs that were arranged in coffee-klatch fashion in the corner. The armchairs, like the rocking chairs in the guidance waiting room, had been installed with the intention of soothing distraught parents, though their calming effect was probably offset by the head-spinning decor of the office. Every nook and cranny of this space was festooned with the diverse emblems of Fenimore achievement. There were trophies for athletic meets, math, and chess team championships, and framed certificates for debate, public speaking, and community service. Amid this welter of accolades, the most notable was a large plaque inscribed "Blue Ribbon Award for Educational Excellence," a much-coveted prize that Vince had wrestled to the ground last year. All mention of the school, even the most pedestrian, was now qualified by reference to this award, as in: "Fenimore High School, Blue Ribbon School of Westchester County, will be closed today due to inclement weather." The plaque occupied the place of honor over Vince's desk, where parents could gaze at it during awkward moments in the discussion of their children's latest foray into delinquency.

"We're in up to our necks with this college thing this year." Vince sighed heavily now, as he dropped into the chair opposite Anne. "I have three parents already on my case about getting their kids into Middlebury, Colby, and Georgetown. I know you want Felicia Desiderio to go to Georgetown, but she's got no parental muscle behind her, and I'd say we need to weigh our options here. I don't see why you couldn't write two strong letters, with a little extra maybe for the Newmans, since Georgetown has a habit of taking only one a year from Fenimore."

"Vince, please," said Anne with exasperation, "I'm not about to undercut Felicia, who has a genuine interest in government and deserves to go to Georgetown far more than Sandra Newman."

"But the Newmans are big," whined Vince. "Newman Developers built all the houses on the west side of town—the ones that Vivian and I can't afford. The Newmans have some gripe about Sandra's junior year with Fenster, and if we don't give her a strong letter, we could be seeing a lawsuit that would up tax dollars, defeat the referendum, and totally destroy the arts program." (Why was it that it was always the arts program, never the athletic program, that was in jeopardy?) Vince's imagination of the far-flung consequences of any given action were not as far-fetched as they might seem; the domino effect was alive and well at Fenimore, where pissing off a powerful parent could indeed have woeful repercussions.

But Anne always argued that giving in to such forces, however threatening, must be avoided at all costs. "I don't care how big the Newmans are," she declared now, "I'm not going to write a stronger reference letter for Sandra Newman than for Felicia Desiderio—and that's final!"

Looking at Anne's face, Vince knew enough to back down. "OK, OK, whatever you say." He waved his hand and moved on to the next item on his agenda. "We also have this new kid coming in that you'll want to have a look at." He flipped open a folder and glanced down at it. "The boy's name is Cutler. Family has lots of money. You know those travel books, *Cutler's Guides to Culture*?"

Anne had turned pale, and Vince stopped speaking and looked at her with concern. "Are you OK?"

She swallowed. "Just some indigestion."

Vince nodded. "Did you have the chopped sirloin for lunch? I don't think it agreed with me either. Of course, three parents were in complaining about Fenster. . . ." He trailed off, obviously unsure as to whether his belly-ache had been caused by toxic hamburger or toxic parents.

Anne was glad to have Vince rattle on and give her a moment to get her bearings. She had mentioned Ben Cutler's name only an hour ago, and the memories had flooded back. Now, to have news that his son was enrolling at Fenimore. She was engulfed by a wave of intense feeling.

"The mother's been in to see me already." Vince returned to the topic. "Single mom. Works for her brother."

"Her brother?" Anne caught her breath.

Vince paused, glancing again at the folder. "Ben Cutler. Very involved in the kid's education. He's listed here as a legal guardian along with the mom."

Anne's felt a weight lift. Of course. She had broken with Ben thirteen years ago, hardly enough time for him to have a son in high school. She remembered there had been a wild older sister who had run off to California.

"They've lived all over the world, working on those travel guides," Vince continued, "but they wanted to settle here for the boy's senior year. We're still waiting for the transcripts from Copenhagen, but I have a feeling he's bright but uneven. Which may cause a problem. It seems the uncle is set on the kid going to Columbia for some reason."

For some reason—Anne had gone to Columbia. Was it her influence that made him want his nephew to go there?

"Did you mention my name?" she asked softly.

Vince shook his head. "But I told him we had a first-rate guidance department that really cared about the students and worked hard to get them into colleges that were right for them. That's what I'm supposed to say, isn't it?"

Anne nodded and braced herself before asking the next question. "Does this uncle have a family of his own?"

"No clue." Vince shrugged. "But he's as rich as Croesus, which means he probably does—or maybe an ex or two and a hot girl-friend." Vince, tied inextricably to Vivian Flockhart and the four young Flockharts, was prone to extravagant fantasies involving less encumbered lifestyles. "Unless, of course, he's gay," he noted pragmatically.

"He's not." Anne spoke without thinking.

"What was that?"

"Nothing," she said, flustered.

"Are you sure you're OK?" Vince peered at her, concerned.

"I'm fine," said Anne, trying to regain her composure. "It might be what I had for lunch—or the Hopgoods this afternoon."

"Double whammy." Vince nodded sympa-thetically, then turned back to the folder in his hand. "Anyway, we'll probably want to see the mother and uncle at some point after we review the kid's transcripts—give them a sense of what to expect, if they're being un-realistic about Columbia. I just hope this Cul-ter fellow isn't one of those pushy rich guys who feels entitled to anything they want. And I sure hope the Newmans are going to be reasonable about Georgetown." Vince heaved a sigh and reached for his antacids. "Jeez," he muttered, "I hate this time of year!"

CHAPTER SIX

ANNE HURRIED BACK DOWN THE HALL, DUCKING past Cindy and closing the door to her office behind her. Her throat was dry, and her hands were shaking. She sat down behind her desk and tried to calm herself. The prospect of seeing Ben Cutler again had affected her more than seemed reasonable. Thirteen years should have blunted any sense of anxiety or excitement, yet it had done nothing of the sort. Not for her. For Ben, she supposed, there would only be indifference or, more likely, aversion to the prospect of seeing her again. The rupture had been her decision and had been effected with a high-handedness that could only have left him feeling bitter and angry toward herself and her family.

She turned to her computer and typed "Benjamin Cutler" into Google. She had done this years ago, at which time she had found, among the clutter about other Benjamin Cutlers, an article that began: "Queens native Benjamin Cutler has parlayed his interest in the literary portrayal of far-off places into *Cutler's Guides to Culture*, a series aimed at the culturally enlightened traveler. A literate, well-written alternative to the standard travel guide." The picture accompanying the article had been of a tall man with unruly hair standing next to a Hindu shrine with a copy of the *Bhagavad-Gītā*. It was unmistakably Ben, and Anne had stared at it for a long time, trying to make out the expression of the eyes. Were they still as angry and sad as they had been when she had last seen him? The article itself had haunted her—bringing home her mistake regarding his prospects and, perhaps more painfully, showing him to be very far away—conclusively lost to her. She had been depressed for months afterward, and a desire not to reawaken such feelings had kept her from Googling him again.

Now, hearing that he had returned to the area, she hardly stopped to think as she typed his name into the search engine. This time a long list appeared on the screen. There were numerous accolades: "Benjamin Cutler receives commendation from Australian aborigines"; "Benjamin Cutler applauded by Pakistani Restaurateurs"; "Benjamin Cutler receives award from French embassy for Unstereotypical Rendering of French Culture," as well as references to articles about his guides: "Cutler's Guides Names Top Ten Museum Restaurants—Whitney in a Snit"; "Cutler's Guides Offers Tips on Motivating Couch-Potato Tourists"; "Cutler's Guides Announces New Travel Trend: Luxury Backpacking," etc. There were even some fairly arcane academic pieces carrying his name: "Travel and the Jolt of the New" (paper delivered at the Conference on the Esthetics of Travel, the City University Graduate Center); "The Figure in the Carpet in Henry James's Travel Writing (*The Henry James Journal*), and "Was Ruskin Right About Work?"

(*Studies in Nineteenth-Century Nonfiction Prose*).

The number and range of references were impressive—impressive but not surprising, Anne thought. Ben Cutler had been an impressive person before he had accomplished anything, and she ought to have had the courage and imagination to realize that he would succeed.

Though she knew it would make her feel worse, she took out her compact and scanned her face in the little mirror. She had always been fair, but with a healthy glow— "apple-cheeked," Ben had once said admiringly. But her complexion was pale now and, with the shock she had had, appeared ashen. She looked down at her body. Had it changed so much in thirteen years? Her weight had not changed—if anything she weighed less, but it was the thinness that comes with forgetting to eat or having no one to eat with. It was not the same body that Ben had known. At thirty-four, she was not the person she had been at twenty-one.

It was 2:45, and she realized that if she left school now, she could be at her grandmother's in time to watch *General Hospital*. Winnie was a great fan of the soap opera and liked nothing better than to talk about whether this one would end up with that one. ("Of course they'll fall in love," she always concluded, "but it won't last.") What Anne wanted more than anything else right now was to sit next to Winnie and let the soap opera, with its artificial turmoil, distract her from the real turmoil inside her head.

But leaving in time for *General Hospital* was apparently not in the cards. Cindy buzzed. "It's Mrs. Greenbaum," she announced in a bored voice. "She says she absolutely needs to see you."

Anne was used to Mrs. Greenbaum's "absolutely needing" to see her. If Jen Forsythe was a "guidance groupie," Eleanor Greenbaum was a "helicopter parent"—so-called because she hovered above her progeny ready to make a rapid, vertical landing at the slightest provocation. Only to be in the vicinity of Mrs. Greenbaum was to feel the sharp blades of a propeller whipping close to your face.

Eleanor Greenbaum was the mother of Jeremy Greenbaum, a sophomore, and the recently graduated Caroline Greenbaum. One might have thought that having learned the system with Caroline (and having shoehorned the girl into Johns Hopkins), Mrs. Greenbaum would be more relaxed about Jeremy. This, unfortunately, was not the case. It was the classic scenario of the more you knew the less you felt you knew—but unlike Socrates, for whom greater knowledge brought humility and wisdom, Eleanor Greenbaum became neither humble nor wise. Instead, she became, if possible, more pushy and anxious.

"I hope I'm not intruding," said Mrs. Greenbaum in a meek tone that Anne knew masked a fierce tenacity of purpose. Despite having been told numerous times to make an appointment in advance, Eleanor Greenbaum insisted on showing up between errands (buying Jeremy tube socks seemed to be the principal one), voicing the clearly rhetorical hope that she was not intruding. "I had a small issue I wanted to discuss," she explained. "It will only take a few minutes."

Eleanor Greenbaum's few minutes invariably lasted an hour, destroying all possibility that Anne could get away in time for *General Hospital*. But, then, Eleanor Greenbaum was a *General Hospital* in herself. It was amazing the amount of drama she could stir up around the most seemingly inconsequential elements of high-school life. She had, for example, spearheaded a write-in campaign on the need for more bulletin board space in the halls ("How else can our children learn about special activities and enrichment programs?") and had staged a "Take Back the School Year" vigil when a teachers' committee had proposed shortening the academic calendar by half a day for an in-service workshop ("Our students must not be cheated of their right to a full and complete education!"). Members of the school board were known to have changed their phone numbers for the sole purpose of avoiding calls from Eleanor Greenbaum. And there had even been the case of a teacher with a long and illustrious career who, when he learned he would have a Greenbaum child in his class, had decided to cut his losses and take early retirement.

In short, Eleanor Greenbaum elicited one predominant response in those she dealt with: extreme irritation. This was not a point in her favor under normal circumstances, but for Anne, at this moment, it had the virtue of driving Ben Cutler from her mind.

"It's regarding the computer programming course that Jeremy took freshman year," continued Mrs. Greenbaum as she settled herself primly in the chair in front of Anne's desk. "I'm told that they made it an honors course this year, which, if I may say so, is a change long overdue. Jeremy only got an A- in that course, which means that it was very challenging."

"Needless to say," said Anne.

"Therefore," said Mrs. Greenbaum, gaining momentum, "I believe the change to honors status should be retroactive." (In the world of Eleanor Greenbaum every change should be retroactive if it could benefit her child; if it would be less than beneficial, then, of course, her child should be grandfathered into the previous policy.)

"Making the change retroactive would pose logistical problems," explained Anne. "Besides, when a course is changed to an honors course, the syllabus changes."

"But not in this case," announced Mrs. Greenbaum triumphantly. "I have the syllabus from this year and from last year right here." She reached into her large purse, rummaged among the packages of Jeremy's tube socks, and extracted two photocopied sheets, which she waved in front of Anne's nose. "As you can see, they're exactly the same."

There was no point questioning the evidence. No one was more versed in the minutiae of the Fenimore curriculum and related matters than Eleanor Greenbaum. This included her knowledge of the number of sick days Mr. Fenster had taken last year (seventeen) and the difference between the grade point average of Ilene Gupta and Aaron Finklestein, the two aspiring valedictorians (.02). Besides, Anne knew that Mr. Simonides, who taught computer programming, was incorrigibly lazy. He had probably not altered the syllabus in his ten years of teaching, and wasn't about to do so just because the curriculum committee had turned his course into an honors course. "It's computer programming, for godsakes," he liked to say, "not nuclear physics. Gimme a break."

"You can ask the curriculum committee to take it up," Anne suggested in a reasonable tone.

"That wouldn't be practical," Mrs. Greenbaum responded quickly, as though she had anticipated this suggestion. "It took them two years to drop Caroline's gym grade after her disability was diagnosed." (Caroline's severely flat feet had, after much lobbying, been deemed a disability that exempted her from gym—allowing her to take another AP course and raise her GPA accordingly.) "Jeremy may graduate before they reach a decision."

"Oh well," said Anne. "Jeremy has excellent grades. The difference in his GPA would be negligible."

"I beg to differ," said Mrs. Greenbaum emphatically. "An A- in an on-level course will murder his GPA."

"I think it would take more than an A- in an on-level course to murder Jeremy's GPA," said Anne, driven to mild sarcasm.

"Every fraction of a point counts," insisted Mrs. Greenbaum.

"I understand your concern," said Anne, taking another tack. It was no use arguing with Mrs. Greenbaum on what it meant to murder a GPA; for Eleanor Greenbaum, murder was a very relative thing. "But to change the weight of a grade, one must go through established channels." There was something about Eleanor Greenbaum that drove people to speak like officials in a totalitarian state.

"But that won't help Jeremy's GPA," Mrs. Greenbaum persisted.

"I don't think Jeremy's GPA needs help," said Anne. "But if you like, you could contact the school board."

"I already did. They said I had to go through the curriculum committee."

"Then I'm afraid that settles it."

"It most certainly does not!" declared Mrs. Greenbaum with sudden stridency. There was a Dr. Jekyll and Mr. Hyde aspect to Eleanor Greenbaum that Anne had seen before. Last year, Mr. Hyde had lobbied fiercely for Caroline's flat feet; now, here he was again, making an appearance on behalf of Jeremy's GPA. The idea of her son losing even the slightest boost to his GPA had transformed the woman from a meek supplicant into a fierce advocate. "Jeremy deserves that fraction of a point!" Mrs. Greenbaum protested shrilly. "He worked for it. It is his right!"

"That may be true," said Anne, "but sometimes the system doesn't quite cooperate. Life, as Jimmy Carter once said, isn't fair."

"I don't see what Jimmy Carter has to do with it!" exclaimed Mrs. Greenbaum, from whom any attempt at lightness was bound to ricochet. "I won't stand for my child being cheated. If necessary, I'll sue to obtain justice for Jeremy."

There it was—the inevitable terminus. Whenever a parent, used to getting his or her own way, reached a seemingly insurmountable roadblock, there was always the final threat of legal action. Lawsuits against the district had risen by 36 percent in the past eight years as applying to college had become an increasingly frenzied and trauma-ridden process. One notorious case had hinged on the faulty calculation of a GPA: An honors English course that was supposed to be worth an additional .5 on one student's transcript had not been properly weighted, with the result that the final grade point average had been off by a fraction of a point—a fact that the parents maintained had kept their child out of Dartmouth, "the school on which [as the mother soulfully put it] she had set her heart." The case had been settled out of court for six figures, and the guidance counselor responsible for the miscalculation had been let go. From what Anne heard, he was finding it difficult to land a job; the blot on his record seemed to be viewed as comparable to a conviction for child abuse. For Eleanor Greenbaum, it might, given her earlier reference to this crime, be equivalent to murder.

Anne found the parental lawsuit to be a particularly egregious form of bullying. She could foresee a time when schools would suffer under the same fear that doctors currently did—and teachers would have to take out malpractice insurance (social studies teachers would probably pay higher rates than math teachers in the way gynecologists paid more than dermatologists). It was the sort of thing she felt she should oppose at all costs.

"I hope it won't come to a lawsuit," she said in an even tone. "Personally, I would advise against it. It might antagonize some of the people you might rely on to write Jeremy's letters of recommendation." She said this while looking Eleanor Greenbaum squarely in the eye.

There was a moment of silence as Mrs. Greenbaum weighed her options. "I wouldn't want to do that," she finally said, coming down on the side of the reference letters and returning to her former Dr. Jekyll–like tone. "Jeremy likes everyone so much." She looked at Anne unctuously. "Especially you."

"I'm sure he does."

"I'll speak to the curriculum committee and cross my fingers that they'll work quickly." She crossed her fingers by way of illustration, and Anne, feeling she was expected to show support, did the same. "Thanks so much for squeezing me in," said Mrs. Greenbaum.

"My pleasure," said Anne.

CHAPTER SEVEN

LIBERATED FROM ELEANOR GREENBAUM, ANNE proceeded to clear her desk, locking all stray papers in the filing cabinet and in the pad-locked bottom drawer of her desk. Security precautions had been issued by Vince last year after he saw a movie in which a bunch of kids broke into a guidance office and changed their transcripts. Vince took all movie renderings of high-school life seriously and was especially sensitive to portrayals of boob-like principals, whom he suspected he resembled.

Having completed the lockdown, Anne was about to walk out the door when the phone rang. Cindy had bolted at 3:01 exactly, so she picked up.

"Hey, it's Carlotta," said a haughty voice on the other end. Carlotta Dupre worked for Anne's sister, Allegra, at *The Widening Gyre*, a poetry magazine of allegedly great critical reputation but very small readership. Carlotta was currently subletting Anne's apartment in the city while Anne was staying in Westchester to care for her grandmother after a minor stroke.

Carlotta was a unique specimen: She combined considerable physical beauty and extreme intellectual pretension. The result: a truly insufferable personality. Carlotta's mother had been a Spanish movie actress, who had suffered a fatal fall several years ago when running down a steep marble staircase in stiletto heels in front of a large film crew. Her father was a French intellectual—a respected job description in France, though not necessarily an income-producing one. As a result of her pedigree, Carlotta had cultivated the ability to sponge regally off others.

"There's a dearth of hot water," Carlotta announced now. "I simply can't tolerate a cold shower." Anne had an image of Carlotta melting away like the Wicked Witch of the West upon contact with cold water.

"Call the super," said Anne in exasperation. Carlotta was continually telephoning her to complain about minor problems with the apartment—a "dearth of hot water" (not surprising given that Carlotta took very long showers, some alone, some with guests) or a roach in the kitchen (also not surprising, given that she was prone to leave unwrapped chocolate babkas on the counter).

Anne had tried to explain that such things as "a dearth of hot water" were par for the course in New York City apartments. Perhaps it was different in Paris and Barcelona, where Carlotta had also lived (or rather squatted). There was nothing she, Anne, could do. But Carlotta seemed to think otherwise.

"*You* could call the super," she countered. "If I call, he might think I was here, like, illegally, and that could be really bad news for you. This real-estate lawyer at Paul, Weiss— who wanted to get in my pants but who was just too nasty to think about—said that your subletting to me might violate the rent code and could result in your eviction."

"It's kind of you to worry about my eviction," said Anne. "Meanwhile, may I remind you that you owe me two months' rent?"

"I haven't forgotten," said Carlotta brusquely. "I just need some hot water."

"Well, maybe the hot water is waiting for you to pay the rent," observed Anne.

"Seriously," continued Carlotta, unamused, "I have to take a shower. I promised to drop by the French consulate tonight. The anti-globalization people will all be there, and they might be interested in my anagram poems—the ones that spell out 'American Fascist State' if you read the first letter vertically in the style of Verlaine. Or maybe someone from Lagerfeld will consider hiring me for the next Chanel show." Only Carlotta could put political poetry and high fashion modeling in an either/or combination.

"I'm sorry, Carlotta," said Anne, "but I just don't have time to call the super right now. I've got to get to Scarsdale to check on my grandmother. I suggest you take a cold shower. It will perk up your nipples, which might help with the modeling gig—if not the Fascist America poems. Meanwhile, I really need the rent."

Carlotta was silent for a moment, letting

the remark pass. She often said that in France, where she spent her formative years, it was vulgar to talk about money—a statement that translated into its also being vulgar to pay debts. "I must say this isn't what I had in mind," she finally said in a miffed tone. "Allegra said your place was sweet—but then Allegra is so busy with the journal and with Zack, I can't say I blame her for exaggerating."

Anne hung up without responding. She was annoyed with Carlotta for her smug posturing but, on a deeper level, she was annoyed with her sister. Anne had thought she was immune to Allegra's ability to exploit and manipulate, but obviously she still had "more work to do on this issue," as Marcy put it. Why else had she agreed (in violation of her lease) to sublet her one-bedroom, rent-controlled apartment in Murray Hill to her sister's protégée, a preening ingrate, while Allegra lived in spacious luxury uptown? Couldn't Allegra have found room for Carlotta in her apartment?

But then her sister had perfected, even more than the insufferable Carlotta, a profound and unshakable sense of entitlement. She had, following her graduation from college, moved into the immense Upper West Side apartment that had belonged to the Ehrlich family for generations, then proceeded to assign each room a function that had somehow become immutable. There was her own bedroom, decorated in a minimalist white on white, "like a nun's chamber," as she liked to say—ignoring the fact that she shared it with her boyfriend (though perhaps he slept on the floor); there was the living room, done in Duchess of Windsor style (lots of chintz, used as if in quotation marks), where she held her literary soirees; and there were two bedrooms renovated as studies—one for Allegra and one for her boyfriend (a role currently occupied by Zack Zimmerman, a stylishly angry literary critic who contributed to many unknown online journals).

The fourth bedroom was reserved for their father when he chose to spend the night in the city. Elihu Ehrlich and his older daughter were close, both having an abiding contempt for anyone who was not themselves. Elihu's bedroom was in the Ralph Lauren "English country gentleman living in Manhattan" style. There was lots of dark furniture, mohair throws, and tartan comforters, with an adjoining bathroom, renovated to Elihu's specifications with a state-of-the-art pulsating multi-jet shower.

As arranged, there was no room in this spacious four-bedroom apartment for Carlotta Dupre. Indeed, there was no room in it for Anne Ehrlich, who, technically speaking, had as much right to it as Allegra, since it had belonged to the family, according to the complex provisions of Elihu's great-grandfather's estate. But Anne had no interest in staking that claim. She was content to occupy the modest one-bedroom apartment in Murray Hill, acquired when she had worked in the city years ago. Its small size had never bothered her until now, when the question of where her grandmother would live after the Scarsdale house was sold weighed on her mind.

Anne didn't like to dwell on the unfairness of her sister's usurpation of family property. It was one of her strengths that she didn't fight for things that didn't matter to her. Still, she knew that this strength was connected to the great failure of her life: not having fought for something that did.

CHAPTER EIGHT

THE HOME WHERE ANNE HAD GROWN UP AND where her grandmother still lived was a large rambling Tudor in the affluent Westchester suburb of Scarsdale. It was an impressive edifice, full of dark wood paneling and oak floors, tall leaded windows, and a multitude of nooks and crannies: pantries and butler closets, maids rooms and sewing rooms. During the early years of Anne's childhood, there had always been a gaggle of children rushing in and out, houseguests coming and going, and a slew of servants continually changing the sheets. Anne thought of the house during those years as a suburban

Jewish version of what Virginia Woolf and Vanessa Bell might have experienced growing up in their country estate in England. Certainly, her grandmother had been a charming hostess, a highly literate woman, and not without the funds to attract cultural luminaries from the city. Beverly Sills had stopped by for lunch a few times in gratitude for a nice bequest that the Mazur family had given to the Metropolitan Opera; and George Plimpton had been there quite often to thank the family for its generosity to the *Paris Review,* a journal in which Allegra had published a few early poems.

But that was years ago. Her grandmother had passed control of the property on to her daughter upon her marriage, who had left it, in standard fashion, to her husband, so that, though the house was originally Winnie's, she now lived in it on sufferance from her son-in-law. Without going so far as to grudge his mother-in-law occupancy, Elihu Ehrlich was not one to feel he owed her anything more. And Anne knew she had no influence with her father. Part of the reason that she maintained her small rent-controlled apartment in the city was because she could pay for it herself and not have to depend on his goodwill—or whatever facsimile of this there was.

She arrived today just as Elihu, who had spent his morning on one of the nearby golf courses, was leaving for the city.

"Hi, Dad," said Anne as she watched her father, dressed impeccably in a crisp cotton shirt and linen jacket, monogrammed on the breast pocket, saunter across the lawn to his car. "How's Gram doing today?"

"Afraid I haven't had a chance to look in," her father said brightly. It was one of Elihu Ehrlich's characteristic qualities that he lacked all sense of embarrassment at not doing what a normally thoughtful person would do. "Played nine holes with Paul Faber, retired from pulmonary at Mount Sinai—looks a wreck, poor fellow. I'm back to the city now to do some errands. Must pick up that sports jacket at J. Press that I'm having altered. They promised to do it this week so I'd have it in time for Allegra's 'do' on Saturday. I must say your sister knows how to throw a party. Word has it that John Updike may turn up, which would certainly be a coup, though I must say the man's complexion might put me off my dinner."

Anne said nothing. She was used to her

father's self-centered ramblings. Given their financial straits, his purchase of the sports jacket was an outrageous indulgence. But what could she do? The situation was too dire to fight about. They were bankrupt—the fact had come home to her several weeks ago when she had finally seen the extent of the damage. He had left his bank statements lying on his desk and the top drawer open containing the bills, no doubt intending them to be found and somehow taken care of. It was clear from a cursory look at the statements that the large assets were gone. But the greater catastrophe were the bills, some with messages indicating a second or third notice.

Anne had seen no alternative but to sell the Scarsdale house (selling the New York apartment was not an option, since it was subject to complicated restrictive covenants put in place through the prescience of Elihu's great-grandfather). She had spoken to her father about the sale, and he had shrugged, as he normally did at anything unpleasant or untidy. "If you think it best," he said lightly. "I spend most of my time with Allegra or at my clubs anyway. The homestead has its sentimental associations, but it's gotten to be rather a burden of late. One doesn't want to spend one's golden years patching a leaking roof. Do what you think necessary, my dear—I leave it all in your capable hands."

It was typical of her father to sidestep responsibility this way. He had squandered the family fortune—which is to say, Winnie's money—on his club memberships, bespoke suits, round-the-world cruises, and investments in dubious business ventures: a line of bow ties with club and college insignias; a line of personally engraved fountain pens; a line of handcrafted billiard balls—all "class ventures," as he put it, that had failed miserably. More distressing was his apparent disregard of what Winnie, who had lived in the house for sixty years, would do once it was sold.

After watching her father drive away in his Jaguar, Anne went inside to look for her grandmother. She had delayed telling her about the need to sell the house, but she could hardly put this off any longer; there were decisions that had to be made about where Winnie would live. This, she knew, should preoccupy her above all else, but the news of Ben Cutler's appearance in the area had distracted her. Now she tried to banish the thought of him from her mind.

She found her grandmother in her bedroom. It was a room Anne imagined that Jackie Kennedy might have inhabited—large and airy, with green flocked wallpaper and a few tasteful, expensive pieces of furniture picked up long ago with the help of some top designer, now deceased. There had been a time when Winnie was as close to Westchester royalty as one could get, and it saddened Anne to think how things had changed. Not only was there no money left, but all the people who had admired her grandmother—that once large and glittering social circle—were gone too.

Winnie was sitting in an armchair reading a book. When she saw Anne, she reached out a very thin but still surprisingly strong arm and clasped Anne's hand in hers. Anne felt her grandmother's love pass through her.

"Edna St. Vincent Millay," said Winnie, letting Anne's hand go and holding up the book for inspection. "I thought I ought to look her over again before reading the new biography they reviewed in the Times a while back. I knew her, you know. A difficult woman, not very nice, but interesting."

Anne gave a strained smile. She was pleased to see that her grandmother was her usual cantankerous self.

"You look like something's on your mind, dear," said Winnie, putting aside the book.

Anne realized that she was almost glad that the news about the house made it possible to avoid any mention of Ben Cutler. "I've had to put the house on the market, Gram," she announced simply.

"I see," said Winnie, nodding. "Don't worry. Things will work out."

"Perhaps you could move in with Allegra." It had occurred to Anne that this might be a solution. With a bit of reorganizing (the reclamation of Zack's study, for example), Winnie could have her own bedroom.

But her grandmother merely snorted at the suggestion. "It's out of the question!" she declared derisively. "Your sister would be unwilling to have me, and I would be unwilling to be had!"

Winnie had long ago placed Allegra in the same category as their father. "The two deserve each other," she often noted. "They're both impossibly selfish, vain people. Selfish and vain aren't bad in their place, especially if there's a degree of wit involved. But those two are wanting in that department. I can't say that I don't have a certain affection for your sister, who does have some of my blood in her veins—though I suspect it's been diluted to a point where it's more like Mercurochrome. As for your father, I don't think he has anything resembling blood; if you cut him, he'd probably bleed cologne, though only private label, mind you."

"But what will you do?" Anne asked.

"I'll go into one of those senior facilities."

"But you hate those places! You've always said so!" There had been a time when Anne had urged her grandmother to spend a few hours a day at one of the Westchester senior centers, but Winnie had rejected the idea out of hand. "Old people babbling about their grandchildren and great-grandchildren!" she had scoffed.

"I'm sorry about the absence of great-grandchildren," Anne had responded, "but you could babble about me."

"I don't need to babble about you. I can talk to you, which is what most of those poor souls never get to do."

"You wouldn't set foot in one of those

places before"— Anne spoke accusingly now—"and you're saying you want to live there?"

Winnie shrugged, obviously not inclined to defend her change of mind.

"You know you can always move in with me. IKEA has some nice futons that I wouldn't mind sleeping on."

Winnie sniffed. "That will be the day when I make my granddaughter sleep on an IKEA futon. But we have plenty of time to plan my future. Maybe I'll enroll at NYU and get one of those cut-rate dorm rooms in the Village."

Anne laughed. She could actually see Winnie in a dorm, chattering the night away with a bunch of undergraduates.

"Or I'll find a rich man to take me under his wing. Too bad Mort Feinberg died last year. Had I known he would die so soon, I might have taken him up on his offer."

"Gram!"

"What? I'm only being honest. Marriage is a gamble. If we knew certain things in advance—like how long someone would live—it would make things much easier. As it is, since we don't know, it's a wonder anyone gets married at all."

Anne was quiet a moment, then observed: "You and Grandpa worked out well enough, and you barely knew each other before you married."

"That's true. But he came highly recommended by my parents. In those days, we put great stock in that sort of thing. Not that it was any guarantee. Look at your mother. Elihu seemed like a good enough match, but thank God Franny never lived long enough to realize what an insufferable fool he was."

Winnie's capacity to cut to the quick of things—even when the quick was disturbing or embarrassing—never ceased to amaze Anne.

"As I said, marriage is always a risk," continued Winnie, "and sometimes you have to shut your eyes and jump." Then, realizing that she had touched on a sensitive point regarding her granddaughter's past, she changed the subject abruptly. "I'm glad to report that you didn't miss anything on *General Hospital* today. I was hoping we might find out who the baby's father was, but I think they'll drag that out for another month. I'd rather hear about your day anyway—it's better than a soap opera. What's become of the boy who carried you down the hall on his shoulder? He sounded like a lively fellow."

This was a reference to Joey Pelosi, who had performed this feat in a Superman cape on a dare from his basketball buddies. "And how's the little girl who's always crying that the teachers hate her? Reminds me of how my friend Sarah Rosenthal used to carry on. Her father was off making crooked real-estate deals and her mother was too busy drinking everything in the liquor cabinet to notice her, poor thing. But such a crybaby—used to drive me mad with her incessant boo-hooing."

Forgetting momentarily about Ben Cutler and their dire financial straits, Anne began to laugh. There was no denying that Winnie Mazur, even at eighty-seven years old, was excellent company.

CHAPTER NINE

WHEN ANNE ARRIVED AT SCHOOL THE NEXT DAY, a young man, dressed all in black, was sprawled in one of the guidance rocking chairs. Anne recognized him as the speaker who had whipped the parents into a frenzy during Back to School Night. Now, fortunately, he appeared mellower—perhaps he was back on his Ritalin.

"I'm Curtis Fink," said the young man, giving Anne an appreciative once-over. "I'm here on behalf of Trevor Hopgood." Had Anne not known better, she might have thought that Trevor had committed a felony and that this man had been retained to defend him.

"I'm afraid I don't have time—"

"It'll only take a minute." Curtis Fink unfolded himself from the rocking chair and sidled up to her as she walked into her office. "I wish all the guidance counselors were as foxy as you are," he drawled.

"Flattery will get you nowhere," said Anne, giving the young man an amused look. Curtis Fink, despite his success as an Ivy packager, had the kind of pleasant, wrongheaded air characteristic of many of her male students—which made it hard for her to be angry with him. She had had the same response to Joey Pelosi when, as she had described to Winnie, he had thrown her over his shoulder and run with her down C Hall, dressed as Superman. Mr. Tortoni, the assistant principal, had wanted to suspend him, but Anne had interceded and gotten this reduced to three Saturday detentions and a community service.

"I don't think Trevor should apply to Williams," Anne asserted succinctly once Curtis Fink had taken a seat in her office. "I don't think he can get in."

"But there, you're wrong!" Fink declared

confidently. "He's a third-generation legacy, his father is a generous donor, and he has excellent SAT scores. What more could you want?"

"How about good grades?"

"A minor glitch," pronounced Fink. "We can spin bad grades."

"And how, pray tell, do you spin bad grades?"

"Simple. Our research shows that under-achievers with a unique hobby or interest are currently a desirable commodity at elite schools."

"But Trevor doesn't have a unique hobby or interest."

"Not yet, but he will!" said Fink cheerfully. "So far, we haven't found a taste for Thomas Pynchon or Gregorian chants, but our field research shows that he listens to the Grate-ful Dead, and we're hoping to package him as a Deadhead *après la lettre.* We did it last year with a kid who liked Bob Dylan—titled his college essay, 'It Ain't Me Babe—Get Off My Case, Mom and Dad,' and made it a modulated rant about how he wouldn't buckle to parental pressure, had his own agenda, wanted to find his own voice, yada yada yada yada. The colleges ate it up. That kid's grades were worse than Trevor's, and we got him into Tufts." Fink delivered this exposition glibly and then gave Anne a moon-eyed look: "Do you have a boyfriend?"

Anne ignored the question. "Are you saying that a taste for the Grateful Dead can cancel Trevor's bad grades?"

"Absolutely!" declared Fink. "If anything, the bad grades can work in his favor. Schools want diversity. Word gets out at some college that everyone is always in the library, no one gets drunk or blows off classes, and, hey, soon no one wants to go. That's what happened to the U of Chicago. We're working with them now. The goal is to get some frat boys in to trash some of the dorm rooms, maybe some slackers to fall asleep in class. You don't want everyone to look too wide awake. Turn it into the new party school: the Duke of the Midwest."

"Has Trevor decided to apply to the University of Chicago?"

"No," said Fink. "The dad wants Williams; that'll take more legwork, but we're optimistic. Once we get this kid on paper, you won't recognize him."

"But isn't the point to relay the real Trevor?"

"Real? What's real?" queried Fink, as though this knotty metaphysical question posed no problem for him. "Our job is to pitch these kids so the colleges think they're hot stuff. Say he spends the summer working as a junior counselor and one of the campers wets the bed?—that's 'experience with troubled youth.' A shlepper at the local rec center?—'an internship in sports management.' Mows the lawn?—'work in landscape architecture.' You get the idea."

"It seems dishonest," noted Anne.

"Not at all," protested Fink. "It's marketing."

"Do you have an MBA?"

"No way. I was an English major. I learned how to bullshit writing term papers." Fink veered off. "Do you want to go out?" He stared at her soulfully.

"No," said Anne curtly.

"That's cool," said Fink.

"It wouldn't be professional," Anne added more gently.

"Hey, no problem," said Fink, as if her rejection was all in a day's work. "Where were we?"

"Trevor Hopgood."

"Right. Just remember the sound bite: 'marches to the beat of a different drummer.' Try to use it in your reference letter. If you want, we'll take care of the letter for you. Some of the guidance counselors appreciate the work we can save them."

Anne looked annoyed. Fink might have a daffy charm, but what he proposed was flagrantly unethical. She stood up. "I can write my own letter and come up with my own sound bite, thank you."

"OK, OK," said Fink, "don't shoot me. But don't shoot the poor kid's chances at Williams either. You may be beautiful, but you don't look heartless."

"Good-bye, Mr. Fink." Anne gestured toward the door.

"Strong principles. Very good. But you might have to tangle with the dad. He isn't pretty."

"I'll manage."

"Tough lady, more power to you," said Fink, giving her a thumbs-up. "I'll be in touch."

"Please don't," said Anne.

CHAPTER TEN

AFTER CURTIS FINK LEFT, ANNE HAD TREVOR Hopgood called out of his sixth-period study hall and told to report to the guidance office. Trevor was the least consulted party in this case, though his life happened to be at issue. This struck Anne as sad. Why couldn't parents love their kids for who they were and not for who they wanted them to be? Trevor's father—like her own—was a particularly egregious example of this mistake, yet all parents were guilty of it to some degree. It was the dark paradox of parental love—that it came tangled up with oppression and disappointment.

"So what are your thoughts about college?" she asked after Trevor had shuffled into her office and seated himself morosely in the chair opposite her desk.

He scowled and said nothing.

"I've spoken to your parents and your college consultant," Anne continued in a soothing voice, "but I really wanted to talk to you."

"Why?" asked Trevor glumly.

"You're a senior, and you need to start work on your applications."

"That guy is taking care of everything," muttered Trevor.

"Taking care?"

"He's doing my Williams application."

"Trevor"—Anne sighed—"you know it's not right to have someone else do your college applications for you."

"Everyone does it."

"That's not true."

"According to that guy, it is."

"It's still wrong. I know you have the moral sense to realize that," said Anne, changing direction. It had been her experience that most adolescents did have a feeble moral sense that was definitively killed off only later in life.

"I don't like having him do my application,"

mumbled Trevor, supporting this supposition, "but nobody asked me."

"Why do you need to be asked?" asked Anne sternly. "Why don't you tell them?"

"Yeah, right!" Trevor sneered.

"You think they wouldn't listen?"

"I know they wouldn't listen."

"Well . . ." Anne considered this for a moment. "*I'll* listen. Why don't you talk to me?" She waited, leaning forward slightly, but Trevor remained silent.

"So what are you interested in?"

"Nothing."

"Nothing?"

"Yeah. I hate everything."

"O-K," said Anne. She had heard kids speak this way before and knew not to take it too seriously. No doubt they *did* hate everything at the moment, though in an hour they might like quite a few things.

"Hating everything is a start," she noted. "You're stating a position, even if it is a negative one. Which is good. And hating everything has the advantage of leaving your options open. Which makes you an especially good candidate for a liberal arts college like Williams." She threw this out.

Trevor grimaced. "I don't want to go to Williams!"

"You don't?"

"No! Williams reminds me of Fenimore. I hate Fenimore!"

Having already announced that he hated everything, Trevor had forfeited some credibility here. Still, Anne thought, he had a point. If you didn't like the bucolic affluence of the Westchester suburbs, why would you want to spend four years in the bucolic affluence of Williams College?

"OK, then." Anne nodded. "Here's what I'm going to do. I'm going to give you a list of schools that are all very different but which have a wide range of offerings and which I think you'd have a good chance of getting into. I want you to read about them on the Internet and see if any of them appeal to you."

Trevor shifted uneasily in his seat. "My father will kill me if I don't apply to Williams."

"I doubt that," said Anne.

"You don't know my dad."

Anne didn't say that she had a pretty good idea. Instead she said, "I know you're young to have to counter a man like your father— who of course wants only the best for you—

but you need to have a say in this. After all, it's your life."

"But it's his money," noted Trevor, realistically.

"True, but if your father refused to pay, you could always declare yourself independent and apply for financial aid on your own."

"I could?"

"Yes. It's a drastic step, but it could be done."

"Neat," said Trevor, perking up a bit. He paused, ruminating on the idea for a moment. "I could just tell my dad I'm going to do that. It would probably be just as good."

"I suppose . . ."

"He wouldn't want people to think I would do something like that. He might let me do what I want just to keep from being embarrassed."

"I don't know . . ." said Anne warily.

"It would be like blackmail," Trevor concluded.

Anne coughed. "I wish you wouldn't use that terminology. It makes me nervous."

"Hey, I don't have to tell him I'm blackmailing him; I just have to do it."

"We'll talk more in a few days."

"Blackmailing my dad—that would be way cool!" exclaimed Trevor as he left the office, looking much more cheerful than when he came in.

CHAPTER ELEVEN

"'I HAVE ALWAYS HAD A GREAT INTEREST IN THE science of governance, and Georgetown University would allow me to study this fascinating subject with which I am so enthused, while observing the political process first-hand in our nation's capital. The university also has a beautiful campus with a fascinating atmosphere that I think would further enrich my education and add greatly to my development as a person.'

"I used 'fascinating' twice," said Felicia Desiderio after reading this paragraph of her college application essay aloud to Anne. The essay went on for another page and a half, but Anne had asked her to stop. She got the idea.

"Sometimes it's better not to use so many adjectives," said Anne, not knowing where to begin.

"I know it's awful," groaned Felicia, who had followed Trevor as Anne's last appointment of the day. This was the third rewrite of her essay, and it was, Anne thought, as awful as ever.

Most students wrote awful essays—whipping out their thesaurus to expound windily about aspirations and goals, lifelong friendships, and the joys of learning that the particular institution (changed for each application) would uniquely fulfill. The sample essay that had been distributed by one of the educational testing services had been awful as well: It explained how the student's experience climbing a mountain had brought into view the academic, social, civic, and economic heights to be scaled in the years ahead. The essay, which had hammered out this stultifying metaphor with as many big words as could be crammed into the smallest possible space, had come with a tag line saying the student who wrote it had gotten into Harvard, Dartmouth, and Cornell—

proof that an awful essay might not be an impediment to admission to a top college.

Indeed, if Felicia Desiderio had received a perfect score on the SATs or been a nationally ranked soccer player, her awful essay would in no way count against her. If, for that matter, she had received a presidential citation for her work helping an indigenous people reform their voting practices or spent her summers in Washington solving the budget deficit, an awful essay might also have been overlooked. But Felicia had nothing of that dramatic order to show for herself. Her extracurricular activities were of a sustained, unglamorous sort. She was a fixture at Fenimore town council meetings, where she could be counted on to have a copy of *Roberts Rules of Order* at the ready and know the names of all the minor officials in local government that no one else knew. She was a longtime intern for the League of Women Voters, prized for her ability to cajole the area's nursing home residents to forgo bingo and get out and vote. She was also the chair (and sole member) of the Fenimore High School Elections Committee, arranging for students to vote for class officers in Mr. Tortoni's office and not, as had previously been done, in their homerooms (where teachers, preoccupied with taking roll and giving bathroom passes, had been unable to prevent rampant bullying and ballot-box stuffing).

Felicia had also deployed her mathematical abilities (which were thankfully greater than her expository ones) to civic ends: She had devised a program to predict, within a two-day margin of error, when Fenster would give a pop quiz, and she had conducted a survey, based on a well-constructed homeroom sample, proving that no one ate the carrot sticks in the Bargain Buster lunch. The former calculation had allowed countless students to thwart Fenster's desire to fail them, and the latter had saved the school money and prevented many injuries from carrot-stick projectiles.

In short, Felicia had devoted herself in small but significant ways to forwarding democracy, civic peace, and fiscal responsibility. She deserved to go to Georgetown.

"Can't you be more specific about 'the fascinating experience that taught you to see the greatness of the democratic process in action'?" Anne had taken the essay from Felicia and just read the sentence: "'Working on a political campaign was a fascinating experience that taught me to see the greatness of the democratic process in action.'"

"God," moaned Felicia, "I used 'fascinating' again."

"That's not the real problem," noted Anne. "You've worked on five local campaigns and seen how local government works; you must have some good stories or insights about the experience."

"Most of what I did was very basic," said Felicia apologetically, "getting coffee and Xeroxing. Nothing really challenging. Not that I minded," she hurried to explain. "I thought it was interesting being so close to the process."

"OK." Anne nodded encouragingly. "But what does it mean to be so close to the process? What was so interesting about it?"

"It's just fascinating to see people working to make things happen," said Felicia.

"You need to be more concrete," said Anne, realizing that Felicia's tendency to speak in clichés was probably a surefire recipe for success in politics, but not necessarily for getting into Georgetown University.

"I guess I need to try harder," said Felicia sadly.

"Think about it some more," Anne conceded.

"OK, I'll bring you a new draft tomorrow."

"You don't have to bring it tomorrow," Anne hurried to assure her. "Just relax and let your mind wander. Sometimes it's better not to try so hard."

"I always try hard," said Felicia. "I can't help it."

"That's your assignment, then," said Anne. "Try not to try so hard. Watch TV, go to the mall, veg out."

"I'll try," said Felicia doubtfully.

"Do you know Trevor Hopgood?" Anne asked on a whim.

"He's in my history class."

"Have you ever talked to him?"

Felicia considered this a moment. "I asked him for a homework assignment once. I don't think that's really talking—" Then, with surprising enthusiasm, she added: "He doesn't get much credit for his ideas because he mumbles and Ms. Fineman doesn't have patience for that. Like she was looking for a mint in her purse the other day when he said something really good about Hitler and Chamberlain, so she probably didn't hear it."

"I see," said Anne. She knew that Marcy's

limitation as a teacher was a certain distract-
edness, the result of thinking too much
about what she wasn't going to eat for lunch.
"I'll tell Ms. Fineman to listen more closely in
the future. Meanwhile, I wonder if you could
do me a favor and talk to Trevor a bit about
the college application process. You can say
I suggested it. I'm giving him some Web
sites to look through, but you might be able
to help him sift through the rhetoric the
schools use and get at the reality of what
they offer—sort of what you would do in fig-
uring out the real policies of a candidate
when you listen to a campaign speech."

"OK," said Felicia, obviously pleased by
the idea. Perhaps the notion of dealing with
propaganda, even if it took the form of college brochures, appealed to her political interests. Or perhaps she had a crush on
Trevor Hopgood. Anne knew that there was
no predicting where adolescent affections
might land.

When Felicia left, Anne felt she had done
a good day's work. Not only had she penetrated Trevor's surly demeanor, setting him
on course, albeit one that might involve
blackmail, but she had steered Felicia in the
direction of Trevor, which might assist his

college search and do something for the girl's love life.

The thought of Felicia's love life made Anne's mind revert again to Ben Cutler. She had glanced at the folder Vince had been holding the other day and noted that Ben's sister was renting a condo about a mile from the school. She wondered whether he was living there too. Despite her efforts not to care, she was agitated by emotions that she didn't like to admit, even to herself. She wanted desperately to know about his life— but she was also afraid of what she would learn.

CHAPTER TWELVE

ANNE ARRIVED LATE TO SCHOOL THE NEXT DAY. She had met with the Realtor that morning, a depressing ordeal that she knew she could not put off. The house had to be sold, and given the state of the grounds, not to mention the roof, the walls, and the floors, she knew she was lucky that Sally Solomon, the premier real-estate agent in Westchester County (where good real-estate agents are on a par with movie stars), had undertaken the sale.

Sally had agreed to do so because she had not forgotten the excellent college recommendation that Anne had written for her son, Spenser Solomon, when he was a student at Fenimore eight years ago. Without said excellent supporting letter, Spenser might never have been admitted to Penn, gone on to NYU law school, and to a career as a prosperous tax attorney. Instead, he might have become a deadbeat like his father. Selling a measly house seemed the least Sally could do to thank Anne Ehrlich for averting such a dire outcome.

"I have to be frank," Sally said this morning (Sally was known to be frank about houses the way cosmetic surgeons are frank about faces, making her ability to sell them way over market price that much more miraculous), "the place is a dump. I mean your bathrooms are from hunger. Where's the Jacuzzi? Where's the 'his and her' sinks? Where's the towel warmer? And your kitchen! There's no island. A kitchen without an island sinks the market price by twenty percent. And the grounds! No landscaping. For God's sake, no grass. Then there's the driveway—when did you have the thing paved, fifty years ago?" Anne said that was about right.

Sally squinted at the property as she stood on the broken flagstone in her red

four-inch heels with her matching red um-
brella. "The place will look better in the
spring," she observed. "Sunlight is a great
accessory. We could bill the weeds as an
English heath."

Anne said waiting until spring was not an
option, and Sally clucked and said that
would make it harder to squeeze every last
cent out of a prospective buyer—but she'd
see what she could do. Forms were filed,
and Sally went out into the jungle of life to try
to sell Anne's dump of a house for three million dollars.

When Anne finally arrived at school two
hours later than usual, she found Gus Dex-
ter, one of Fenimore's two other guidance
counselors, talking to Cindy. Gus was just
out of college, and it often struck Anne as
ironic that someone who, only a few years
earlier, would have sat cluelessly in her office, tapping his pencil against the chair and
staring into space, was now administering
sage advice to boys only a few years
younger than himself. And yet that was the
wonder of the educational process: It could
have a renovating effect on individuals like
Gus. Indeed, Gus was actually a very good
guidance counselor, particularly with some

of the lazier students, with whom he had an affinity: "Come on, man, you don't want to be working in the 7-Eleven for the rest of your life!" Such nuggets carried weight, since Gus freely admitted that he had been only a step away from the 7-Eleven himself, saved, during his junior year, by seeing one of his idols, Stu Parker, four years his senior and once "a really cool guy," working there. "Scared the crap out of me," admitted Gus. "Do you know what it's like making those Italian junior subs all day long? Or refilling the decaf for like the thirtieth time in an hour? I mean reading poetry isn't as boring as that." The lazy student, when faced with such vivid testimony, would stop fiddling with his eyebrow ring and pay attention.

When not administering this kind of advice, however, Gus was generally leaning over the ledge in front of Cindy's desk, engaged in a seemingly endless, muffled exposition, punctuated by loud bursts of giggling from Cindy. Even in her office with her door closed, Anne was able to hear the laughter coming from Cindy in response to the low, indecipherable murmur of Gus. The exchange had so intrigued Anne (what could he be saying that could so riotously amuse?)

that she had finally managed to eavesdrop one day while pretending to look for the Syracuse catalogue on the College Materials Shelf behind them.

She discovered that their conversation consisted principally of Gus's teasing Cindy about such things as how she held her pencil and the way she marked off appointments with different colored markers for different days (details which, by virtue of his noticing them, translated into his finding them adorable). The two also seemed to spend inordinate amounts of time in mock arguments about whether Cindy looked better with her hair up or down (Cindy argued for up; Gus, down) and about whether Justin Timberlake's latest album was really awesome (Cindy) or pure crap (Gus).

Today, however, Anne had no time to eavesdrop on Gus and Cindy. Before she had finished hanging up her jacket, Daphne Morgan motioned to her to come into her office.

Daphne, Fenimore's third guidance counselor, was the most senior if also the most wifty of the three. The fact that she wanted to speak to Anne was a novelty in itself. Mostly, Daphne preferred knitting and meditating to speaking. Until recently, her method of dealing with the college admissions frenzy had been to tell students to chill out and take a year off. Then, after Vince had a talk with her, she had taken to playing Indian music and giving them an oatmeal cookie.

"I wanted to let you know that a man was here this morning who knew you," said Daphne now as she sipped from a mug of herbal tea.

Anne felt her pulse quicken. "A man?"

"Yes. Cutler, I think his name was. He's the uncle of a new student." Daphne began to fumble through the papers on her desk but quickly gave up. Names and dates, not to mention board scores and GPAs, had a way of slipping through Daphne Morgan's fingers, a fact that many parents found terrifying.

"Ben Cutler?" Anne prompted Daphne now.

"Who?"

"You said this man Cutler was here this morning."

"Oh, yes," said Daphne. "Mr. Cutler. He was very nice."

"And?"

"Well, he came in to talk about getting his nephew into Columbia. I said I wouldn't presume to give advice there. My area was more on the order of Bard or Hampshire. Though I don't know that I'm quite up on those schools anymore either. Anyway, when he said Columbia, I mentioned your name and said he should speak to you. That's when he jumped."

"He jumped?" Anne felt slightly faint. Fortunately, Daphne didn't notice—but then, Daphne didn't notice much of anything.

"Well, he didn't literally jump, dear. His feet didn't leave the floor. But he did seem surprised. It took him a moment to recover. I gave him some herbal tea. It seemed to do the trick."

"And then," said Anne softly, "what did he say?"

"Not much, dear. He mentioned something about knowing you once a long time ago and not realizing you worked here. That's all. But he seemed a very pleasant sort of man, not someone you need to worry about—though I'm no expert, of course." Daphne was known to prefer women to men, and cats to both.

Anne left Daphne's office and went into her own, closing the door. She could hear Gus and Cindy giggling in the waiting area.

She buzzed Cindy. "Would you remind

Gus that he has to pick up the Colgate recruiter at the station this morning."

"Ms. Ehrlich says to remind you that you have to pick up the Colgate recruiter this morning," Anne heard Cindy say to Gus in a coquettish singsong.

"He's not due in till eleven," she heard Gus say, "but I guess I better mosey over to my office and get a little snooze in before I have to go." There was laughter again, and Anne hung up the phone. She sat at her desk for a moment, trying to clear her brain. Ben Cutler knew she was at Fenimore. Would he want to see her, she wondered—or not?

CHAPTER THIRTEEN

By popular demand (which is to say lots of pressure from parents), Fenimore held a college fair on the last Saturday morning in September. Most schools had college fairs in April or May, which Fenimore did too, but someone on the Home and School Committee had suggested that if one was good, two would be better—a quantitative philosophy that operated everywhere in the college admissions process.

The fall fair was generally a lackluster event, since most schools waited till spring to send a representative. This did not prevent the Home and School Committee, not to mention local real-estate brokers, from trumpeting the fact of the fair as another example of Fenimore's pedagogical excellence.

The fall fair, like the spring fair, took place in the school gymnasium, where school dances were also held. This was apt, since the fair was like a school dance. The popular colleges got all the attention; everyone else just sort of sat around and watched.

This year, there were some thirty schools represented in the gym, but students were clustered around only a few. A large gaggle stood shmoozing with the Duke representative, a fashionably dressed black man (chosen perhaps to counteract Duke's Southern cracker associations), while Dickinson and Denison reps sat overlooked off to the side. Most of the reps from the smaller, less well-known schools had become reconciled to slim pickings and brought a book or did a crossword puzzle. The Denison rep was reading *The Sound and the Fury*. A student approached the table curiously: "I never heard of your school," he said.

"And you probably never heard of William Faulkner either," noted the rep, looking up scornfully from his book. This rep was known to be caustic and had been dressed down a number of times by Denison's dean of admissions—though some in the admissions office thought that his disdainful attitude spurred the interest of certain students. This appeared to be the case now.

"So what kind of school are you?" asked the student, who seemed disinclined to reveal if he had heard of William Faulkner.

"We're known as a fine small liberal arts college," snapped the rep. "But only by those who care about such things." He returned to his book, while the student dawdled a moment at the table, took a brochure, and wandered off.

Anne noted that this year there was a representative present from Flemington College, a traditionally black school with high academic standards. She approached the rep and introduced herself. "I have to tell you," she said frankly, "most of our best African-American students are inclined toward the Ivies. I don't know if you'll find much interest here."

"That's OK," said the recruiter, a young woman in a business suit and cornrows. "We're marketing Flemington to whites. We're aiming to sell them on the novelty aspect: what it feels like to be a minority." The young woman gave her a business card. "Please have any students interested in something different give me a call—but be sure their grades and scores are up to par. We don't have affirmative action."

Across the gym, a large cluster of students stood around the Columbia rep. Columbia was always represented at Fenimore's fall fair, since all they had to do was to put someone on the commuter train. In this instance, the rep, a nerdy-looking young man who appeared to be basking in attention that he did not otherwise get, was intoning that Columbia was "very, very selective," a statement that appeared to fan the flames of the students' desire. "Are 2200 SATs good enough?" asked a pretty blond-haired girl. The rep, who had been rejected by more girls who looked like this than he could count, seemed to relish the idea that he might, metaphorically at least, reject this girl. "Take them again," he said smugly.

Most of the students at Fenimore were ambivalent about Columbia. It had prestige, but it was also right next door. This had the drawback and advantage of placing them within the proximity of their parents, who would be on hand to nag and swoop down unexpectedly, but who could also be used in a pinch to do laundry and take them out to dinner.

On the other side of the gym, the Stanford rep, who had been in the area to visit an ailing aunt, had a collection of students gathered around him. They had heard that Stanford was the Harvard of the West and thus worth considering, at least as a safety school. Since those who went to school in California never came back, an observer might have viewed the recruiter as a kind of pied piper in deep cover, luring unsuspecting students to a faraway place where they would rarely see their parents again.

Many of the booths were manned by local alumni, who enjoyed the idea of representing their alma maters but knew next to nothing about the college application process and almost as little about the schools themselves. Quite a number of these were retirees, who tended to be hard of hearing, dim of sight, and imbued with ancient tastes and prejudices.

"How many SAT IIs do you have to have?" asked a student of an elderly man wearing a Boston College cap and blazer, who looked like he had gone there when the Jesuits founded the place.

"SAT IIs?" said the man, befuddled.

"That's what they call the Achievement tests now," said the Denison rep helpfully, looking up from *The Sound and the Fury.*

"Ah!" said the alumnus, who clearly couldn't recall the Achievement tests either. "It's all in the brochure," he assured the student. "Great school, BC. Good Catholic school. Great football team. You ever heard of Doug Flutie?" The student, looking frightened, fled the table.

Another alum in green plaid pants and a green blazer was expounding loudly to a collection of students about the merits of Yale. Many of these students had thought they wanted to go to Yale until meeting up with this alumnus.

"Those road trips to Holyoke, let me tell you; we had a grand old time. You should look into Mount Holyoke," he said to a girl in the group.

"Yale is co-ed," said the girl.

"So it is," said the alum. "But Mount Holyoke is a damn good school too. My wife went there."

On the other side of the room, a very old Williams alumnus was talking to Jeffrey Hopgood, who, having graduated only twenty-five years ago, was more knowledge-able about the place and was filling him in. Trevor had slunk off to the corner with his iPod, while Mrs. Hopgood was showing a polite interest in the materials of the nearby Vanderbilt rep, a young woman with a perky disposition that seemed to cheer her up.

"Has your son considered Vanderbilt?" asked the Vanderbilt rep.

"I don't know," said Mrs. Hopgood, eyeing Trevor and wondering if she should try putting this question to him. "We're thinking of Williams at the moment."

"Excellent school," said the young woman, "but cold. Does your son like the cold?"

Mrs. Hopgood did not know the answer to this question either and glanced over at Trevor, wondering if she ought to probe him on the subject of temperature.

"Warm weather would be nice," said Mrs. Hopgood wistfully. "I would have liked to go south to school."

"Never too late," said the rep. "Where did you go?"

"SUNY at Oneonta." Mrs. Hopgood sighed. "Very cold."

"Well, you might consider a graduate degree. What field are you in?"

Mrs. Hopgood appeared to consider this question for a moment. "I was a psychology major," she finally said.

"We have a great clinical psych program," chirped the girl. "Take a brochure." Mrs. Hopgood took a brochure.

A large gaggle of students stood around the University of Pennsylvania table, where the mother of one of the more popular senior girls was manning the booth. She was trying to convince them to consider Penn. "It's my first choice, Mrs. Steinberg, after Harvard, Yale, Princeton, and Dartmouth," said a girl in an Abercrombie & Fitch miniskirt.

"I think Philadelphia is awesome," said another girl.

"It's the cradle of our country," said Mrs. Steinberg, who took her recruiting position very seriously.

"My mom went to Penn State," said another girl, known to be the least swift of the group.

"That's not the same thing," said Mrs. Steinberg.

"You're so lucky you're a legacy," said the girl in the Abercrombie skirt to Hilary Steinberg, Mrs. Steinberg's daughter. "At least you have a good chance of getting in."

"I know," said Hilary, "but I really want to go to Duke." She glanced furtively over at the group around the Duke rep. "Don't tell my mother."

Anne walked through the gym, taking brochures from some of the schools and chatting for a few minutes with the lonelier-looking reps.

"Hello, Miss Ehrlich," said the SUNY Binghamton rep, an ancient alum, who liked to drop by the guidance office on a weekly basis. He had a way of popping up just as Anne was about to do something important, wanting to fill her in on new developments at the university. He read the college newspaper on the Internet and thus always came prepared with some small nugget of information (the student cafeteria had added a salad bar, the student union would be closed for a week for renovation, Professor Simkus—whoever he was—had not gotten tenure, etc., etc.). What he really came to talk about was his blood pressure medicine and his deceased wife. It was, Anne realized, an important therapeutic part of his week and she tried not to begrudge him, though given the frequency of his visits, she wondered if she ought to be paid a social service fee on top of her salary.

"See you next week," he called out. "Have some interesting new developments to tell you about the interlibrary loan policy."

"I'm looking forward to it, Mr. Crane," responded Anne as she made her getaway.

CHAPTER FOURTEEN

SHE WAS WALKING BRISKLY DOWN THE STAIRS OF the gym, wondering what inconvenient time next week Mr. Crane would show up, when she saw Ben Cutler walking toward her. He looked older—which of course he was—but he also looked the same. It was the familiar lanky figure: tall, the body a bit more substantial than it had been, but with the same slight slope to the shoulders and the same dark hair, now flecked here and there with gray. The hair was cut more stylishly than she remembered, but it was still thick and a bit unruly, curling unevenly at the bottom.

He was walking up the steps with a

heavyset woman and a boy of about seventeen who looked uncomfortable in their company, the way boys of seventeen tend to do. The woman looked cheerful and was talking animatedly, while the boy was making every effort to lag behind.

Ben Cutler's expression was pleasant. Anne could understand why Daphne had made a point of saying he was nice; he had not lost the look of optimism and goodwill that had always characterized him, despite a less-than-privileged upbringing. It was that quality that should have given her confidence in his future, had she had more confidence in herself.

What was markedly different about him now was his dress. The jeans and sweatshirt had been replaced by what Anne could tell was a very good if casual suit and the kind of soft, expensive loafers that she associated with European men. It occurred to her that, having spent a good many years abroad writing his cultural guides, he would have developed cosmopolitan tastes. The woman beside him, whom Anne guessed was his sister, was dressed expensively too, though rather garishly in a pink wool suit with a large pin and a good deal of makeup.

They had arrived within a few feet of each other on the steps. She could tell that he had seen her a few moments earlier, since he had stopped talking to his sister and was looking straight ahead.

"Anne—" he said, stepping forward and shaking her hand. She felt the warmth of his palm in hers, a feeling that sent a familiar shiver through her body. Had it really been thirteen years since she had had his hand in hers?

She tried to maintain her composure and speak casually. "I heard that your nephew had enrolled at Fenimore. It's quite a coincidence."

"It is," he said. She felt he was looking at her for what seemed like a long time, though it couldn't have been more than a few seconds. "I didn't know you worked here, of course," he finally said.

He said "of course," she thought, because, had he known, he would never have come to the area.

"That amusing woman I met at the school told me that you were head of guidance," he continued. "It wasn't the career I would have imagined you'd go into."

Anne supposed he had expected her to pursue a more glamorous and high-powered career, given her family's wealth and status at the time. And suddenly she knew what he was thinking: that if he had never imagined her as a high-school guidance counselor, she had never imagined him as a successful businessman. She had not trusted him to do something with his life, and he had proven her wrong.

She saw his face flush slightly as the thought passed through his mind, but then he turned away quickly and began making introductions. "This is my sister, Pauline," he said, motioning to the woman in the pink suit. "And this is my nephew, Jonathan." He put his hand affectionately on the boy's shoulder. "This is Anne Ehrlich." He gestured stiffly toward Anne. "I knew her years ago. It turns out she's head of guidance here at Fenimore."

Pauline put out her hand cordially. "I always say it's a small world," she declared in the manner of someone who never suspects more than what is said. "How nice that you're in guidance. Jonathan needs guidance."

Ben gave a short laugh. "Pauline doesn't beat around the bush. It's true that we've dragged Jonathan with us around the world, and he's retaliated by paying no attention to us." He glanced over at the boy, who had moved off to the side and begun reading a book. Ben's face registered concern, and Anne imagined that he felt responsible for his nephew and perhaps guilty for any difficulties the boy may have suffered as a result of their moving so much.

"I'm sure he gained a lot from traveling," said Anne quietly. "He may not realize it now, but later he will."

Ben nodded slightly, as if he thought so too. "I hope your family is well," he said suddenly in a low voice.

"Everyone is fine," she replied, trying for a cheerful tone. "My grandmother had a minor stroke a few months ago, so I'm staying with her, but she's recovering nicely. And my father and sister are the same."

"That's good," said Ben without inflection.

Anne turned to the boy to cover her discomfort. "I hope you're going to like Fenimore," she said. "I know you're only here for your senior year, but it's not a bad place, all things considered. I hope you'll feel free to drop by my office if you have questions—or even if you don't."

"Sure," said the boy, looking up from his book indifferently.

"Mrs. Ehrlich knows Uncle Ben, so maybe she'll give you special attention," said Pauline in that clueless parental way that Anne knew tended to drive kids crazy— though Jonathan appeared to take the practical tack of ignoring her.

"It's Ms. Ehrlich," corrected Anne.

"Miss Ehrlich," said Pauline, nodding. But Jonathan had returned to his book and did not look up. "Jonathan, sweetie, it's not nice to read in front of people," she said, then turned to Anne apologetically, since he was not paying attention. "What can you do? Even Ben can't get him to say much, and if Bennie can't, well . . ."

Anne thought that in that line alone she saw the entire dynamic of the family. She could tell by the way Pauline spoke of Ben that she not only relied on his help but saw him as the font of all wisdom.

"I've never been particularly good at convincing people to do things they don't want to do," noted Ben wryly. She could feel his eyes on her face, looking at her closely now, perhaps noting how she had changed. She recalled how he had looked at her with so much undisguised admiration the first time they met. How different from the clinical assessment she felt in his gaze now.

"It's nice that Jonathan likes to read," Anne said, trying to hide her embarrassment.

"Yes, but he reads all the time," complained Pauline. "We want him to stop reading a little bit and start paying attention to what's going on around him. I don't think he noticed half the places we lived. He might as well have been in Queens, right, Ben?" She looked to her brother, as Anne surmised she often did, to elaborate on what she had said.

But before he could respond, a tall blond woman in a colorful silk dress came running up the steps. She was very pretty, with the air that only a few lucky women have of looking at once impeccably put-together and entirely natural. "I'm awfully sorry I'm late, my darling," she said in a breathless, slightly accented voice. She gave Jonathan a peck on the cheek and hugged Pauline quickly, then lifted her head to kiss Ben lightly on the mouth. "I had to stand in line for an hour, but I got the theater tickets you wanted for this weekend. Aren't you pleased?" The woman then turned to look at Anne with curiosity.

"Kirsten is my editorial director—and my fiancée," said Ben quickly.

"Not in that order, I hope." The woman addressed Anne with a laugh. "I am resigned to coming second to his sister and his dear nephew, but I insist on coming before his business. It would not bode well for the impending nuptials."

Anne tried to smile, but felt a painful tightening in her chest. So there it was. Ben was engaged to someone who looked like a fashion model and was not without a sense of humor.

The woman put out her hand. "I'm Kirsten Knudsen. I met this motley crew in Copenhagen a year ago, and I've been tagging along ever since."

Anne tried to keep her voice steady. "I'm Anne Ehrlich," she said, then hesitated as she tried to clear her head and find the right words to present herself. "I'm Jonathan's guidance counselor, though I knew his uncle years ago," she finally added.

"Ah," said Kirsten, as though, unlike Pauline, she was extremely gifted at understanding what wasn't said. "Jonathan is a lucky boy!" Anne saw Ben's eyes flicker.

There was a moment of awkward silence.

"I don't want to keep you from the college fair"—Anne began to speak, hardly knowing what was coming out of her mouth. "I'm not sure why they call it a fair—I think of ferris wheels and cotton candy. Though you can pick up some pens and refrigerator magnets with college logos, and the Home and School Committee did make brownies. . . ." She was babbling, she realized, and she stopped herself. "It was so nice to meet you all"—she nodded to Pauline and Kirsten (Jonathan wasn't paying attention)—"and to see you again," she added as her eyes grazed Ben's face. She forced herself to smile, and then, holding herself very straight, she walked briskly down the stairs of the gym without looking back.

CHAPTER FIFTEEN

Their first date had been at a coffee shop on Broadway. After Ben had booked her trip to Italy, he had said he had something she should read before she went; he would bring it if she'd meet him for lunch the next day. Noon: that's when he had his lunch break. She had had to leave her Western Civilization class early, though she hadn't told him that.

When she arrived at the coffee shop, he was already there, and as she walked toward the back where he was sitting, she saw his face brighten. It was the sort of pleasure that people rarely show, but Ben Cutler had never been inclined to hide his feelings. Whether it was pleasure or, later, disappointment, it took over his face completely. In this case, his obvious pleasure in seeing her made her feel free to express hers in seeing him. She smiled back and her whole face and even her body seemed to relax. So much of her growing up had been about masking or repressing feeling. Even her grandmother, who had loved her unequivocally, had been guarded—unwilling to let on how much the loss of Anne's mother had meant to her, and not wanting Anne to feel that loss too strongly.

"I'm glad you came," he said, as if admitting that he had worried that she wouldn't.

"Of course I came," Anne said. "I always keep my promises. Besides, you said you had a book I should read to prepare for my trip."

Ben laughed. "I knew you were the self-improving type." He said this as though she had passed some sort of secret test—not only of showing up but of wanting whatever it was he had to give. "Order something," he said. "It's on me. Next time, it can be on you." It had made her exceptionally happy to hear him refer to a next time. Then, he took a paperback out of his pocket and handed it to her.

"*Italian Hours* by Henry James. Heavy stuff," said Anne, examining the book. It was tattered, as though it had been carried along in a hip pocket and read in subways and probably in coffee shops like this.

"Not really," said Ben. "It's more an appreciation than a dissertation—a lot of gushing about beautiful places. But it seems to me that when you travel you want to go all out and admit that the stuff is beautiful. I've never been anywhere, but when I finally go, I want to do it the way James did, with enthusiasm—and reverence."

"You make traveling sound like a pilgrimage."

"I guess I think of it that way. It's a chance to see things fresh—not so much because it's so different somewhere else, but because you haven't gotten used to seeing it yet. Sometimes I try to turn the corner and make believe that I've never been on 113th and Broadway before. And sometimes I can actually do it, but it only lasts a second or two. When you go to a new place, I imagine you can hold the feeling longer."

143

"That's a neat way of putting it," said Anne. "I hope you get to travel."

"I will," said Ben simply, "but for now, I can do it through Henry James."

"And through me," she offered. "I'll save you my impressions. It will only be two weeks."

"You can have a lot of impressions in two weeks," he said.

"I meant that I'll be back in two weeks."

"I know," he said, "and I'll be waiting for you."

CHAPTER SIXTEEN

ANNE TRIED TO CONCENTRATE ON THE ROAD AS she drove the few miles from Fenimore to Scarsdale, but she felt slightly sick. She had finally learned what she had feared to learn—that Ben Cutler was attached to someone else. It was an idea that she had entertained hypothetically, but now she knew it as a fact—and it was all the more painful because the attraction she had felt thirteen years ago was still there. How was it that after so much time had passed, she still felt her heart beat faster and her head grow light when she looked at him?

She arrived at the house at noon, as she

had promised Winnie she would. Ever since she could remember, she had saved one Saturday afternoon every month for shopping and lunch with her grandmother. The ritual had been put on hold after the last stroke, but lately Winnie had begun to say she felt "cooped up," a sure sign of recovery. And so, they decided that today, after the college fair, they would spend the rest of the afternoon together, browsing Scarsdale's main shopping street. To facilitate the outing, Winnie had volunteered to give up her cane for a wheelchair, a major concession.

"I was attached to the cane," she acknowledged, "but I fear I've outgrown it. The logical progression would be to one of those hideous walkers. But under no circumstances will I succumb to such a thing. It's not only unsightly, it gets in everyone else's way. Old age is scandal enough without having to inflict it on other people."

Anne told Winnie that she was being rather hard on walkers, but was secretly glad for the convenience of the wheelchair. As it turned out, they were able to maneuver with relative ease in and out of shops, where some of the merchants remembered Winnie from the years when she had been a dominant force in Westchester society. In the sixties and seventies, she had bullied and cajoled them to lend their support to her various charities and political causes, and in the eighties, she had repaid them by helping to fund the "Save Main Street" campaigns for this part of Westchester County—a movement that had kept the area towns limping along despite the incursions of the nearby malls. Many of the original merchants from that period were gone, but those who remained treated Winnie like royalty.

Although they went into almost a dozen shops, they concluded that there was nothing to buy—a fortunate conclusion since they had no money. They seated themselves in the little restaurant that had always been their favorite. There was still the lunch to pay for, and Anne was appalled to see that the grilled chicken salad now cost $16.95. "I remember when I got that here for six-fifty!" she exclaimed.

"Now, Anne," Winnie said reprovingly, "I'm the old lady, and I should do the complaining. Sixteen ninety-five is what you have to pay if you want the restaurant to stay in business. And there's a fruit salad on the side, which makes all the difference. Besides, it's my treat."

"And how is it your treat?" asked Anne.

"I have my resources, don't worry."

"You probably sold another piece of jewelry!" Anne looked at her grandmother accusingly. She knew that Winnie had recently had a visit from an area antique dealer, which would account for this sudden acquisition of disposable income.

"And if I did, that's my own affair," sniffed Winnie. "As it happens, you can thank your grandfather. He was, as you know, a generous man, and every occasion that rolled around—birthday, anniversary, Valentine's Day, you name it—there was another bracelet. I made believe I was thrilled, but of course, I said to myself, 'Not another one!' I don't blame the poor man, mind you. He was just doing what men do. They hit on something you like—a bracelet, for example—and then they insist on buying it for you over and over again. I never had the heart to tell him that one bracelet was good, but two was less good, and that ten was really not good at all. But in the end, you see, it turned out for the best. It's nice to have a few extra bracelets on hand for a rainy day."

"Gram, you're terrible!" Anne laughed.

But Winnie, who had delivered her discourse on bracelets in a breezy tone, now grew serious. "Something's been on your mind, dear. I knew it ever since the day you told me about selling the house. I'm sure that's part of it—but there's more. I know you too well."

Anne was silent.

"Out with it!" ordered Winnie.

"It's nothing really, Gram," said Anne grudgingly. "But if you must know, it's that I've had a bit of a surprise. You remember Ben Cutler? It seems his nephew has enrolled at Fenimore. The family recently moved back to the area after spending time abroad. I think I've mentioned that he publishes those popular travel guides."

"Yes," mused Winnie. "The fellow did very well for himself, after all." She looked at Anne probingly. "So he's back?"

"He's engaged to be married," Anne murmured.

Winnie's gaze lingered on her granddaughter. "I'm sorry," she said simply.

Suddenly, Anne felt tears running down her face. Now that things were clear—she had seen Ben Cutler and he was lost to her—she felt an uncontrollable need to cry. Winnie reached out and took her hand. They sat that way for a while: the granddaughter crying, the grandmother gazing across at her helplessly. Then, finally, Winnie spoke. "You know, my dear," she said with determined cheerfulness, "I think I'll have the grilled chicken salad after all. With a nice glass of red wine. And the chocolate torte for dessert. I suggest you wipe those tears and do the same. No point spoiling a perfectly good lunch. As I said, it's my treat—and you have your grandfather's lack of imagination to thank for it."

CHAPTER SEVENTEEN

ALLEGRA'S PARTY THAT EVENING WAS FOR *THE Widening Gyre,* the poetry journal that relied on the kindness of socialites with literary pretensions to keep it afloat. Both Allegra and Carlotta Dupre, Anne's temporary tenant, wrote clotted verse for the journal that Anne, despite her undergraduate degree in English, could not decipher. Allegra also wrote the journal's editor's column, usually on the subject of how the populace would never be able to appreciate poetry. Anne had once asked her sister if she would be willing to lead an after-school poetry workshop at Fenimore, and Allegra had raised a finely arched eyebrow and said that she didn't "do high school"—as if she were speaking about some perverted sexual practice.

"But high-school students grow into adult readers," Anne had argued. "It might be worthwhile to help form their taste."

"I'm not into missionary work," asserted Allegra disdainfully. "Besides, it's my belief that poetry can't be taught. It either inhabits the individual at the core or it doesn't. And it's a waste of time talking to high-school students about anything."

Like their father, Allegra was inclined to make remarks that ignored the sensitivities of her respondents. It would never occur to her that Anne spent her day talking to high-school students or, if it did, to edit herself in consideration of her sister's feelings.

Although Anne had long ago given up trying to convince Allegra to "do high school," she occasionally went to her sister's parties in the hope of snagging someone who would. Given the number of doctors, lawyers, advertising executives, and financial analysts who visited the school to talk about the art of making money, it seemed like a good idea to have someone come in once in a while to talk about art in its purer sense. It was her belief that a poet was a valuable role model for high-school kids, even if the poet wasn't very good.

This year, for example, she knew that one of Allegra's guests would be Peter Jacobson, a recent winner of the Pitzer Prize of Westchester County, an award whose major recommendation was that it sounded like the Pulitzer Prize, if you weren't listening closely. Peter had the distinction of being half Irish and half Jewish, a combination that might have been the deciding factor in his winning the award. Last year, it had gone to a black lesbian, a more high-profile but less practical hybrid, given that the population of Westchester County had more Jews and Irish than blacks or lesbians.

Anne had settled on a gray skirt and white silk blouse for the party this evening, an outfit that she believed too unassuming to be faulted. But as soon as she entered the foyer and peeked into the living room, she saw she was wrong. Allegra was standing near the fireplace, wearing a pair of pre-faded jeans and a pumpkin-colored designer T-shirt. Her boyfriend-of-the-moment, Zack, was standing in the opposite corner, wearing a pea-green, artfully rumpled button-down shirt. They were both talking to people in faux-worn ochre garments. In the context of so many distressed earth tones, Anne felt her gray and white looked positively vulgar.

In a corner, Anne could see that her cousin, Rachel Kramer, aged twenty-six, was speaking to an older man who probably had some connection to the theater. An aspiring actress, Rachel was the daughter of Elihu's much younger half-sister, who had married a dentist and lived in a split level in New Jersey, a fact that both Elihu and Allegra found extremely déclassé. Allegra had been trying, in the interest of the family's reputation, to steer her cousin to a job with an underfunded Off-Off Broadway repertory company. Rachel, however, was resistant to her efforts. She wanted a more mainstream career and had, to the dismay of Elihu and Allegra, recently been cast in a commercial for sinus medicine. "Pornography would be classier," Allegra had said, rolling her eyes.

Looking around the room, Anne saw that her father was standing in the corner and speaking with more than usual animation with Carlotta Dupre, who was fingering the lapel of his new cashmere sports jacket.

John Updike, despite Elihu's fearful prediction, did not appear to be present.

As she stood at the door to the living room, surveying the guests, she saw a very tall, thin man, whose pale flyaway hair made him resemble a scarecrow, whip out a sheaf of crumpled pages. One of the staples of Allegra's literary parties was at least one dramatic reading, carefully orchestrated to appear spontaneous. The scarecrow figure had apparently been assigned the role of providing this, since he began reading from the crumpled pages with the requisite suddenness:

"The two bodies twisted in the summer heat, the sweat dripping from their labile limbs, entwined in a fearsome knot on the daybed. Mario drew his hand slowly over Albertina's supple buttocks . . ."

Anne stood uncomfortably at the entrance to the room as the reading continued for perhaps ten minutes until finally subsiding into artful anticlimax. "The sun beat down. It was summer . . ." As the reader's voice trailed off, he gazed around the room dramatically, obviously taken with the power of his own words. There was a smattering of half-hearted applause. Anne wondered whether

anyone besides herself had felt uncomfortable during this protracted if pompous exposition of graphic sex.

No one apparently had, since everyone
went on talking as though the scarecrow's
reading had been pleasant background
noise. The exception was a young man sitting on the couch in the center of the room,
who was fiddling nervously with his napkin.
As Anne looked more closely, she recognized the young man, whom she had seen
interviewed on a cable morning show, as Peter Jacobson, winner of the Pitzer Prize.

Anne walked over to the couch. Peter Jacobson was in his early thirties and was
wearing a light blue sweater and a pair of
corduroy pants, an outfit that had the advantage of making no apparent sartorial statement. "I'm Anne Ehrlich," she said simply, "I
saw you interviewed on *Wake-up Westchester* last week."

"It's nice to know someone was watching
at five-thirty A.M.," Peter said. His speech
was slow and somewhat lugubrious, though
it was clear that he was glad to talk—though
perhaps he was only glad that the embarrassing reading was over.

"Five-thirty is when I get up," explained

Anne. "I work as a guidance counselor in a public high school where we have to report to work before seven. I have to say that you sounded like the kind of poet who would interest our more literary sixteen-year-olds."

"Oh?" said Peter, looking rather insulted.

"I mean that as a compliment," Anne hurried to explain. "Unlike those TV executives who say that sixteen-year-olds are morons whom they're obliged to cater to, I tend to think that this age group is quite discriminating. I suspect the TV executives are confusing them with older people more like themselves."

"An interesting distinction." Peter nodded, smiling wanly. "You've convinced me to be flattered that I would interest the sixteen-year-olds at your high school."

"So, given your renewed respect for sixteen-year-olds"—Anne proceeded directly to her point—"we happen to have a Poetry Day coming up next month, and I wonder whether you'd be willing to speak at the school?"

"Sure," said Peter, as though he didn't need to give the request a second thought.

"We would obviously pay you something for your time. Though I'm afraid it wouldn't be significant."

"What's significant?" Peter shrugged. "Short of a few million, nothing's significant. I don't care about money. If you want me, I'll come."

Anne looked at Peter with more interest. Physically, he had a lot to recommend him: He was of medium height but powerfully built, with a mop of dark red hair and a handsome, lightly freckled face that seemed refreshingly lacking in arrogance. She noted that he looked in need of cheering up. He had told the reporter on *Wake-up Westchester* that he had recently lost his girlfriend, a fellow poet, to a rare blood disease.

"I'm sorry about your loss," Anne said now.

Peter sighed, his blue eyes doleful.

"At least you have your work—your writing," she suggested gently. "That must help."

"It does, a little," he acknowledged, "but I still feel empty. I know there are plenty of people out there"—he gave a wave to the room—"women, and men too, if I were inclined that way—who would keep me company. But it's not what I'm after. These aren't the kind of people I feel comfortable with." He gave her a long, probing look.

"I understand," said Anne, wondering whether he was after a relationship with someone like her, since she didn't resemble the other people in the room.

She decided to return to the main subject: "Anyway, I hope you'll keep your promise and speak at my school. I came expressly to ask you when my sister told me you'd be here." She gestured to where their hostess was standing across the room. "Allegra's my sister, you know."

"I didn't know," said Peter, surprised. "You don't look anything like her." Most people would have agreed. Allegra had the extreme fairness and aquiline features that came from the Ehrlich side of the family, while Anne's hair and eyes were dark, her eyebrows rather thick. Elihu used to tell Winnie to "please have those bushy things plucked," but her grandmother had known enough to ignore him. Anne's eyebrows had the effect of balancing the sweetness of her mouth, so that people found her at once strong and comforting. If Anne was less immediately striking than her sister, whose shimmering blondness always created a stir, she was the one they tended to remember at the end of the evening.

"We aren't much alike," Anne acknowledged to Peter now. "And I have to admit that this isn't my scene either. I came because I wanted to pitch you on the high school appearance. Since I succeeded, it was worth it."

Before he could respond, Allegra, as if on cue at the mention of her name, flitted over, gave Anne a perfunctory air kiss, and grabbed Peter's arm to lead him to Zack who, she gushed, was dying to meet him. Zack was actually planning to write an article for an obscure online journal about why the Pitzer Prize should not have gone to Peter but to a homeless Bosnian refugee living in the Mamaroneck train station.

Like a lamb to the slaughter, Peter dutifully followed his hostess to the other side of the room—though not before writing his number on the napkin and pressing it into Anne's hand.

"Call about your Poetry Day—or anything else," he called out plaintively as Allegra dragged him off.

CHAPTER EIGHTEEN

ANNE SPENT MONDAY MORNING ON THE PHONE. It was her practice to devote a few days during the fall term to calling those colleges which she felt would be an especially good match for certain students. Many guidance counselors didn't bother making these calls. It took a lot of time, and it was always a challenge to convince admissions officers that the kids one was advocating for were somehow different from the kids at other schools who, on paper, looked exactly the same.

"Sean Dunne isn't on staff any longer," explained a harried Amherst admissions officer when Anne asked to speak to this person. "He quit to do bodybuilding. Can I help you?"

Anne felt a drop. She had been cultivating Sean Dunne for ages, and had even indulged in an annual flirtation over drinks at the Marriot during the National Association of College Admissions Counselors. The result had been a record number of admissions to Amherst for Fenimore students over the past five years.

"I'd like to discuss a few of our students who I think would be good prospects for Amherst," she explained now, knowing that if it had been Sean Dunne, they would have spent twenty minutes playfully teasing each other and then segued into a brief but serious discussion of each of the three students she had in mind for Amherst.

"We don't talk about students at this stage of the process," said the officer curtly. "If we have questions about an application, we'll call." And there went five years of cultivating Amherst over margaritas down the drain.

This sort of thing made Anne particularly sensitive when she was on the receiving end of calls. Like the one she got after lunch that day from an intrepid admissions officer at Molson College, a little-known institution somewhere in the Midwest, who had been calling Anne once a week since school began. While the guidance counselors called the more popular colleges, the less popular colleges called the guidance counselors. It was just another version of that age-old law of social dynamics that happens to find its purest manifestation in a high school cafeteria.

The Molson admissions officer had some of the annoying tenacity of a telephone marketer—which, in a manner of speaking, he was. Molson had been trying for several years to claw its way from a third-tier position in *U.S. News & World Report,* the bible of college ranking, to a low second-tier position—an aspiration that Molson's president had articulated to the Board of Trustees alongside his other visionary goal: to amend the name of the institution from Molson College to Thomas Molson College, thereby mitigating its evocation of a certain brand of beer.

"I'm calling about Toby Tucker," said the admissions officer now.

Anne knew that Toby Tucker was being courted by many third-tier schools, less because of his grades and scores, which were unimpressive, than because he was "cool."

This value used to have the limited function of getting someone a date for the prom and the adulation of underclassmen, but it had now become a marketable commodity, at least in the view of certain lesser-known colleges. For these schools, the student was seen as a valuable trendsetter, who could entice other, perhaps better, students to go where he did. How colleges like Molson determined the coolness factor of students like Toby Tucker was anyone's guess, though Anne suspected that they resorted to consulting middle school yearbooks, flagging the "Most Popular" and "Cutest Couple" honorees, and checking local newspapers for names of underclassmen elected to the prom court.

Just the other day Toby Tucker had come into Anne's office holding a bunch of letters. "All these schools want me," he announced.

Anne looked at the letters. Each was a personalized pitch by schools of minor reputation who had somehow gotten wind of Toby's coolness. Some of them were offering full scholarships and additional stipends if he agreed to come.

Toby, to his credit, was too cool to care about any of this. He had come to Anne because his mother had told him to. He wanted to go to Franklin and Marshall, where his older brother had gone. "I wish they wouldn't send me these things," he complained, "because now my parents won't let me go to F&M unless I get a scholarship." The lure of a free ride—or, at least, a reduced fare—posed difficulties for many students, whose parents might otherwise not have thought twice about paying full price.

Anne felt that there was a certain irony in the fact that being cool, while it had gotten Toby many invitations, might now prevent him from going to the party he wanted to go to.

"This Tucker kid is a ripple kid," said the admissions officer on the phone, implying that Toby was likely to inspire others to follow him, like ripples in a stream, wherever he chose to go. "We can promise Tucker a full scholarship and a starter position on the baseball team if he comes, but we can't keep admitting kids who are going to blow us off."

"I really don't know Toby's plans," Anne said warily.

"And if you did, you wouldn't say," concluded the admissions officer.

"Well, it's not my place to say," said Anne.

"But you know."

"I didn't say that." She switched the subject. "What about Paul Wasser? His grades are just as good as Tucker's." What she really meant was that they were just as bad. "And he definitely wants to go to Molson." Paul actually did want to go to this lackluster school: He had an uncle who lived nearby, and he liked cold weather. Before Molson had begun to claw its way toward the second tier, this would have been recommendation enough.

"Which means that Tucker doesn't want to go?" deduced the admissions officer.

"I didn't say that. I just said that Paul is very gung ho about the place."

"But Wasser isn't a ripple kid."

"He's a very nice boy."

"Nice won't get us squat."

Anne was silent for a moment. "I don't think that speaks well for your values."

The officer cleared his throat. "Tell you what," he said slyly. "You tell me the truth about Toby Tucker, and I'll guarantee that this Wasser kid gets in, no matter what."

"That's blackmail," said Anne, recalling that Trevor Hopgood wanted to resort to this tactic with his father, and wondering if she had spotted a trend.

166

"It's negotiation," corrected the admissions officer.

"I'll get back to you," said Anne.

If she could find out if F&M was going to offer Toby a scholarship, she could tell Molson that he wasn't interested and ensure Paul Wasser's place. It wasn't exactly the sort of thing that appealed to her, but there was an understandable logic behind it. No school wanted to accept someone who would ruin their "yield" (the number of students admitted who agreed to go). And no school wanted to be the garbage dump for the college-bound, the place for those who would spend four years griping about how they'd really wanted to go somewhere else. Hence the willingness of the Molson admissions officer to do some under-the-table deals to make sure that things worked out in their favor.

The whole thing had a definite cloak-and-dagger feel—and no doubt the mob would soon have a piece of the action, if it didn't already. Meanwhile, Anne got on the phone with F&M.

CHAPTER NINETEEN

AFTER RECEIVING CRYPTIC ASSURANCE REGARD-
ing Toby Tucker's scholarship ("Don't quote
me; don't even say you spoke to me," whispered the F&M admissions officer in a con-
spiratorial tone), Anne spent the afternoon
meeting with a parade of students about
their college choices.

First came Aurora Mendelson, a bright but
timid girl who, Anne suggested, should apply to Smith. It had been her experience that
girls who had a hard time opening their
mouths in high school blossomed in an all-
female environment, though sometimes with
the adjunct of a nose ring and a butch hair-

cut. The first lines of Aurora's college essay suggested she might be a good candidate for such a transformation: "There's a famous ad that reads: 'I am woman, hear me roar.' I, Aurora Mendelson, want to go to college to learn to roar."

Next came Chelsea Beemer, a star field hockey player, who was being courted by a number of top schools.

After pondering why Chelsea was coveted above, say, Skyler Landow, Fenimore's resident math genius, Anne had concluded that an action shot of Chelsea in her shockingly short field hockey skirt would look better in college promotional materials than a photo of Skyler working out a formula in a library carrel.

"I have a real problem," said Chelsea, furrowing her blond brow. "Stanford and Dartmouth both really want me, and I really like them both." She might have been referring to two attractive guys who wanted to take her to the prom. "Dartmouth is really pretty, but Stanford is in California and has really nice weather." Chelsea appeared genuinely confused by these competing attributes. Anne observed that "weather" might have the advantage over "pretty" if you played field hockey, which seemed to shed sudden light on the matter for Chelsea, who realized that she had favored Stanford all along.

Next came Cal Minuti, who was an officer in junior ROTC. "I want to go to Yale because it is an excellent school and has an excellent ROTC program," his application essay began. The only problem, as Anne pointed out, was that Yale didn't have an ROTC program.

Cal was followed by Kyra Pearlstein, who wanted to apply early to Bowdoin, but had already prepared her backup applications to Antioch, Bard, Middlebury, F&M, Gettysburg, Skidmore, Hampshire, Bennington, Emory, Wesleyan, Haverford, Carnegie-Mellon, Rice, and the University of Virginia.

"Don't you think you should eliminate a few of your backup schools?" suggested Anne. "The application fees alone are going to mount up."

"I like to be well covered," explained Kyra, "and I'll pay the fees from my bat mitzvah money. I saved it for a rainy day, which I figure this is." There was no arguing with this sort of reasoning.

Kyra's essay was in the fulsome style characteristic of girls who were told, from an early age, that they had a creative flair (often to compensate for their abysmal math skills):

"When I was a baby at my mother's knee," began Kyra's essay, "I did not have goals, aspirations, or dreams. Like a puppy, I rolled and tumbled, knowing no reason or purpose for my actions. However, as I grew, I began to aspire to more. I began to study and question. In time, a dream began to take shape. That dream was to go to Bowdoin (Antioch, Bard, Middlebury, etc.)."

"Very nice," said Anne, who saw no point in trying to change this sort of essay (it would be like editing air).

After Kyra came Albert Odoms, whose application essay began: "A young boy went to the top of a mountain and said: 'Lord, I am seeking an education. Help me to that education, Lord.'"

Albert's top choices were Brandeis and Yeshiva.

"Brandeis and Yeshiva?" asked Anne, mystified. Albert was the son of the Reverend Charles Odoms, pastor of Fenimore's First Baptist Church, a black evangelical congregation.

"My dad wants me to choose a college where God is respected," explained Albert.

"He doesn't care about race or religious affiliation, so long as there's a spiritual component. Brandeis and Yeshiva are very spiritual, and they're both offering me full scholarships."

Anne commended this open-minded approach, but suggested that Brandeis would be the better choice. The predominance of forelocks and black hats at Yeshiva might strain even the most ecumenical spirit.

After Albert came Sophie Kwan, a sophomore, who announced her intention of transferring to Yonkers for the rest of high school: "If I transfer I could be, like, salutatorian. Plus there aren't as many smart Asians in Yonkers, so I'd stand out." Anne told Sophie that these were not good reasons to transfer.

Finally came Lyle Peterson, her last appointment of the day. Lyle was one of those superserious students who keep track of their GPAs the way dieters keep track of their calorie intake—no sooner did a teacher return a quiz than out came his calculator. Most parents wished they had kids who were more scrupulous and focused, but Lyle was an example of why you should be careful of what you wish for.

"I want to apply to a college that will get

me into a top medical school, so I can get into a top internship and residency program, and then into a top fellowship program in cardiothoracic surgery," announced Lyle as soon as he sat down. He extracted a spread sheet from his briefcase (kids like Lyle Peterson never carried backpacks). "I've already compiled the average MCAT scores, the availability of summer internships, and the percentage of premed students who go on to earn seven figure incomes for twenty universities. I've narrowed my top choices down to ten."

Anne was momentarily speechless. Most kids could barely plan beyond the next day, which was why the so-called "long-term senior project" might just as well be named the "night-from-hell senior project." Most everyone wrote it the night before—except kids like Lyle, who started working on it in the ninth grade.

"Don't you think you're jumping the gun a little bit in thinking about medical school and residency programs when you haven't even started college?" asked Anne. "You might discover you don't want to be a doctor."

Lyle looked at her as though she were crazy. "My dad's a cardiothoracic surgeon and I want to be one too," he asserted firmly. "I've been a cardiothoracic surgeon for Halloween ever since the first grade."

"O-K," said Anne slowly, "I guess that means you're really serious about being a cardiothoracic surgeon."

"I am," said Lyle bluntly.

"Then why don't we discuss some quality-of-life factors. Do you think you'd be happier in a small school or a large one? Do you prefer an urban environment or a quieter, more rural setting?"

"That stuff doesn't matter," Lyle pronounced dismissively. "I'll just be in the library and the lab all the time anyway."

"All the time?" asked Anne, dazzled by this image of relentless industry.

"I suppose I'll have to go to a party now and then in order to meet a girl," he conceded. "My dad says it helps your concentration if you're married by the time you go to medical school."

What could she say? Anne found Lyle's humorless tenacity of purpose unnerving, but she could imagine that someday she wouldn't. One spoke of people growing into their nose or their feet; Lyle would doubtless grow into his personality. Which only went to prove that weirdos in high school could one day grow up to become highly respected cardiothoracic surgeons.

As Anne prepared to leave for the day, she glanced down at the blotter on her desk and was jolted to see the name she had traced, without thinking, in the course of the afternoon. It was the sort of thing silly high-school girls did, reflexively writing the names of their crushes in their notebooks as the teacher droned on. Now, here she was, a grown woman, engaging in the same sort of ridiculous behavior. She tore off the sheet of blotter paper and crumpled it in her hand. She would not be haunted, she told herself. She would not succumb to mooning over a man she had not seen in thirteen years, who was engaged to someone else.

CHAPTER TWENTY

As Anne was about to leave the office, Cindy looked up from her murmurings with Gus about whether she should get another piercing in her left ear.

"Oh, by the way, Ms. Ehrlich," said Cindy, "I was just going to ring you. Dr. Flockhart called to say the mom of that new student, Cutler, is coming in tomorrow morning and wants to meet with you and Dr. Flockhart. It'll be at nine A.M. in Dr. Flockhart's office. He said there'd be bagels." Cindy looked over at Gus, who gazed adoringly at her for being able to impart so much information so accurately.

"Thanks," muttered Anne. But instead of hurrying past the main office as she usually did on her way out of the school, she stopped and went in. Gwendolen, the principal's secretary, had left, and Vince was sitting at the front desk, trying to get a handle on the school's tardiness policy. He looked grateful to see her. "I can't get this straight," he said. "Is it three latenesses equals a Saturday detention—or two? And is it an after-school detention if the kid skips homeroom? And do they go to the nurse with the late slip after ten A.M. or to the main office?" The rules in running a high school were labyrinthine, and it sometimes seemed as if no one actually knew them.

After Anne had helped Vince wrestle for a while with the fine points of the policy, she interjected casually: "What time is Pauline Cutler coming in tomorrow?"

"The Cutlers are coming at nine," said Vince.

"Cindy said the mom was coming in."

"The mom *and* the uncle. He called this morning, suggesting that you be in on the meeting—kill two birds with one stone, so to speak."

Anne was silent, wondering if this was

Ben's way of getting her input while not having to meet with her alone.

"We just got the transcripts from the boy's previous schools," continued Vince, taking a file from his desk. "Here you go"—he handed it over. "Not exactly strong in some areas, as you can see."

Glancing at the transcripts, Anne could see that, indeed, Jonathan Cutler had received mostly B's and a few C's in math, and had hardly done better in science, though he had consistent A's in English, history, and philosophy (a course taught at the American high school in Calcutta). "Problematic," said Vince. "We might get him into Bennington or Bard, but I don't know about Columbia."

"We'll see," said Anne, ruminatively. "Perhaps Columbia wouldn't be the best fit."

"But this guy's got his heart set on it. He mentioned it to me again on the phone."

"Yes, but *he's* not going," Anne reminded him.

Vince sighed. "I know, I know. It's what you always say. And I'm not saying that you're wrong. Only we can't all be as high-minded as you."

"I'm not so high-minded," protested Anne.

"You are," insisted Vince, with a mixture of

annoyance and admiration. "You're the Jiminy Cricket of Fenimore, and I'm Pinocchio." He touched his nose—which was actually rather flat, having been broken twice on the football field.

Anne laughed but returned to the point. "Don't you think it's our responsibility to stand up for the kids when the parents start to bully them? I'm not saying I entirely blame the parents, but they lose perspective. The least we can do is help them get it back."

"I'm not disagreeing with you," said Vince in a harried tone. "Only there are other factors to consider. Some of these parents have a lot of clout. You remember what happened to Fliegler when he criticized the new sidewalks in town in his biology class? Didn't get tenure. Are you going to tell me that there wasn't a relationship between Fliegler's not getting tenure and the fact that Tim Iorrio is on the board and has the paving contract for Fenimore Township?"

"Yes, I am," said Anne. "Fliegler pinched Julia Sheffler's behind as she was leaving his bio lab. I think that was rather good cause to deny him tenure."

"Possibly," said Vince, "but still . . ."

"Vince," said Anne, with some fervor,

"you're a fine leader. You've put Fenimore on the map in so many ways: academically, athletically, in terms of the quality of guest speakers"—she added this as a reward for his having agreed to a generous honorarium for a guest poet for Poetry Day (which meant that she could call Peter Jacobson with a formal invitation). "You have an impeccable reputation. You don't have to buckle to anyone!"

"OK, OK, I'll do what I can." Vince was always inspired by Anne's pep talks—until he got another call from an irate parent, who usually argued better (or at least yelled louder) than she did, which put him back to square one. "Just be sure to be there to back me up tomorrow. By the way, do you like sesame or poppy seed bagels?"

"Sesame," said Anne.

Vince made a note for Gwendolen, popped an antacid into his mouth, and waded back into the swamp of Fenimore's tardiness policy.

CHAPTER TWENTY-ONE

BEN WAS STANDING INSIDE THE MAIN OFFICE when she arrived at school the next day. She could see through the glass door of Vince's office that he was leaning forward to take in what Gwendolen was saying, and the posture reminded her of what a good listener he had always been. She had once been the one he listened to most, before she had been exiled—or had exiled herself—from the charmed space of his attention. Now, watching as he listened to Gwendolen, she felt the stab of being on the outside looking in.

She hesitated for a moment before opening the door to the office. When she did, he turned and held her eyes for a moment. She moved toward him and they shook hands, her line of vision meeting his directly as he arranged his body into the slight slouch that she remembered, which brought him closer to her height.

As she gained her bearings, she could see that his sister stood next to him, dressed this time in a bright blue-and-white striped pants suit that gave her the look of a high-end prison guard. If Pauline Cutler did not have the most elegant taste, she did have a zestful sense of color and style. She was smiling broadly, and Anne was struck by the neediness beneath her effusive manner.

"Hello again," said Pauline as she shook Anne's hand. "You're a doll to meet with us like this. I thought we could wait until Jonathan was more settled, but Bennie wouldn't hear of it. He likes to stay on top of things." She patted Ben's arm affectionately. "Of course, he's a genius," she noted proudly. "He was tested when he was a little boy and his IQ was off the chart. Jonathan takes after him. I want them both to join that group, what's it called?— MENSA—where they get together and talk about the things geniuses talk about."

Anne laughed, relieved that Pauline was doing such an excellent job of embarrassing Ben that she didn't have to think about her own embarrassment. "As I recall, Ben was always very bright," she agreed. "And obviously he's turned his intelligence to good use in his business."

"You can say that again!" exclaimed Pauline, pleased to expound on what was obviously a favorite subject. "Everyone knows *Cutler's Guides to Culture.* I don't think I'm telling a secret when I say it's made us rich. Did you know that one of those magazines named Bennie one of the world's one hundred most eligible bachelors? The calls he got! That was before he met Kirsten."

Ben flinched slightly, but Pauline continued on, happily oblivious: "I always thought he was a good catch, but, needless to say, I'm prejudiced, being his sister."

Ben interrupted here: "Pauline, we didn't come here for you to extol my virtues."

"But I like to!" protested Pauline. "I haven't had the best luck with men," she confided to Anne, "so I'm glad Bennie is my brother. Otherwise, I'd think they were all rotten."

"Pauline!" said Ben somewhat sharply. "Why don't you see if Dr. Flockhart has all the papers on Jonathan. Especially the transcript from Copenhagen. Make sure his junior-year grades are there, including the ones from the spring term, when he got the A-plus in English." Pauline dutifully went over to Vince and began chattering, though it didn't seem to be about Jonathan's Copenhagen transcript.

"I'm sorry," said Ben, turning to Anne, though not meeting her eyes. "She's a good sister, but she can get carried away."

"It's nice that she thinks so highly of you," said Anne quietly. "And that you've done so much for her and Jonathan."

"They're my family," he said, as though this was explanation enough. Then, he cleared his throat and looked at her directly. "I saw your house was on the market. We were talking to real estate brokers in the area, and I couldn't help but recognize the listing. That house is a family heirloom, isn't it? Why would you want to sell it?"

"Why do people ever want to sell family heirlooms?" said Anne dryly.

"I see." Ben nodded. She felt him looking at her more closely, perhaps trying to discern signs of poverty. It was ironic that the tables had turned so completely. She had once been the privileged one, with the expensive education and the opportunity to travel. He had had nothing, except his curiosity about life—and the confidence that he would one day gratify that curiosity.

The day after she returned from Italy, she had gone back to the travel agency, trying not to admit how much she was looking forward to seeing him again. Just as she had hoped, he had been sitting behind the desk as if waiting for her.

"Tell me all about your trip," he said. "Every detail. Make it so I can see what you saw." And she had spent the rest of the afternoon telling him everything she could remember—and then, many more afternoons and evenings and mornings after that, telling him everything else.

He couldn't possibly know, she thought, as she stood opposite him now in Vince's office, how much of her he possessed. Even though it had been thirteen years since she had seen him, she had never spoken as frankly, never been so fully herself, with anyone since.

They stood a few seconds without speaking until they were interrupted by Gwendolen, who brought out a tray of bagels and cream cheese and rolled over the coffee urn; then she proceeded to prepare coffees according to their specifications. "Black with lots of sugar," said Ben. But Anne had remembered before he said it—as she remembered so much else about him that she had no business remembering.

Vince and Pauline had now crossed the room to join them. "I was telling your sister that my wife and I love your Cultural Guides," said Vince, shaking Ben's hand vigorously. "We used *London Theater: A Cornucopia* during our trip to England last year. Really helped us out—especially the after-theater snack section."

"Thanks." Ben laughed. "But you should really thank Pauline and Jonathan for that. They did most of the sampling. I was never much of an expert on food, though our travels at least raised my consciousness beyond peanut butter and jelly."

Anne wondered if this was spoken for her benefit. "You come from culinary royalty," he used to say. "You've grown up on those fancy Jewish meals. In my house, we were satisfied with peanut butter and jelly, spaghetti, and an occasional meat loaf." Anne had responded that Jewish meals were not generally associated with royalty but that she saw his point. Winnie cooked with a regal respect for the savory potential of a good brisket or chicken stock. She had the time and, in former days, the help to make the classic Jewish dishes to perfection, and they had not been the least of the attractions for the many illustrious visitors who used to frequent the Mazur home. Ben's sorry knowledge of food had been emblematic of all the advantages she had had that he didn't. Was he trying to say that he now had them too? But his words brought other thoughts to mind— images of meals prepared on the hot plate in his studio apartment in Queens and of peanut butter and jelly sandwiches slapped hastily together—pathetic attempts at nourishment, she called them, that became part of the climate of their desire. She could see the room in her mind's eye, shabby and crammed with books, delightful because it was his. She looked at him quickly, wondering if the image had occurred to him, but his eyes were fixed on Vince. No doubt his words had meant nothing but what they said. If the past lived in his memory, it consisted of scenes that rankled and that he preferred not to dwell on.

"It's great to have your nephew on board for his senior year," Vince continued expansively. "I'm sure he's going be a great addition to the Fenimore team."

"I don't know," worried Pauline. "Jonathan isn't into teams. I couldn't even get him to play soccer in Brazil, and it's practically all they do there. He isn't outgoing like me; he's more into books like Ben. But Bennie was always so good with people."

"Not really," muttered Ben.

"You were," insisted Pauline. "You weren't wild the way I was, but you always had lots of friends. Everyone loved you. But Jonathan doesn't have many friends. Of course, we've moved around a lot. Not that I'm complaining. It was an education, traveling around the world. And Ben's been like a father to Jonathan. Better than a father."

Ben intervened here, obviously concerned that Pauline was about to embark on more embarrassing praise. "We've traveled a good deal," he asserted, "and it's probably taken its toll on the boy."

Gwendolen clucked softly and muttered, "A child needs a settled home," under her breath.

"I think that's true." Ben nodded, catching

the remark. "When I was his age, I was dying to get out of Queens. But there are advantages to staying in one place—even Queens." He half-met Anne's eyes. "We're hoping that college will help him develop more confidence and a greater sense of belonging. I'm planning to stay in this area for a while, and Pauline and I were thinking that Columbia, being in the city and with an excellent curriculum and lively campus life, would be just what was called for—" He stopped, perhaps realizing that he sounded like a college brochure.

Anne picked up the thread. "Jonathan seems like a serious student, at least in some areas," she noted gently. "But given the fact that you've moved around so much, you might consider a smaller college in a less hectic environment."

"His math and science grades aren't the strongest," Vince piped in.

"We think Columbia would help fill in some of his gaps," Ben persisted.

"It might," acknowledged Anne. "But maybe you shouldn't view him as having gaps. Why don't you concentrate on his strengths. There are many colleges that might take advantage of those."

Vince jumped in here: "Bennington, say, or Bard."

"Artsy schools," said Ben with irritation.

"And what's wrong with artsy?"

"I want Jonathan to get a solid education, not fritter away four years playing the zither."

The remark surprised Anne. She would not have thought that Ben Cutler, at least the Ben Cutler she had known, would be so dismissive. But, then, she also knew it was common for people to be less tolerant of interests and ideas that had once defined them, especially if they had been betrayed in some way by their former selves.

They looked at each other a moment and she felt he knew what she was thinking. "I admit that I want Jonathan at Columbia," he said in a milder tone, "but I also realize he might not get in and that he might be happy—happier even—elsewhere. He's a sensitive boy—quiet, inclined to isolate himself, which isn't surprising, given that he's lived in places where he didn't speak the language. It would be hard on any kid, and he's never complained outright, which I see as a sign of his character. He also has an intellectual intensity and a capacity for concentration that's rare, I think, in someone his age."

"He sounds like an unusual boy." Anne was struck by the thoroughness of Ben's analysis and by the affection and concern reflected in it.

"I want Jonathan to have all the advantages I'm in a position to give him," he continued soberly. "I've watched him grow up, and though I'm not his father, Pauline knows I love him like one and want only the best for him."

"Ben's been more than a father to Jonathan," Pauline repeated, looking gratefully at her brother.

"Well, we'll see," said Vince, who had limited patience for the psychodramas of Westchester families, a fact that probably saved him from being completely suffocated by them. "Let's start by taking a look at the transcripts and making sure everything's in order. These European schools can be sloppy, so we want to double-check." With this high-handed pronouncement (the irony of which did not escape Anne, given Fenimore's GPA fiasco several years ago), Vince ushered Ben and Pauline into his private sanctum, leaving Anne in the outer office with Gwendolen.

"Now, there's a good man," Gwendolen

asserted knowingly, after Ben had left the room. "Not many men would foot the bill for a nephew, no less take that kind of interest. You don't see many like that, I can tell you. And he has nice eyes."

CHAPTER TWENTY-TWO

ART WILEY WAS WAITING FOR ANNE WHEN SHE returned to her office after her meeting with the Cutlers. Art was the director, CEO, and sole instructor of the Wiley Way, an SAT review service. Fall was prime SAT review season, when underclassmen were limbering up to take the tests for the first time, and when upperclassmen still clung to the dream of lifting their scores by an additional 150 points.

SAT test-taking had spawned an enormous supporting industry in Westchester County. There were shelves of study guides (options in bookstores had proliferated in the manner of panty hose in drugstores), legions of tutors (mostly out-of-work Ph.D.s), and enrichment courses (summer programs for "gifted and talented youth," not to mention more expensive sojourns at the London School of Economics and the Sorbonne). Stanley Kaplan and the Princeton Review had multiple franchises in the area, and everywhere you looked there was a boutique course "tailored to the special needs of your special child." In Art Wiley's case, "boutique" might not seem like the right word for the raucous sessions held in the basement of his ramshackle split-level in New Rochelle—but many members of the Westchester community swore by them, as evidenced by the Mercedes and Lexuses lined up in front of his house every evening.

Art was a large unkempt man in baggy jeans and a misbuttoned shirt. He slouched into Anne's office this morning with a stack of flyers for the Wiley Way.

"As lovely as ever," said Art, kissing Anne's hand. It was his habit to pay elaborate court to her, comfortable in the knowledge that his affection would remain unreciprocated. Art Wiley was the kind of guy who would never seriously contemplate a relationship with anyone, since it might require him to get up before noon and take a bath more than once a week.

"Thank you, you're looking well yourself, Art," said Anne, trying for the flip tone she generally took with him, though her voice sounded strained to her own ears—she was still recovering from her encounter with Ben Cutler. "What's new in SAT prep at the Wiley Way?" she asked quickly.

"Well, I've got a new course in the pipeline on crafting the SAT essay," Art announced proudly, pointing a rather dirty fingernail at an item on the Wiley Way flyer. "That was a real curve ball they threw us when they added the writing section. No matter how much I drilled the kids in the five-paragraph essay, most of them just sat and stared at the paper—that deer in the headlights sort of thing. Let's face it, these kids don't think in the narrow, plodding way that the guys who make up these tests have in mind. Ask them to come up with something creative—say, cementing a golf cart in the middle of the school courtyard or removing the doors from the faculty bathroom stalls in the middle of the night—and they can manage it, no problem, even if it involves high-level calculations that might challenge a seasoned engineer. But a twenty-five-minute extemporaneous essay on some topic of no interest whatsoever? Forget about it. So I was stumped there for a while. But I'm glad to say I've finally figured the thing out. With my method, even the dyslexics and the serious cases of ADD can score above the eightieth percentile on the essay."

"Really?" said Anne. She never ceased to be intrigued by Art's abilities to beat the test. "What's your secret?"

"The key," said Art, "is in the prep. You have them decide what they're going to write about ahead of time. Maybe even draft the essay and memorize it."

"But how can they do that? They don't know the question," protested Anne.

"True." Art nodded. "But that doesn't matter. You teach them to make the essay answer the question. Simple rhetorical technique: goes back to the Disputatio of Aquinas. Read the language theorists— Chomsky, Peirce, Wittgenstein. Watch celebrity interviews, political debates. It's tried and true."

"Can you give me an example?" prompted Anne.

"Sure. Let's say the kid prepares an essay: 'Why I Love My Dog.' We review the general run of possible questions: meaning of life, gender roles, democratic process—all the big topics—and teach them to transition 'Why I Love My Dog' into the response. Ideally, of course, you'd want something more complex than 'Why I Love My Dog,' but some of these kids can't do much better than that, so you work with what they have. With my method, even the ones that don't have a dog and have to go with why they love video games can do respectably on the sample. The rest of the time we spend on grammar and sentence structure. That's my secret ammo. Most of these kids were so busy 'finding their voice' with those freewriting exercises in grade school they never learned how to use a comma—they just sort of sprinkle the thing around like some sort of all-purpose seasoning. Let me tell you—correct use of the comma goes a long way with some of these test graders."

Anne nodded. Art had none of the slimy polish of Curtis Fink, but he did hold a B.A. in philosophy from Swarthmore, a Ph.D. in physics from MIT, and had worked for a short, unhappy period for the defense department, surefire credentials for deconstructing the SATs. He often took the test as many as six times a year and spent hundreds of hours tabulating results, which he kept in rows of loose-leaf binders above his bed.

The courses themselves were conducted by Art in the manner of a progressive nursery school. Fifteen or twenty kids would sit in lawn chairs in his basement, eating Cheez-Its and drinking Dr. Brown's celery tonic (pretty much what Art Wiley subsisted on), while he expounded on the major components of SAT-taking, which he divided into five principal categories:

1. Scientific guessing.

"To guess or not to guess, that is the question!" Art would intone, before proceeding to teach an elaborate series of probability formulas. In some cases, the calculations regarding when to guess were more difficult than the problems on the test, so that students came away from his courses knowing more math than they had learned in four years of high school.

2. Linguistic tonality.

"Listen for the voice of the test," Art would advise, as if teaching a high-level course in poetics. "Anything that sounds too right is probably wrong and anything that sounds too wrong is probably wrong too. Keep away from any answer that has that smug teacher's tone—they're trying to trip you up. And don't ever choose an answer that reads 'a kind of liqueur.' The underpaid social studies teachers who like to pretend they own a country estate and a smoking jacket like to throw that one in."

3. Motifs and patterns.

"All life," Art opened this section of his course by saying, "is built on pattern. The SATs are no exception. Remember, the guys that write these tests usually only know one or two things well. Maybe it's predatory animals. Maybe it's precipitation. Maybe it's the life cycle of the fruit fly. Whatever it is, once you get hold of the motif, hang on and you'll start to see the pattern. It's like a game of concentration. Any kindergartner can do it."

4. Practice.

"At the heart of good test-taking," lectured Art, "is practice. No one likes to practice; it's boring. But with the SATs, remember: the more bored you are, the better you'll do. You want to take the test over and over again. In time, you begin to think like the test. Fortunately, I've only known a few cases where this thinking persists beyond high school, and those people go into politics." Art's biggest disappointment with regard to practice was when the SATs eliminated score choice. "Used to be I'd send these kids in to take the SAT IIs six, seven times if their folks could afford it. There's nothing like the adrenaline rush of sitting in a big overcrowded classroom with some kid farting in front of you and some Nazi in charge of watching the clock. Eventually, no matter how lamebrained you are, you get the hang of it. Now, all the scores show up on the transcripts, so you can't take the test more than three times, max. It's a shame. I try to simulate the test situation for their practice tests—but let's face it, there's only so much I can do."

5. Keep the five SAT commandments.

"If you don't do anything else, you can get a 600 on a section if you keep my commandments," Art said, gesturing to a list in Gothic font posted over the Ping-Pong table in his basement. Art often closed his sessions by expounding a bit on each commandment:

• **Thou shalt not eat junk food the night before the test.**

"Who can do quadratic equations with gas?"

• **Thou shalt not clutter thy brain.**

"The night before the test, watch TV, listen to really bad pop music, play Candy Land with your little brother. Don't under any circumstances read a book or engage in substantive conversation. The key to SAT-taking is not to think; the people who write these tests don't and you want to keep on their level."

• **Thou shalt not forget Kleenex.**

"You'll never get through those long, boring reading samples with a runny nose."

• **Thou shalt not let thy eyes wander.**

"Seeing that hot girl in the cutoffs will make you forget all about the Constitutional Convention. Plus you never know when one of those mean gym teacher types who's monitoring the test will get bored and want to accuse someone of cheating. Don't let it be you."

• **Thou shalt not read the questions too closely.**

"The key to SAT-taking is to skim. If you start to concentrate on what the questions really mean, you'll realize how stupid they are and never get anywhere."

Since Art's teaching of the SATs was connected to a deep-seated contempt for their content, Anne sometimes wondered if it was advisable for kids to take his courses. But in the end, she concluded that his approach was not so much against the system as in the interests of the students. Indeed, his sympathy for the downtrodden and scruffier element of that population gave him a special status as the Robin Hood of SAT review, especially since he was willing to waive the fee if a student couldn't afford it. As he explained to Anne, "SAT review isn't just a job, it's a calling. Everyone should have the chance to work the system, not just the rich and powerful. My dream is to have every kid who slept through half of high school ace the test." Even if Anne did not find this the most laudable goal, she had to admit that Art was one hell of a good teacher.

"I have about a half dozen kids I'll be steering your way this term," said Anne, after Art had given her the flyers and the spiel about "Why I Love My Dog." "Two of them are financially strapped."

"Don't worry about it." Art waved a hand.

"You're a good man, Art."

"No. I'm just in love. Do I have a chance?"

"I'm afraid not."

"I guess your heart's already taken. Just my luck."

Anne looked away, her eyes suddenly filling with tears, and Art, who was smart enough to know he'd hit a nerve and kind enough to be sorry about it, said gruffly, "Don't worry, it'll work out." He hesitated, considered saying more, and decided against it. ("If you really haven't got a clue about an answer, leave it blank" was his advice to his students.) He stood up and arranged the pile of Wiley Way flyers carefully on the desk. "Just tell those kids to give me a call," he said gently. "I'll fit them in sometime next week."

CHAPTER TWENTY-THREE

ANNE SAT FOR A MOMENT AT HER DESK, WONDER-
ing what had gotten into her. Someone says
a few words about the state of her heart and
she starts "boo-hooing," as Winnie might
say. "Pull yourself together," she scolded herself, "you're not sixteen." She wiped her eyes
and put on some lipstick. Then, remembering that an "Athletic Scholarship Information
Session" was about to begin in the auditorium, she got up and left the office.

If one segment of the Fenimore student
body was focused on SAT prep, another was
focused on athletic prep. The idea—increasingly prevalent as competition for col-

lege admission had heated up in recent years—was that muscles offered an alternative to brains in getting into college.

This morning's talk was by one Ted Wackowski, a former coaching pal of Vince's. Ted had founded Blitz Athletic Recruiting, a consulting firm aimed at what he liked to call "the non-academic athlete"—more commonly known as the dumb jock.

The audience consisted of a group of befuddled parents who were hoping to turn their kids' ability to throw balls or wave around sticks to some sort of advantage. Over the years they had been told that these athletic activities were invaluable: that they would build character, hone leadership skills, and develop judgment. If pressed, however, they would have admitted that what their kids had mostly learned was how to take Tylenol without water and wrap an Ace bandage at record speed. Meanwhile, their homework had been forced to take a back seat, squeezed into the small window after the knee had been iced and the uniform put in the dryer. As a result, many of these kids needed all the help they could get, and their parents were eager to hear more from Blitz Athletic Recruiting.

Ted opened his PowerPoint presentation with a colorful graphic of a youth throwing a ball through a hole in a mortar board, over which was superimposed the slogan, "Blitz Your Way to College."

"Now, if your guy is NFL or NBA material, then he doesn't need me," Ted clarified at the outset. "And if he's got good grades and scores, he doesn't need me either. I'm here for all the other guys—and gals too (with Title 9, there's a goldmine in this for the ladies). Your kids want to go to college because, hey, they don't want to spend their lives working in McDonald's, and, more important, because they want to play college ball. I can make it so they can do that without costing you, Mom and Dad, an arm and a leg."

The parents nodded hopefully—this was precisely what they were after: not paying an arm and leg to send their kids off to play college ball.

"What we at Blitz do is simple," continued Ted. "First, we collect the names of all those schools you never heard of that can't afford to scout for players." Ted clicked on the PowerPoint presentation so that the screen read: *Compile list of schools no one heard of.*

"Then," continued Ted, "we get those lesser-known schools interested in your kid." Ted went on to the next PowerPoint: *Get lesser-known schools interested in kid.* "We do that," explained Ted, "through personalized, individualized letters." Again, he clicked: *Write personalized, individualized letters for kid's signature.* "We write these personalized, individualized letters so that the coach thinks your kid wrote them," Ted spelled out. "This piques the interest of the coach." He clicked to the final PowerPoint screen: *Peaks interest of coach.*

"This is terrible," Anne whispered to Vince, who was standing with her in the back of the auditorium. "He's suggesting something blatantly dishonest. And he can't spell."

"For God's sake, Anne, why can't you give the jocks a break for a change," responded Vince with surprising vehemence. "I don't think Ted's doing anything the Ivy packagers don't do, only he's being more simple and direct about it. Besides, he's a nice guy and just trying to make a living."

Anne thought Vince had a point and kept her mouth shut for the rest of the presentation.

CHAPTER TWENTY-FOUR

AFTER LEAVING THE BLITZ RECRUITING SESSION, where a gaggle of parents had crowded around Ted, trying to ascertain whether a modest talent for soccer or basketball might indeed qualify their son or daughter for a scholarship to a school no one had ever heard of, Anne escaped to the faculty cafeteria where she found Marcy staring at her Caesar salad.

"I can see about ten kids actually taking advantage of Blitz Athletic Recruiting and getting themselves a scholarship somewhere," Anne launched forth as she sat down. "Then, I figure we have about ten more elite athletes likely to get commitments from the better schools over the next two weeks. That'll leave a mere 130 to thrash things out based on brain power alone. Some of these won't pose a problem. They'll simply choose schools for the predictable reasons: location—skiers to Vermont or Colorado and surfers to California; tradition—wherever Mom and Dad went, even if it's Southwest Boondocks State; then, there are the financially savvy who will opt for the best financial aid package, even if it means going to a Bible college in Wyoming. That leaves maybe seventy-five who will drive me nuts for the next few months looking for a designer school—which is to say, the right decal for their car."

Anne thought this was a pretty good riff, but Marcy wasn't listening. She wasn't even picking the croutons out of her salad. Something was definitely bothering her.

"A guy named Curtis Fink called me yesterday," she finally said glumly. "He asked if I was up for writing a reference letter for Trevor Hopgood."

"Really?" Anne looked surprised. "I didn't realize Trevor did well in history."

"He didn't," said Marcy. "I told this guy that

Trevor got a B-minus in my American history course last year and he's not doing much better in Euro history now. So I wouldn't be in a position to write a very strong letter."

"And he said?"

"He said I should think again. He could give me some points about how Trevor marches to the beat of a different drummer or something like that."

"I see," said Anne, remembering that Curtis Fink had mentioned such a sound bite to her. "And you said?"

"I said I didn't feel comfortable saying that," said Marcy. "I haven't really seen Trevor marching anywhere. He just sort of sits in class and mumbles sometimes." She paused. "And then this Fink person said that maybe I should think again—that I might want to help the Hopgoods out—given my problem."

"Your problem?"

"Yes," said Marcy, sighing. "He seemed to know all about my food issues. That I spaz out if anyone eats anything, say a cookie, in my class." (Fink, who did extensive research to "verify" potential references, had obviously gotten wind of Marcy's unresolved anorexia and tried to use it to some sort of advantage.)

"He said that!" exclaimed Anne. "The nerve of that—Fink!"

"Well, I *do* tend to spaz out when someone eats a cookie," said Marcy sadly.

"And if you do, what business is it of his? How dare he try to blackmail you!" When, Anne wondered, had blackmail become such a pervasive tactic in the admissions process?

"So you think he's going to tell the school board that I spaz out over a cookie?" asked Marcy despondently.

"If he does, we'll report him!" asserted Anne.

"To whom?"

"I don't know—the school board. Or we'll sue the pants off him. Very tight ones, I should add. But you're being silly. What do you care what Curtis Fink says? You have tenure; the kids like you; and you have a record for high AP scores, which speaks volumes to the parents. So you have a problem with food. Half of Westchester has a problem with food."

"That's true," acknowledged Marcy, "*Self* magazine says nine out of ten women have a problem with body image, though some of them want breast implants. That's never been my issue."

"Thank God for that," said Anne, pleased to see Marcy returning to her old self.

"I probably could listen a little better to Trevor Hopgood," acknowledged Marcy. "I think I may have dismissed him too quickly. He does try to participate, only he mumbles."

"Well, tell him to speak up," advised Anne. "But ignore Curtis Fink. If you were single, he'd probably hit on you. That's what he tried with me."

"Really?" said Marcy, perking up. "Was he cute?"

"Marcy!" exclaimed Anne. "I can't believe you'd want me to go out with a blackmailer like Curtis Fink. Besides, I already have some romantic prospects." She knew this was a surefire way to get her friend's attention.

"Really? Why didn't you tell me? I want to hear every detail!" Marcy grew animated and began to pick excitedly at her salad. "Did you say 'prospects'—are you speaking in the plural? Where did you find them? Did you try J-Date, like I suggested? Or did you meet them in the supermarket? I read in *O* that the supermarket is a good place—it's unthreatening, and there's the conversation piece of the food. You can ask, say, what kind of mustard he recommends, or whether he's ever tried the extra-lite virgin olive oil."

Marcy had forgotten Curtis Fink and even Anne's romantic life, as she fell into a reverie about what you could find in the aisles of the supermarket.

CHAPTER TWENTY-FIVE

WHEN ANNE RETURNED FROM LUNCH, SHE found Jodi Fields' mother, Mandy, in the guidance waiting room, deep in conversation with Cindy. Cindy had admired Mrs. Fields' Louis Vuitton backpack and had thereby opened up a cornucopia of topics relating to designer goods and where they could be purchased at so-called discount (though still exorbitant) prices. Along with the Louis Vuitton backpack, Mandy Fields was outfitted in a pink cashmere jogging suit, a pair of pink-and-gold flip-flops, and a matching diamond necklace and bracelet—

routine casual wear in certain parts of Westchester County.

After Mrs. Fields had jotted down the addresses of several designer discount outlets for Cindy, she followed Anne into her office and perched excitedly on the edge of the chair: "Guess what?" she announced, "Jodi has ADD!"

"Excuse me?" said Anne.

"ADD! You know. Attention Deficit Disorder."

Anne said she knew what ADD was.

"Well, Jodi has it!" exclaimed Mrs. Fields.

"Are you sure?" Anne asked doubtfully. Jodi Fields did not seem like someone with ADD. She seemed like an average underachieving student, for whom studying fell somewhere between depilating leg hair and putting on makeup.

"Oh yes," Mrs. Fields assured her. "She definitely does. We just had her tested."

"But why did you wait till the fall of her senior year to have her tested?"

"We were hoping she'd outgrow it. She's such a fun-loving girl, we didn't want to bother her."

"But didn't the ADD bother her?"

"Oh no, it was no bother at all," said Mrs. Fields, as though the disability were a guest that had behaved well. "If it weren't for Jodi's grades and test scores, we would never have known."

Anne would have liked to explain the difference between ADD and old-fashioned sloth, but she feared that Mrs. Fields would not follow such an explanation. It was possible that Mrs. Fields was the one with ADD. Still, her response was understandable. The diagnosis carried well-known advantages, and Mandy Fields was simply doing what she thought was best for her daughter.

Anne recalled the Corcoran case, the sine qua non of what a Westchester family was capable of in working the system on behalf of its progeny. Several years ago, Faith Corcoran, daughter of a wealthy and influential local businessman, had received an entire phalanx of disability diagnoses late in her sophomore year that had given her access to special tutors, extra SAT time, and exemption from gym (a non-honors course that would have lowered her GPA). As a result, she had graduated first in her class, forcing the class's genuine genius, Melinda Wong, into the salutatory position. During graduation, a near riot had developed, in which Faith, in the middle of her valedictory address, had been pelted with eggs hidden under the caps of the graduating seniors. The result had been humiliating and messy, with the Corcorans suing the school for pain and suffering to the tune of two and a half million dollars. Fury over the suit (with its likely effect on property taxes) had sent a posse of parents to the Corcoran home to throw eggs at it too, causing the family to sue the township for an additional $3.5 million. Princeton University, where Faith had been admitted, apprised of the situation by an outraged Fenimore citizen, had revisited her application and discovered that her essay on the plight of itinerant tobacco farmers in California had been lifted wholesale from a back issue of *Progressive Labor*. The admission had been rescinded and the Corcorans' suit against the school settled out of court for a lesser sum that left nothing to speak of for the Corcorans once the lawyers had been paid, but still raised taxes in the district by 2 percent. The Corcorans, fearing for their lives, had decamped the town and were rumored to be living in Tuscany, where Faith was enrolled at the University of Siena.

But though the Corcoran case was frequently invoked by area citizens as a sorry tale (especially since Mrs. Corcoran was rumored to find Tuscany boring and to miss the malls of Westchester County), many felt that the Corcorans had erred less in kind than in degree. No one argued with working the system in moderation. But the Corcorans had overreached. They should have been satisfied with one or two disability diagnoses and a salutatory spot, instead of insisting on the whole shebang. The lesson, in short, was that one should bilk the system more discreetly, which meant that cases less dramatic than the Corcorans' cropped up all the time. That was why Mandy Fields was sitting in Anne's office right now.

"As I said, it's rather late in Jodi's high-school career for an ADD diagnosis," Anne explained patiently.

Mrs. Fields eyes opened wide. "Will that count against her?"

"Well, it's unlikely that our child study team will approve the diagnosis at such a late date, which means she wouldn't get extra time on the SATs."

"But Jodi needs extra time," protested Mrs. Fields. "You should see how long it takes her to pick out an outfit in the morning. She has to try on fifteen tops until she's satisfied. All of them are left inside out on the floor for Rosalee to pick up. And she doesn't even put her underwear in the hamper. I tell her it's disrespectful to leave dirty panties lying around for the maid to pick up, but she just can't seem to do it."

"Mrs. Fields," said Anne, "this really doesn't have bearing on Jodi's diagnosis."

"I thought that it reflected her difficulty getting things done and keeping on task," said Mrs. Fields. "I haven't even told you about the makeup and the shoes. There must be ten pairs of shoes that she tries on before she chooses one that I usually don't like. It's a wonder she gets herself out of the house at all."

"She could lay her outfit out the night before," suggested Anne, finding that she had somehow been drawn into this bizarre discussion of Jodi's wardrobe issues.

Jodi's mother nodded. "You think I don't suggest that? But she ends up laying out five outfits, saying you never know the weather or if something will make your legs look fat."

"And you believe this problem getting dressed is connected to her ADD?"

"Absolutely. She's always been a dawdler."

"Dawdling and ADD are not one and the same," noted Anne, "though they both have *d*'s in them," she couldn't resist adding.

Mrs. Fields looked at her blankly. "Are you saying she doesn't have ADD?"

"I'm saying that the diagnosis looks suspicious coming at this time late in her high-school career. And noting it on her college application might raise a red flag."

"Are you saying ADD won't help her?" asked Mrs. Fields in a more incredulous tone.

Anne shook her head wearily. She wanted to say that she thought Jodi was spoiled, lazy, and possibly dumb (although with a highly developed fashion sense inherited from her mother) but restrained herself.

"Why not think the diagnosis over and consult with your husband?" suggested Anne.

Mrs. Fields waved her hand; apparently, this creature labored in the coal mines of Wall Street and was rarely at home.

"Or talk to your clinical social worker," Anne amended. "The diagnosis, if it lacks proper backup, might give colleges the wrong impression—they might think that Jodi was taking advantage of the system."

"I thought that was the point," said Mrs. Fields, "to take advantage of the system if you can."

"No," said Anne slowly, "that's not the point. And it certainly won't help if the system sees it's being taken advantage of."

Even Mrs. Fields seemed to grasp this point.

"So talk it over with your social worker. Maybe she can help you decide whether it's better to present Jodi as a fun-loving girl with a large and varied wardrobe or a victim of ADD who can't dress herself in the morning. I leave the final decision to you."

CHAPTER TWENTY-SIX

"HELLO, PETER, THIS IS ANNE EHRLICH. WE met—"

"You don't have to say where we met," interrupted Peter. "You're the beautiful, sad guidance counselor."

Anne was momentarily taken aback. That he found her beautiful was flattering. But sad? She had always thought of herself as a rather cheerful person—all things considered.

"I wanted to call you," Peter continued, "but I didn't have your number and I didn't know anyone at that party. I know practically no one. I spend most of my time in bed or at my desk, trying to write. Lately, I've had some bad writer's block." He said this as though he were talking about a case of athlete's foot or indigestion.

"I'm sorry," said Anne.

"Don't be. It's not your fault. Though I did have a dream about you."

"You did?"

"Yes, I was consoling you for your loss."

"But you're the one who had the loss."

"I know; it was strange. Even in the dream I remember thinking: 'I'm the one who had the loss.' But there was no arguing with the dream. And I suppose when I met you I sensed you'd lost someone, at some time, which was part of what drew me to you."

"Well," said Anne, feeling that the conversation was making her uneasy, "I'm calling about Poetry Day at Fenimore High School. If you remember me, you'll also remember your promise. You volunteered to take part in our attempt at high-school literary uplift. We hold the event during the last week of October, which lets us coordinate with the Edgar Allan Poe unit and have the kids dress up as their favorite poets in the spirit of Halloween."

"How charming," said Peter doubtfully.

"Actually, it is. There's something refreshing about seeing high-school kids trying to figure out whether the shy girl in the back is Emily Dickinson or Elizabeth Barrett Browning. We always have our share of boys in tights as Shakespeare, and of course an assortment of Edgar Allan Poes, with capes and stuffed birds. And we have the more original efforts too. Last year, a kid came as T. S. Eliot, in black-rimmed glasses with his hair parted down the middle. And there was an Allen Ginsberg with beads and a hashish pipe. A few years ago, we had an excellent Byron: he wore a smoking jacket, walked with a limp, and strolled through the halls holding his sister's hand."

"Sounds neat," said Peter without much enthusiasm. "Unfortunately, they won't know me."

"But they will, once they read your poetry. They'll be hailing you as the next Shelley. We may even have a few who want to dress up as you."

"They can hold a box of tissues and a bottle of Prozac."

"Oh dear," said Anne. "But if that's how you're feeling, I promise we'll cheer you up. I can begin by offering you a five-hundred-dollar honorarium, pried from the rapacious grasp of my principal. You see, he was impressed—not, I'm afraid, by your poetry—he's too busy to read—but by the Pitzer Prize. He thinks we can publicize it in our *Newsforum.*"

"That's very kind," said Peter laconically. "But you don't have to pay me anything."

"But that wouldn't be right," Anne objected.

"Why not?"

"It would set a bad precedent."

"You mean other Pitzer Prize winners might want to come for nothing?"

Anne laughed but hesitated before responding. "It would look too much as though you were doing me a personal favor."

"And if I am? But if you'd feel better about it, I'll accept the money and donate it back to your school's arts program. Not that five hundred dollars would make much difference, but it would look good in your *Newsforum.*"

"It would," agreed Anne. "I accept your donation."

"Thank you." Peter sighed, as though the conversation had worn him out. "And now that we've settled that, how about going with me to the exhibit of nineteenth-century mortuary sculpture at the Met this Sunday? It's only there till the end of the month."

Anne paused, overtaken suddenly by a

wave of memory. She and Ben used to go to the Met on Sunday mornings when the place was relatively deserted. On one outing, perhaps three months after they met, they had stood for almost half an hour in front of a portrait by Titian.

"He looks like you," Anne said.

"Not at all," said Ben. "He's haughty and proud."

"It's just his posture. He's really very nice. You see there around the eyes; they're kind, like yours." She had pointed to the portrait and then turned to touch Ben's eyes gently.

That's when he grabbed her hand and pulled her toward him: "Do you know what?" he said. "I love you."

"Are you there?" said Peter.

"Yes," said Anne, pushing away the memory. "I'd love to go with you to the Met on Sunday. I'm just dying to see some good mortuary sculpture."

CHAPTER TWENTY-SEVEN

FOR THE OCCASION OF HIS SIXTIETH BIRTHDAY, Elihu Ehrlich had reserved a large table in the dining room of the Princeton Club in New York City. The club was one of Elihu's favored hangouts, possibly because it was as vain as he was. The rooms were festooned everywhere with the school's colors; there were banners and shields, emblazoned with the school insignia, and statues and portraits of the school's founders and famous alumni. Yet it would be wrong to single Princeton out in this. All colleges, even the more lackluster ones, were given to lavish self-promotion, which extended to a wide array of customized merchandise: T-shirts and pens, ties and mugs, bed linen and even toilet paper.

Anne often thought that colleges performed a dual function in American life. On the one hand, they were sites of intellectual enlightenment, bastions of important research and original thought. On the other, they were the breeding ground for a highly conventionalized identity, fostered by a rah-rah spirit and a profusion of regalia and commodity items. If her father was any indication, one could keep these two functions entirely distinct. Elihu Ehrlich had majored in economics at Princeton, but his grasp of this subject was extremely weak. By the same token, the school had also taught him to indulge expensive tastes, a lesson he had learned extremely well and that had helped to bankrupt the family. Indeed, Anne sometimes thought that she might be justified in sending the bills in her father's desk drawer to the Princeton alumni office.

Tonight, Elihu sat in state at the head of the table under a large orange and black banner. Allegra was to his right and Carlotta to his left. Why Carlotta was there at all puzzled Anne. She was not a relative or even a particular friend of the family, having only recently begun work on *The Widening Gyre*. She had been hired based on her ability to flatter Allegra and her alleged affiliation with the famed Iowa Writers' Workshop (in reality, this had consisted of her sharing the bed of one of the "writers in residence," making her a "girlfriend in residence," so to speak).

Opposite Carlotta and next to Allegra sat their cousin Rachel Kramer, who looked tired. She was holding down a waitressing job as she continued to audition for soap operas and commercials. Allegra's boyfriend, Zack, was absent. Presumably, he was stuck with a deadline for his piece trashing Peter Jacobson in favor of the Bosnian poet living in the Mamaroneck train station. But Anne suspected that Allegra had dumped him. Her sister liked to discard her boyfriends suddenly, as if in a fit of creative whimsy, though these decisions were usually planned, like the dramatic readings at her parties, to appear spontaneous.

Anne arrived last, having traveled in from Westchester, where she had kept her grandmother company over an early dinner. She now took her place next to Rachel at the end of the table. As she sat down, she could hear her father loudly summoning "the somme-lier" to bring them wine. The sommelier was actually a harried-looking waiter.

"What do you suggest, monsieur?" said Elihu, looking at the waiter without expecting an answer, which was fortunate. "I think we will start with a few bottles of this lovely Chardonnay. How is your fish this evening, monsieur?"

"It's good," said the waiter.

"I will have the sole, then," said Elihu. "I want it light on the butter sauce, Pierre." The waiter's actual name was Pedro. "As you know, I watch my waistline. The fish is quite well prepared here," he announced to the group seated around him, "though not on a par with La Chanterelle. Now, *there* was a restaurant that knew fish."

He was unable to expound on La Chanterelle's knowledge of fish, since no one was listening. Carlotta was busy adjusting her bustier, and Allegra was trying to convince Rachel to audition for a Pinter play in some obscure hole-in-the-wall theater downtown.

"I don't understand what it's about, so I couldn't try out for it," said Rachel.

"You don't have to understand it," said Allegra with irritation. "You just have to read the lines. The director will tell you what to do."

"But it's such a small part," protested Rachel, "and it doesn't look like it would be any fun."

"Fun?" exclaimed Allegra in an incredulous tone. "What does fun have to do with it? If you're looking for fun, you might as well join the circus."

"I'm not saying I'm *just* looking for fun," persisted Rachel, "but if it's no fun, I don't think I'd want to do it. I mean, I might as well do something that's less, like, hard to break into—like teaching." Rachel, to her credit, glanced over at Anne at this. "No offense," she said. "I'd actually like to be a kindergarten teacher. I'm just saying that acting is, like, my dream, and I wouldn't want to do it unless it gave me some, like, satisfaction."

"Pinter is possibly the greatest living playwright," pronounced Allegra, on whom this logic was lost. "Are you saying that it wouldn't give you satisfaction to perform in the work of a living legend?"

"I don't know," said Rachel with some confusion. "I mean, even if he were a dead legend, I don't think it would help me like him more."

"Taste requires cultivation," interjected Elihu, who, as was typical of him, had been half-listening to the conversation while gazing around the table and sniffing the cork of the wine that the "sommelier" had brought. "One isn't born with the taste for a fine wine"—he held up his glass—"one develops it through attention and practice."

"But I don't want to develop a taste for the kind of play you're talking about," said Rachel, holding stubbornly to her line of thought. "It's boring."

"Ennui. The scourge of youth," intoned Elihu.

"Henri? I probably wouldn't like his play either," declared Rachel. Anne refused to catch her father or sister's eye and, instead, proceeded to ask her cousin when her sinus commercial was going to air.

"They decided not to use it," said Rachel sadly. "They said my nose looked too red."

"But wasn't your nose supposed to be red?" asked Anne. "After all, it was a sinus commercial."

Rachel sighed. "I know, but they said it was red in the wrong way. They thought I looked like I'd been drinking, not like I had hay fever. It wasn't my nose's fault; it was the makeup artist. But it was still a bummer." She sighed again and Anne noted that Rachel, far from looking red, looked extremely pale. She was obviously being worn down in pursuit of her life's dream.

At this juncture, Elihu, who had been fingering his wineglass and looking around the table in vague anticipation, interrupted Allegra's conversation to whisper: "Don't you think we should have a toast?" He would not ask Allegra to give the toast, since no one ever presumed to ask Allegra to do anything, but he obviously felt she could get someone else to give it.

Allegra shrugged and looked lazily around the table. Anne wished she could leave the room. It would be just like her sister to say: "Anne, why don't you give Dad a toast?"—and Anne knew she would never have the nerve to start a fight by answering, "Why don't you?"

Fortunately, before Allegra could say anything, there was a bustle of activity at the front of the table as Carlotta stood up, adjusting her bustier again and smoothing down her micro-miniskirt. She raised her glass.

"Tonight, we are celebrating the birthday

of a very special man," she began, looking down at Elihu tenderly, who looked up at her—or rather, at her ample décolletage. "In an age of vulgarity, Elihu Ehrlich is an emblem of elegance, refinement, and taste."

"Hear, hear," said Elihu on his own behalf.

"This is a man who understands good food, good wine, and good company," Carlotta continued. "He knows how to wear his clothes, choose his cigars, and treat his women. He is, quite simply, a gentleman. And it is a pleasure—nay, an honor—to celebrate his birthday with him tonight."

After Carlotta sat down, Elihu, raising his hand in mock modesty, rose, as if under duress (though no one seemed the least interested), and held up his glass. "How do I begin to survey the span of so many years?" he asked, and looked around, as if waiting for an answer. When none came, he continued: "Not easily, I assure you. Others have experienced joys and sorrows, but I believe I can boast a greater share of life's pleasures and vicissitudes." (Rachel furrowed her brow at "vicissitudes.")

"I find myself now in the bosom of loved ones, feeling both the whisper of my mortality and the call of life still to come. What can

I say? The outpouring of affection here leaves me speechless."

Anne cringed in the face of her father's inflated verbiage. She was back in the realm of the college admissions essay where there was a similar tendency to sever words from any reality to which they might conceivably correspond. Her hope was that the "sommelier" would soon bring out the birthday cake, and she would be able to make a quiet escape and go home to bed.

CHAPTER TWENTY-EIGHT

THE APPEARANCE OF FELICIA DESIDERIO AND Trevor Hopgood at the door of her office the next day gave Anne a start.

"We don't have an appointment," said Felicia, "but your secretary said you were in and that we could ask if you would see us."

Felicia looked different. Anne realized that she was wearing makeup. Trevor seemed changed too. He didn't look surly.

"We thought it might save time if you saw us both at once," continued Felicia. "We both have stuff to talk about and, since we sort of worked together, we decided to come in together. Also, since we're sort of going out"—

this was added as an afterthought, though it was clearly the item of most pressing importance to Felicia.

"That's so nice," said Anne. She stopped herself from saying more. Extensive experience with high-school romances had taught her to smile and nod and act as though the thing, no matter how bizarre it might seem, was entirely to be expected.

"We talked about a couple of schools for Trevor," Felicia explained excitedly. "He has lots of interests, so he could go lots of places."

"Is that so?" said Anne, recalling that Trevor had said he had no interests.

"He especially likes music," added Felicia.

"Yeah," said Trevor, "I'm really into music. My grandfather owned this music store in Maple Shade, New Jersey. I guess I got my love of music from him. He was great."

"But he died," proffered Felicia.

"I'm sorry," said Anne.

"It's OK. He was really old," said Trevor.

"Trevor has an awesome music collection," continued Felicia. "Like a million CDs."

"Not that many," noted Trevor modestly. "But a lot. And some records: Led Zeppelin. The Grateful Dead."

"Ah!" said Anne. Curtis Fink had not been entirely off base after all.

"So . . ." Trevor looked at Felicia, who nodded encouragingly. "We talked about it, and I decided that maybe I want to own a record store someday. Like my grandfather's, only bigger."

"That sounds like a commendable goal," said Anne. "It means you'll want to take music courses but maybe major in business. Do I have this right?"

"Yeah." Trevor nodded.

"He's thinking George Washington University," said Felicia. "It has a good business program, and it's in D.C." The proximity to Georgetown was not lost on Anne.

"And Drexel University," said Trevor. "It's in Philadelphia, which is only two hours from D.C." He offered this for Felicia's benefit, then continued: "Drexel has this really neat co-op program that lets you work at what you want to do while you go to school."

Anne nodded. "Northeastern has a co-op program too," she suggested. "It's in Boston."

"Boston is too cold," asserted Felicia.

"Yeah," said Trevor. "I hate the cold."

"Then cross off Boston," agreed Anne. "But GW and Drexel sound like good choices. You can start working on those applications now, and maybe look around for some others. Anything else?"

Felicia, who had been waiting patiently for the conversation to get to her, now burst out: "I think I have a better handle on my Georgetown essay!"

"That's wonderful!" said Anne.

"Trevor really helped me. He's really good at spotting trite, fake stuff, and he got me to be more concrete the way you wanted. Listen to the beginning." Felicia began reading from a sheet of paper she had been clutching in her hand:

"'I don't want to be President of the United States. Or a U.S. Senator. Or even Mayor of Fenimore.'"

Felicia paused to explicate: "It was Trevor's idea that I should start with what I don't want to do, as a way of getting attention."

"It's a nice touch," agreed Anne.

Felicia continued:

"'Even though I don't want to run for political office, I do want to pursue a career in politics. My interest has less to do with issues and candidates than with how democracy works. I am fascinated by how a country as large and diverse as ours can coordinate its many functions, and how the local, state, and national governments can work independently and together in the act of governance. I am proud that we can have free elections and maintain a political process that reflects the will of the people.'"

"That's my intro," said Felicia proudly. "I'm not sure about some of the wording, and Trevor said that what happened in Florida during the Gore-Bush campaign contradicts my point a little, but I think the general idea is right and that this has a lot more energy than my other drafts."

"I agree," said Anne, "it has a lot more energy."

"The rest is better too. Trevor and I started talking about the things I do in my volunteer work that seem unimportant but that are, like, necessary to the political process."

"Like the time cards," prompted Trevor.

"Yeah." Felicia nodded. "I have a paragraph about how one of the things I do is hold up the time cards during the League of Women Voters debates (she read from her sheet): "'Timing each speaker represents the ideal of democracy where everyone is held to the same standard. This is an ideal I strongly believe in, that is sometimes infringed upon, but that as citizens we must try to maintain.'"

"Read the stuff about campaign finance reform," urged Trevor.

Felicia continued: "'I have also been involved in the related area of campaign finance reform at my high school. As chair of the Elections Committee, I helped make the rule that kids couldn't use professional ad agencies to make their campaign posters, even if their dads owned the agencies. This is another example of helping to promote the democratic process on a very basic level.'"

"I remember you did that," Anne said, nodding. "That's an excellent concrete example."

"Trevor's going to help me come up with a third example—because I think it's always good to have three. And then I'm going to end with how"—she returned to her sheet—"'Georgetown, by being located in our nation's capital and having an excellent reputation for its coursework in political science and governance, will allow me to learn more about the fascinating political process that I have become interested in through my volunteer work on the local level.'" She stopped suddenly. "Uh-oh, I used 'fascinating' again," she noted. "I may have to edit that. But you get the idea."

"I do," said Anne, relieved. The last paragraph aside, Felicia had finally broken through the clichés that had dogged her writing and arrived at something that, if not earthshakingly profound, at least showed some genuine glimpses of who she was. With the addition of her own letter as head of guidance—not to mention letters from the president of Fenimore's League of Women Voters and various aldermen, councilmen, and assemblymen for whom Felicia had uncomplainingly fetched coffee and stuffed envelopes—Anne felt that the girl now had a good shot at Georgetown.

"It sounds like you and Trevor make a really good team," Anne went on.

"We do," agreed Felicia. "He needs to try harder and I need to not try so hard. We sort of balance each other."

"Well, I'm very proud of the good work you've done," said Anne. "We'll send out your application, Felicia, once you finish editing your essay. Trevor can continue researching colleges and getting his references lined up."

"He spoke to Ms. Fineman and she

242

agreed to write him a letter," volunteered Felicia. "She said that after listening to him this week in class, she thinks she can write something positive."

Anne had suspected that, given a hint, Marcy would see something in Trevor. "This is great," she said, "this is fantastic. But there's still something important left to do. Trevor"—she waited for the boy to look up from trying to get a comfortable grasp of Felicia's hand—"you still have to speak to your father."

CHAPTER TWENTY-NINE

"WE MAY HAVE A WINDFALL!"

It was Sally Solomon, the Realtor, calling Anne one morning about a month after the house had been on the market. She was whispering. Sally's involvement with houses was so intense that she may have believed that other houses under her watch would get jealous if she spoke too loudly.

"There's interest," she whispered excitedly. "I'm not saying it's certain. But you know I have instincts, and my instincts give me a good feeling about this one. I'll want you to be available when they take a walk-

through early next week. So keep your afternoons free. I'll be in touch."

Anne felt a mixture of elation and sadness
at hearing the house might be sold soon. On
the one hand, it was a necessity—the bills
had mounted to a point where she had begun to worry that the gas and water would
be turned off and Winnie would be left
parched and shivering in the dark. But the
loss of the house where she had grown up
was still hard to take in. And it was the idea
of Winnie being uprooted at the very end of
her life that upset her most.

"My dear, stop worrying," said Winnie
philosophically, when Anne relayed Sally's
news. "If need be, I can always go stay with
Serge Freedman in Paris. He's ninety now
and senile, but he's still your grandfather's
cousin and was once in love with me. And
the poor man has more money than he
knows what to do with."

"So now you're saying you're going to go
live with a ninety-year-old senile Frenchman?"

"And why not? A senile Frenchman is
likely to be more interesting than an American with all his marbles. And I'm not saying
I'm going to live with him. I'm just saying I

could. I also have it from good authority that the senior facility in Larchmont is very nice."

"And what authority is that?"

"Harriet Ackerman's second husband was there. He died of a massive coronary last year, poor thing. But they say he was very happy."

"Who said?" pressed Anne.

"Not Harriet, I'm afraid. She died of viral pneumonia three years ago. No, I heard it from someone. Don't ask me who. He's probably dead anyway."

"Winnie, you're terrible!"

"Not terrible, dear, just realistic. Everyone's dead except me."

"Oh Gram!"

"I'm rather proud of it, you know. Besides, it's not your place to worry about me. It's my place to worry about you."

"And why would you worry about me?"

"Because, dear, you are almost thirty-five years old and you're not married. There's nothing wrong with the single life, mind you. My friend Sadie never married and always said it was the best decision she ever made. But some women are meant to be married, and you're one of them."

"I've had plenty of chances to marry."

"Precisely what worries me. You met one man whom you liked and you can't seem to move on. It's not normal. I admitted I was wrong about the fellow and I'm sorry for it. But mistakes happen and one gets past them. I never imagined you'd be so stubborn."

"I'm not stubborn," said Anne. "I've just never met anyone that I liked as much."

"'Liked as much!'" exclaimed Winnie. "For goodness' sakes, all you need is to like someone enough. Life isn't a Jane Austen novel. It's one thing to be long-suffering in a story, where the author can make it worth your while, but in real life, who's going to make sure it ends happily? Just look at what happened with poor Jane Austen. She worked things out for that long-suffering ninny, Anne Elliot, in her last book, but who worked things out for her? The woman probably waited around for her Ben Cutler to show up, which he never did. If you ask me, it's a good thing this Cutler fellow is back in the area. You can take a good look at him and see that he's not Prince Charming. Believe me, my dear, no man is a prince, except in the imagination."

Anne realized that Winnie had been storing up this lecture for weeks. She had sat by and watched as Anne cried over Ben Cutler during their last outing, but she was not about to tolerate any more tears. Life meant reducing expectations and making-do with what one had. What was the point of boo-hooing, as she saw it, when "no man is a prince, except in the imagination"? It was the same thing Marcy had said: "No one is as good as you think they are."

Only Ben *was* as good. Encountering him again had not just confirmed Anne's sense of his qualities but added luster to them. Everything she had once loved in him—his kindness, his intelligence, his imagination—had gone into making him the person he was now. And if that wasn't enough, the attraction she had once felt was still there. He still had the capacity to make her pulse quicken by simply looking at her.

Everything he had become had been inherent in what he had been. Why, then, had she been persuaded to give him up? The reason was simple. She had been afraid to stand up to her family and to trust herself. He had known it. It had been the accusation he hurled at her that last time.

They had been together for eight months and he had met her family, who had pretended to be polite while asking him pointed questions (whose answers they already knew) about where he had gone to college and where he worked. She had hoped that Winnie would engage with him about a book or an idea, but she had spoken to him only briefly, turning aside to discuss a charity benefit she was planning with Allegra. It had been a busy time for her then, and she had always had a tendency to make snap judgments about people. "I can take their measure in a few words," she liked to say. "And I always look at their shoes. Shoes, you know, speak volumes." At the time, Ben owned only a pair of scruffy sneakers, and Anne had wondered what volumes they spoke.

She found out only a few days later, when she joined her grandmother for lunch at a little restaurant on East Sixty-seventh Street. In those days, there had been a car to drive them into the city and some half-dozen unpretentious (but not inexpensive) bistros where the maître d's knew them and always found them a table. Winnie was dressed impeccably that day in a Chanel suit with a Hermès scarf draped around her shoulders and a Tatiana hat perched on the top of her head. She had an appointment later with someone from the mayor's office ("They probably want me to host another gathering for the landmark commission"). From there, she was going on to Mort Feinberg's on Central Park West for a light dinner. "Ever since his wife died, he's been nagging me to marry him; I won't hear of it. But his cook is excellent, so I don't mind having dinner with him."

Winnie had lived with the benefits of money for so long that she had lost track of how much it could blunt and derail judgment.

"I'm not saying your friend isn't a good person," she launched forth once they had settled in the corner of the bistro, "I'm just saying he's not worthy of you. You know I don't usually side with your father, but here I must admit, he has a point. What does the young man have to recommend him? He's good-looking enough, which I suppose counts for something. But believe me, the sexual part doesn't last, and once that's gone, what will you have? I shudder to think what his family is like. Can you imagine sitting around a kitchen table in Queens? And what are his prospects? To ascend to the august position of manager of a travel agency? Or perhaps to lead one of those tour groups that visit eleven cities in ten days? It will be bad enough for you, dear, but think of him. These lopsided relationships are always worse for the men. In the end, it makes them bitter. Gert Rosner married some boy who worked in a deli, and she showed up at my door one day with a black eye. I know you, Anne; you wouldn't like having your husband dependent on you. And he'd feel your disapproval and resent you for it."

It was amazing how Winnie had managed, in a few strokes, to paint a picture that made everything seem so complicated. It was true: Ben had no knowledge of her world and was likely to feel out of place in it. And Anne had no good answers for the questions about his work. What was he going to do with his life? He seemed without clear ambition, content to continue working in a travel agency.

Winnie was so definite that Anne suddenly saw the relationship through her grandmother's eyes: She had a childish crush on an inappropriate person; perhaps she had fallen for him *because* he was inappropriate. A travel agent in a Queens College sweatshirt was her attempt at rebellion. But what right had she to rebel against Winnie, who loved her more than anyone else in the world?

She had spoken to Ben several days later during a visit to the Met, as they stood, as they sometimes did, in front of the Titian. They had been holding hands, but it was as though she were keeping her hand apart. He felt it in the tension of her fingers, and looked at her face for a while as she stared blankly at the portrait.

"What's wrong?" he finally asked.

"I think," she responded, in the quiet deliberate way she had when she finally made up her mind to something, "we should cut it off."

"Cut what off?" he said tensely but attempting lightness. "Are you suggesting we take a hatchet to some part of my anatomy? I was under the impression that you liked it the way it was."

Anne did not smile. She did not even look at him. "Cut off our relationship," she clarified bluntly.

He didn't say anything for a moment. He had recognized the finality of her tone. "Why?" he finally asked.

"We're too young."

"I'm twenty-five."

"I'm too young, then. And you're not—"

"Settled?"

"I suppose that's it," admitted Anne.

"OK, you're too young and I'm not settled. We don't have to get married now. We'll wait till you're older and I'm settled."

"That's not the whole problem."

"Then what?"

"We're just not right for each other."

"Because I work in a travel agency. Because I went to Queens College and my parents have blue-collar jobs?"

Anne was silent.

"Your family thinks I'm beneath you."

"It's my decision."

"Your family thinks so and you agree."

Anne shrugged.

"Your family are fools," he said. "Except maybe your grandmother, and she's living in another world. She'd come around if you took a stand. It's not really that at all. It's that you haven't got the courage to love me. You're afraid to trust yourself."

She did not respond, which seemed to anger him more. "You're a coward!" His voice had grown loud, and the guard near the door looked at them severely.

"Maybe I am." Anne shrugged.

"Then I feel sorry for you!"

"Good. Feel sorry for me. If it will make you feel better."

"Unfortunately," he said softly, "it doesn't make me feel better." For a moment, she met his eyes, where she recognized as much pain as anger. And then, he turned abruptly and walked away.

"You made the best decision you could at the time," Winnie pronounced, pulling Anne from her reverie. "There's no point dwelling on it."

But instead of nodding and changing the subject as she usually did when Winnie took this tone, Anne felt herself stiffen. She was not about to cry this time.

"No," Anne said in a steely tone. "It was *not* the best decision at the time. It was based on stupid prejudices and a false sense of superiority."

Winnie looked taken aback. "But you were so young," she countered, her voice grown suddenly plaintive.

"I was young, but I knew who he was and that I loved him. I shouldn't have allowed you to persuade me to give him up."

"You're blaming me!" Winnie's face seemed to crumple, and for the first time in her recollection, Anne saw tears forming in her grandmother's eyes.

"No, I'm really blaming myself for not having the strength to oppose you. I've tried to teach the kids who come to my office to listen to their parents up to a point—and then to listen to themselves. I didn't do that, and I regret it."

"Regret is a useless emotion," murmured Winnie.

"It's a sad emotion, but it's not a useless one," said Anne resolutely. "You have to regret—even mourn—your mistakes if you're ever going to move on. I made a mistake when I gave up Ben Cutler, and I regret it. Which doesn't mean I can't go on living."

"You deserve a wonderful life," Winnie said quietly.

Anne was silent a moment, looking at her grandmother's proud, worn face. Her anger had subsided, but something subtle had changed in the aftermath of this gust of emotion. She felt oddly alone, even bereft—and yet also strangely exhilarated. "That's not true," she said gently. "I don't deserve a wonderful life. It's not some privilege of birth. Whatever life I get, I have to make."

She had said what she had wanted to

say—what had been bottled up in her for a long time—and having said it, she felt at peace. She bent forward and kissed her grandmother on the forehead. Now, finally, she could forgive Winnie—and herself—and move on.

CHAPTER THIRTY

WHEN ANNE TOLD MARCY THAT BEN CUTLER was in the area but engaged to be married, she took the same view as Winnie: "So now that you've seen him and know that he's taken, you can finally put him behind you. I read in *Psychology Today* that women get a new lease on life when they hear their ex is remarried. It sets them free to find someone else for a serious relationship."

"I don't need to be set free," said Anne testily. "I am free. And I don't know that I want a serious relationship."

"Bullshit," said Marcy. "You need something more substantial to worry about than where the kids at Fenimore get into college."

"You mean like what time my husband is coming home for dinner?"

"That's a low blow," said Marcy. It was true that she often sat, the table set, a low-cal gourmet meal carefully prepared, waiting hours for Rich to get home from work.

"I'm sorry, but I guess I'm getting back at you for setting that awful lawyer on me the other night."

Anne had accepted an invitation to dinner at the Finemans a week earlier, where Harry Furman, the partner from Rich's firm, had been a surprise guest. A short, balding man with an awkward manner, Harry was dressed in a bright green and orange sweater, which he might have hoped would perform some of the work of socializing for him.

Things had not begun well when Anne asked him whether he'd be willing to come to Fenimore for Career Day and he flatly refused. Had she known that he had an abiding fear of high school, the result of being taunted for being bad at sports and bungling his locker combination, she might have been more sympathetic. As it was, she assumed his refusal hinged on not getting a tax write-off for this brand of pro bono work.

During the meal, he stared at her in beagle-like fashion, as though expecting her to draw him out, but peeved, she turned her back on him and proceeded to talk to Marcy about Trevor Hopgood.

As Felicia reported, Marcy had had a change of heart about Trevor. After only a week of listening to his mumbled comments in class, she had found a number of favorable points to include in a reference letter.

"I gave Trevor a second look and revised my opinion; maybe you should do the same with Harry Furman," Marcy reasoned now. "Harry liked you. I'm sure he'll ask you out."

"He didn't like me," said Anne. "We barely spoke more than ten words. Besides, he must be fifty. He's too old for me."

"So maybe you like the poetry fellow better?"

"Peter Jacobson?" Peter had called a few days earlier, asking her to dinner as a follow-up to their mortuary sculpture date, a lugubrious outing in which he had stood for a long time before a plaster representation of death in the form of a young woman in a helmet. Anne had backed off from dinner and instead agreed to meet for lunch, where they could discuss the agenda for Poetry Day a few weeks hence.

"He's too young for me," she responded now.

"Either they're too old or too young, but whatever they are, you reject them. Two men, both good prospects," said Marcy, scraping the cream cheese off her bagel. "I keep telling you: you're just too picky."

CHAPTER THIRTY-ONE

DESPITE SALLY SOLOMON'S "INSTINCTS" THAT the Scarsdale house would be sold soon, it had a new occupant. Anne's cousin, Rachel Kramer, had been evicted from her apartment in the seedier precincts of downtown Manhattan for not paying her rent. The sinus commercial, which had never aired, had not provided her with sufficient income, and the soap opera tryout had not panned out. Owing to an excess of sick days, she had been fired from her waitressing job, leaving her nothing to live on.

When Rachel called to explain her dilemma, it occurred to Anne that the situation might be turned to everyone's advantage. Only a few days before, Winnie had fallen and sprained her ankle. Anne, who had been working on college recommendation letters in the library, had heard a clatter and found her grandmother sprawled on the kitchen floor, looking more embarrassed than hurt. "Don't say it," said Winnie. "I wanted to start marinating the flank steak, and I placed too much confidence in my old friend, the cane. I should have used the walker, but you know how I feel about it. And now, you see, I've been punished for my vanity."

Anne bit her tongue, wanting to scold Winnie for creating yet another complication—and expense, since it would now be necessary to hire a day nurse while Anne was at school and to delay the closing on the house, assuming that it sold soon, until Winnie was mobile enough to climb stairs.

Winnie had finally agreed that she would move into Anne's Murray Hill apartment once the house was sold, under the assumption that she could eventually shame Elihu into contributing something toward a larger apartment. "He'll have three million from the sale, and he wouldn't want it to get around that his daughter was sleeping on an IKEA futon," she reasoned.

But these arrangements lay in the future. For now, Rachel was delighted to help take care of Winnie in exchange for room and board.

"It's great to live with your grandmother for a while," Rachel said with relief. "It gives me time to rest; I've been feeling really tired lately." The missed days that had gotten her fired from her waitressing job had not been a sign of irresponsibility; she really hadn't been feeling well. Anne remembered her cousin's pallor at her father's party and asked if she'd seen a doctor.

"No, I just think I'm run-down—you know, auditions during the day and waitressing at night. If I get some rest and eat better, I'll be fine." Her diet, she confessed, had consisted largely of Krispy Kremes and French fries.

"No wonder the poor girl is ill," clucked Winnie. "She's poisoning herself with junk food! I'll make sure she eats properly, and we can watch *General Hospital* together. It's not Tolstoy, but it has its moments. And who knows, I might eventually get her to read a book."

With Rachel installed in the Scarsdale house, Anne could also move back to her apartment. She was eager to return to the city, to be in her own place, and to get ready for Winnie's eventual occupancy. But difficulties immediately sprung up.

When she called Carlotta to announce her intention to move back, there was silence on the other end of the phone. "I'm sort of settled here," Carlotta finally said. "There's even hot water sometimes."

"That's great news," said Anne. "But my cousin Rachel is staying with my grandmother. So I'd like my apartment back."

"Well," said Carlotta in a ruminative tone, "I don't know."

"What don't you know?" asked Anne sharply.

"I don't know if it's feasible for me to move right now. I'll have to start looking around."

"Please do," said Anne. "I'll give you three weeks—that's a week beyond standard notice."

"Hmm," said Carlotta, "I don't think that will be enough time."

"How much time do you need?" asked Anne, trying to keep her temper.

"It's hard to say," said Carlotta coolly. "I

might not want to leave at all. As you may know, occupancy is three-quarters of possession."

"I also know that my name is on the lease," said Anne between clenched teeth.

"My friend from Paul, Weiss said that sometimes that doesn't matter," said Carlotta.

"Listen," said Anne evenly. "I don't want this to get ugly. I'm telling you that I intend to be back in my apartment by the beginning of next month. If you're not out of there by then, I will be forced to take legal action. You may know someone at Paul, Weiss, but I know my share of excellent lawyers. And with my name on the lease, you haven't got a leg to stand on."

Anne hung up the phone, shaking. It occurred to her to speak to her sister, but she realized that Allegra would refuse to get involved—it was her standard position on everything. As for speaking to her father, there was no telling what was going on between him and Carlotta. Only a few days ago, while riding a bus down Fifth Avenue, Anne had been shocked to look out the window and see Carlotta and her father gazing together into the window of Tiffany's. Carlotta was wearing a chinchilla wrap, which seemed to be constructed out of the tails of a thousand dead animals—no doubt another find from a runway remnant sale. She had her arm tucked complacently inside Elihu Ehrlich's, who was wearing a Burberry trench coat with a matching scarf and hat. Seeing them together, gazing with rapt intimacy at a priceless bauble against the turquoise backdrop of the Tiffany's window, struck a hollow note in Anne's heart. Though she knew that her father didn't have a dime left to his name, there was still the hereditary asset of the Ehrlichs' New York apartment, and there was no telling how much further Carlotta might plunge the family into debt.

Anne imagined Carlotta as a huge boa constrictor, swallowing not just her father and the Ehrlichs' Manhattan real estate (it was conceivable that the woman might procreate simply in order to acquire it) but also Anne's sunny one-bedroom. The image made her shudder. She had a key to her apartment, of course, and could always change the locks—but then it occurred to her that Carlotta might be in the process of changing them on her end. Anne decided to check about this as soon as she could. Meanwhile, she realized, she ought to make good on her threat to Carlotta and consult a lawyer.

Perhaps it would be worth her while to go out with Harry Furman after all.

CHAPTER THIRTY-TWO

ONE MORNING, SOON AFTER FELICIA AND Trevor's visit, Anne was sitting at her desk reviewing senior grade-point averages. This was not a simple task. Gone were the days when all you needed to know was that A's were worth 4.0, B's 3.0, and C's 2.0. Now, not only had pluses and minuses made an appearance, but there were the added weights given to honors and AP courses as schools struggled to situate students in an ever-expanding context of worth. Rumor had it that there actually existed a student at an elite prep school like Exeter or Andover—or it might have been a competitive public high

school like Stuyvesant or Bronx Science—
who had pushed the envelope and achieved
a GPA of 5.3. Many swore they knew someone who knew someone whose cousin had
done it—the equivalent to breaking the
sound barrier, the three-minute mile, and the
record for holding one's breath underwater.
To achieve a mere 4.0 was, in the context of
such dazzling feats, a decidedly lackluster
achievement.

Anne knew that as head of guidance she
was accountable for proper GPA calculation.
The famous miscalculation of a few years
back, in which an honors course had not
been duly weighted and a student's final
GPA was mistakenly reduced by a fraction of
a point, had served as a red light. This egregious error had taken place under the watch
of the former head of guidance, a dour older
woman, who wore tweed suits, had ramrod
posture, and was named Miss Prickett (she
had insisted upon the Miss over the more
politically correct Ms. as a sign that she was
not open to newfangled ideas). Miss Prickett
had weathered many a storm during her
tenure, most notably a scandal involving the
lacrosse team, when fifteen girls had gotten
drunk at the regional meet and trashed an

entire floor of hotel rooms in a Marriott in Ossining. But the GPA miscalculation was of another order of magnitude entirely. In the case of the lacrosse incident, Miss Prickett had required that the team do intensive community service (i.e., making cards for the area nursing home, using glitter paint and calligraphy pens—"really fun," said Jodi Fields, then freshman-class vice president, who had recruited many non-offending students to take part).

But the GPA incident did not allow for any such simple remedy. It was not the students who had sinned but the administration, and no amount of sackcloth and ashes on the part of the guidance department was going to appease parents who believed that their children's future had been irreparably compromised. If one student's grades had been miscalculated, who was to say that the whole lot wasn't tainted? A mad cow–like panic took hold of the school as parents furiously checked and double-checked their children's GPAs.

The incident had not only ended the career of the hapless guidance counselor responsible for the student's transcript (he was now operating heavy machinery in White

Plains); it had also been Prickett's Waterloo. She had folded her tents—or rather, hung up her tweed blazer—and opted for early retirement. At the time, Anne had been at Fenimore for five years and had already distinguished herself by showing uncommon bravery in the face of parental pressure and an innate gift for manipulating Vince. She was thus seen as Prickett's natural and inevitable successor.

As a result, it now fell to her to check not only her own calculations but those of the two other counselors under her watch. After doing this, she then passed the results on to Vince, who, to his credit, was known to stay up till all hours, popping No-Doz and antacids in rapid succession while checking and rechecking the weighted figures, so that, in the baseball parlance he favored for this endeavor, "we pitch a perfect game."

On this particular day, Anne was in the throes of reviewing Skyler Landow's average, wading through the thicket of weighted and double-weighted grades. Skyler was a math genius, enrolled in a nonlinear algebra course at NYU that met three evenings a week as well as Saturday morning— a double-weighted course that was also a double-credit course. The calculation of Skyler's GPA, in short, could make anyone but a high-level mathematician's head spin (perhaps, Anne thought, only Skyler himself was truly qualified to calculate it).

She had paused to determine whether the NYU course needed to be calculated first as a double-weighted course or first as a double-credit course—a question that itself indicated her abysmal abilities in math—when she heard a commotion in the outer office.

Suddenly, Jeffrey Hopgood, his face red, his hair disheveled and tie askew, burst into the room. Cindy had tried unsuccessfully to keep him from coming into the office without being announced but he had ignored her, and his visage appeared so menacing that Cindy stood by the door, mouthing the question: "Should I call someone?"

"It's OK," said Anne. Perhaps naively, she felt confident that she could bring Jeffrey Hopgood under control. "Just leave the door open," she added hastily.

Meanwhile, Jeffrey Hopgood was standing in front of her desk, his hands gripping its edges, glaring down at her. He did not look friendly. He did not, truth be told, look quite human.

"Would you like to take a seat?" asked Anne in her calmest guidance counselor voice.

"No," seethed Hopgood. "I don't want to take a seat. I want you to tell me what you've done to my son!"

"Mr. Hopgood," said Anne, "please calm down. I've done nothing at all to your son."

"Don't give me that!" Hopgood growled. "You know what you've done. You've turned him into a conniving little shit. He was always a little shit—but he wasn't conniving. That's your doing!"

"Mr. Hopgood," reasoned Anne, "I think you do your son a disservice. He has a mind of his own."

"Like hell he does! He never had a mind of his own before. What business has he having one now? I want that little shit to go to Williams, and now he says he won't go. He's even threatened to blackmail me. Says he'll take out loans or something, make me look like a manipulative bastard if I don't support his decision." Hopgood paused, perhaps aware that he did look like a manipulative bastard. Then, apparently deciding that he didn't care, he plunged on: "The little shit wants to go to someplace called Drexel."

"Drexel has an excellent co-op program and a Music Industry Major, which appeals to Trevor."

"A Music Industry Major! What in hell is a Music Industry Major? Since when does Trevor want to go into the music industry? All he ever wants to do is put those plugs in his ears and tune his mother and me out. Williams would at least give him a chance to carry on a family tradition. Who are you to get in the way of family tradition?"

"I'm not trying to get in the way of family tradition," said Anne. "I just listened to Trevor and pointed him in a direction that seemed to suit his interests. It was his idea to pursue a career in the music industry."

"I don't believe you!" said Jeffrey Hopgood, his eyes narrowing. "Trevor never came up with an idea in his life. You told him what to do—you did it to spite me. I know your kind. You don't like men because we get in the way of your hoity-toity feminist ideas." Hopgood had clearly moved into another phase of response that tapped into deeper wells of resentment.

"Mr. Hopgood, please sit down! I really don't know what you're talking about!" She felt herself backing up slightly as Hopgood leaned further forward and eyed the Blue Ribbon School of Excellence paperweight on her desk.

"You don't know what I'm talking about?!" seethed Hopgood. "Well, I'll tell you what I'm talking about! I'll have you dragged into court for this; I'll get you fired; I'll show you what happens when you interfere in private family business; I'll—"

"Calm down," said a voice that seemed to come out of nowhere. It was Ben Cutler's voice. He had entered the room quietly, assessed the situation, and assumed control.

Ben did not look at Anne but walked around to face Jeffrey Hopgood. The two men stared at each other a moment, then Hopgood, as if suddenly deflated, slumped into the chair behind him.

"I want you to take a few deep breaths," said Ben, his voice quiet but firm. "You're obviously angry and you're taking it out on Ms. Ehrlich. You need to go home and think things over, and then, once you get a grip on things, you need to apologize for your behavior." He brought his face close to Jeffrey Hopgood's and looked him sternly in the eye. "Do you understand what I'm saying?"

For a moment, Jeffrey Hopgood sat as if shell-shocked; then, he nodded his head.

"Now go home," ordered Ben.

Hopgood took a breath and rose slowly from the chair. He now appeared more confused than angry, and a look of embarrassment and possibly contrition passed over his features.

"No need to speak now," counseled Ben. "You're too worked up. Go home, think it over, talk to your wife. Then come back when you're ready to give that apology."

Hopgood turned and walked out the door. And Anne stood behind her desk facing Ben Cutler.

CHAPTER THIRTY-THREE

"I SUPPOSE YOU SAVED MY LIFE."

Ben laughed. "I doubt it would have come to that. But he *was* worked up. You always had a way of doing that to people. In any case, it was lucky I dropped by when I did . . . I wanted to talk something over with you."

Anne looked at him. She suddenly realized that, for the first time since she had seen him again, they were alone together. She studied his face—it was the same face, with its strong, familiar planes, and she realized that she wished she could trace them with her hand as she once had done. Their eyes met for a moment, and she knew there was a shared, unspoken remembrance of each other's touch. Then, he cleared his throat and spoke quickly. "It's about your house," he said. "I mentioned that I knew it was on the market. Well, I've been thinking it over, and, to be brief about it, I'd like to buy it. That is—unless you object."

Anne looked stunned.

"I know it seems like an odd thing to do," Ben hurried on. "At first I rejected the idea. I thought you'd be offended, given our—past history and so forth." He hesitated a moment, then continued. "But the more I thought about it, the more I felt it might be a good solution for"—he paused again in order to come up with the right phrase—"all concerned." He waited, giving her a chance to say something. When she didn't, he continued: "Pauline and Jonathan have been looking for a place in the area, and I've been on the lookout for office space in the city, where the rents, as you can imagine, are sky high. Then it occurred to me that I might have my office here in Westchester, which would be convenient for a number of reasons. I remember your house was spacious, with plenty of rooms—I'm thinking that one wing could serve as office space. The old-world charm would fit well with the nature of the guides." He stopped abruptly as though sensing he had been giving information that she would have no reason to care about. He now continued with more deliberation. "Pauline has come to depend on me, as you may have sensed. And Kirsten"—he cleared his throat again—"seems to like the area. As it happens, she also likes old houses and has a knack for renovation. . . ."

Anne felt suddenly as though someone had shaken her awake. She had almost lost herself in the vague idea that Ben wanted to buy the house for reasons that had something to do with her. But with the mention of Kirsten, she was brought back to reality. This was a business transaction, nothing more. She struggled to master her emotions and looked at him, her gaze direct and unflinching. "It's a wonderful place to raise children," she said quietly.

But Ben appeared not to hear and continued hurriedly: "So I thought we could combine office space with living space, which Sally—you know, the Realtor—says wouldn't pose problems with the zoning board. She seems to know all the ins and outs. She told us you're looking to sell as soon as possible." He stopped again, perhaps worried that he was giving the impression that he was doing her a favor, and shifted course: "Not that you wouldn't get a lot of interest, given the charm of the place. And of course, if you object . . ."

"I don't object," said Anne evenly. "It's flattering that you would want to live there." Her voice, she realized, sounded cold, and he looked away again for a moment as if stung. When he looked back she could tell that there was something more he wanted to say.

"Sally told me about your grandmother's fall and the need to put off the closing. From my experience, a sprained ankle in an elderly person can take quite a long time to heal."

"I'm sure the delay won't be too long," Anne said hastily.

"The fact is"—Ben spoke slowly now, laying out the argument carefully, so as to be sure she would follow his reasoning—"our lease on the condo is up at the end of this month and I have a slew of contractors that I'd like to get started on the renovations. Pauline is, as you can imagine, eager to have her own place—and Kirsten too wants to settle down. So it occurred to me that perhaps we could close earlier and your grandmother could stay on with us until she felt better. She could take as long as she needs; the place is certainly big enough. It might be the best solution." He looked at her, his face impassive; whatever emotion he might be feeling was impossible to read.

Anne felt slightly dizzy. Ben Cutler was offering to house Winnie Mazur? The idea of having her grandmother live with the man whom she had persuaded her granddaughter to give up seemed too incredible to take in.

"Think it over and speak to your grandmother," said Ben, his eyes still on her face, "and I'll speak to her myself. Obviously, if you still want to delay the closing, there won't be a problem." His voice now took on an undertone of gentleness. "I have no rancor, you know. There was a time I did, but I don't anymore. In some sense, I feel grateful to you and your grandmother. I don't know if I'd have achieved what I did if you hadn't thrown me over."

Anne tried but failed to detect a note of irony in this speech. "Not that there's anything wrong with working in a travel agency," she said softly.

"No," said Ben, a look of amusement crossing his face, "not that there's anything wrong with that."

CHAPTER THIRTY-FOUR

ANNE COULD NOT HAVE SAID HOW LONG SHE SAT at her desk without moving after Ben left, but at some point Cindy buzzed to say that Peter Jacobson was waiting to take her to lunch. She had forgotten all about their lunch date; the events of the morning had thrown everything else into the background. She now tried to get her bearings as she went into the outer office to greet him.

Peter was seated in one of the guidance rocking chairs, rocking mournfully, while Cindy eyed him with interest.

"I've been looking forward to seeing you

again," he said as Anne came in. "You look really good."

Anne could only assume that he found her slight dishevelment and glazed expression appealing—perhaps they complemented his depressed state. Cindy, meanwhile, looked at her with renewed respect; Peter was extremely handsome.

As they were about to leave the office, the phone rang, and Cindy signaled for them to wait. "Your grandmother's on the other line." She addressed Anne in her best Valley girl lilt. "She, like, really wants to talk to you."

Anne took the receiver. "What is it, Gram?" she said. "I'm just about to walk out the door."

"I hate to bother you at work like this, dear, but I wish you'd stop by right away." Winnie's voice, usually calm and matter-of-fact, contained a note of real alarm.

"What is it? Are you all right?" Anne suddenly felt herself jolted out of the vague disorientation she had been feeling after her encounter with Ben into a state of real anxiety. She imagined that her grandmother was having chest pain or the onset of another stroke.

kitchen, making Rachel a cup of tea. Though Winnie still could not walk, she had grown adept at wheeling herself from the small maid's room behind the library, where she had been sleeping since the accident, to the kitchen, where she managed to continue to cook what she called "a proper meal" for her poorly nourished charge. Anne took a moment to register the irony that the eighty-seven-year-old was ministering to the twenty-six-year-old assigned to be her caretaker.

"She says she's not hungry," said Winnie, after Anne had introduced Peter, "but maybe she can drink something. I've never seen her like this. She was tired before, but now she can't move."

"Where is she?" asked Anne.

"In the living room on the couch. I've called the doctor; he says to bring her to the emergency room if it seems serious."

Anne and Peter went into the living room where they found Rachel sprawled on the sofa, whimpering softly.

"What's wrong, dear?" asked Anne.

"Everything hurts," moaned Rachel.

"Everything?"

"My whole body. I can't move."

"Dull ache or sharp pain?" asked Peter.

"Dull but sharp," moaned Rachel. "I feel like I sprained every muscle in my body." As she spoke, her eyes flickered appraisingly over Peter. Sick as she was, she was not so sick as to be insensible to a good-looking man.

"But why such a sudden onset?" Anne queried Peter, as though he were a consulting physician.

He turned to Rachel. "Did you eat or drink anything last night that might have caused a reaction?"

"No," groaned Rachel. "I ate dinner with Winnie—one of her nice Jewish meals, and a Diet Coke before I went to bed. She doesn't like me drinking diet soda, so I keep it in my room. That's it. But I've been feeling kind of low for a while: tired with aches and pains, sometimes pretty bad, but never as bad as this." She started to cry.

Peter had sat down on the side of the sofa and took her hand. "Just relax," he said. "Pain is a very subjective thing."

"No it's not," wailed Rachel.

"OK, maybe it's not," agreed Peter, "but you can relax into it. I used to help a loved one, who was very sick, deal with pain.

Sometimes, I'd read her poetry—that seemed to have a palliative effect."

Rachel furrowed her brow, and Peter quickly clarified: "It made her feel better."

Rachel smiled weakly. "You could read me poetry, if you think it would make me feel better."

He nodded and took a battered anthology of verse from his pocket. "My tried and true companion," he noted, opened it and began to read:

Because I could not stop for Death—
He kindly stopped for me—
The Carriage held but just Ourselves—
And Immortality . . .

Rachel groaned and Peter stopped reading: "Emily Dickinson may not be the best choice under the circumstances," he acknowledged, thumbing through the anthology and embarking again:

Something there is that doesn't love a
   wall,
That sends the frozen ground-swell un-
   der it,

288

And spills the upper boulders in the sun
And makes gaps even two can pass
abreast.

Rachel appeared more satisfied with Robert Frost's "Mending Wall." She half-closed her eyes, lulled by the cadence of the verse.

"Have you had any other symptoms?" interrupted Anne. Her cousin looked even more pale and worn than at her father's birthday party, and the extreme lethargy and apparent pain were disturbing symptoms.

"I had a rash a few weeks ago," said Rachel. "I was using some new moisturizer, and I figured that caused it. But I can't think of anything else. Oh God," she moaned, "everything hurts." She turned to Peter: "Keep reading."

Peter continued his reading of "Mending Wall."

Winnie had wheeled into the room with a cup of tea, which Rachel waved away. "I think we need to take her to the hospital," Anne told her grandmother. "I'm supposed to be giving career placement tests during fifth period, but I'll call the office and tell them to have the students reschedule."

"Don't do that," interjected Peter, who had managed to follow this conversation even as he was reading Frost's poem. "I'll take her to the hospital."

"You don't have to go to any trouble," said Rachel, looking up at him gratefully.

"It's no trouble at all," Peter assured her. "I'll drive you to the hospital, and read to you while you wait to see a doctor. Your cousin can give her tests and meet us there when she's done."

Anne saw no point in arguing with this. Whatever was wrong with Rachel, Peter (with or without poetry) was better medicine than anything she could offer.

CHAPTER THIRTY-FIVE

"LYME DISEASE. ADVANCED CASE," REPORTED PE-
ter, when Anne arrived at the hospital after
fifth period. He was sitting in the visitor's
lounge while Rachel was having additional
blood work done. "The doctor says they want
to take more tests for a conclusive diagnosis, but the symptoms look pretty classic.
She'll need time to recuperate."

"But how could she have advanced Lyme
disease?" asked Anne. "Up until a week ago,
she lived in downtown Manhattan."

"She thinks that it might have happened
during the photo shoot for the sinus com-

mercial. They filmed it in some meadow in upstate New York. She had to stand around for hours in the middle of a field, rubbing the bridge of her nose. The rash came soon afterward. Of course, it wouldn't have been a problem if she'd caught it sooner."

"But why didn't she?"

"I think she was so run-down that it didn't register. She was going to all those auditions during the day and waitressing at night—she thought it was normal to feel tired. And there was no one to look after her."

Anne realized that this was true. Although Allegra had boasted of taking her cousin under her wing, this had consisted entirely of getting her auditions for Off-Off Broadway plays. Had Rachel not come to stay with Winnie, God knows what would have happened. Anne had visions of the girl lying helpless for weeks in her studio apartment in the Bowery, too feeble to lift herself from the couch.

"They said they'll need to keep her in the hospital for a week or so," said Peter. "I hope she'll let me come by and read while she's here. She's not too familiar with literature, but she's a very receptive person."

Anne wanted to say that Rachel was certainly receptive to him, but a nurse appeared at this moment and motioned to them to follow her. She ushered them into a room where Rachel was sitting up in bed, looking weak but calm. She had received something for the pain, and her face brightened as they entered. Anne hugged her.

"I wish my mother were here," she said suddenly.

"Would you like me to call her?" asked Anne.

"Would you? I'd be so grateful. I haven't spoken to her enough this year. I really shouldn't have built that wall." She looked over at Peter. "I liked the poem you read about building a wall," she said. "I can't tell whether it's saying walls are good or walls are bad—I guess sometimes they're good and sometimes they're bad."

"That's exactly right!" exclaimed Peter.

"I liked having you read me the poetry," she continued. "It made me feel better, even when I felt like shit."

Peter nodded. "I'll come by tomorrow with Wordsworth. He's a very calming poet. We can start on *The Prelude*; it's this superlong poem."

"I'm sure it will have a *palliative* effect," declared Rachel contentedly, settling back in the bed and closing her eyes. "And I'm in no hurry."

CHAPTER THIRTY-SIX

AFTER ANNE HAD RETURNED TO THE HOUSE AND given Winnie a report on Rachel's condition, she took a breath and relayed the news about Ben Cutler's decision to buy the house.

"Is that so!" said Winnie.

"It will serve as his office, as well as a home for his family," Anne elaborated quickly. "That includes his sister and nephew, and his fiancée. She's a very attractive Danish woman, who works with him on the guides."

"Mmmm," said Winnie.

"He said he always admired the house,

and that it would suit his purposes very well," Anne continued, feeling the need to spell this out.

"Of course," said Winnie. "It's a fine house."

"Anyway," concluded Anne, "he wants to close right away and have you stay on until your ankle is better. It's ridiculous, of course, but I thought I should tell you."

"Why is it ridiculous?" asked Winnie.

Anne looked at her grandmother incredulously. "You're not saying that you're going to accept!"

"Well, my dear, we need the money."

"A month isn't going to matter. You'll be walking in a month."

"I may be, but then again, I may not. At my age, it's hard to predict these things. And you live in a third-floor brownstone. God only knows when I'll be able to climb those stairs."

"Then, we'll find another apartment. We're going to do it anyway, so why not now?"

"Because we don't have the money now," responded Winnie bluntly. "I'm hoping to pry it out of your father after the sale of the house, but doubtless it will take some doing, and finding an apartment in Manhattan isn't easy. Sally may be a real-estate genius, but she's not a magician. All things considered, this seems a more reasonable option."

"But how can you stay in the house? You don't know these people. They're complete strangers!"

"I wouldn't say that," said Winnie lightly. "You wanted to marry this Benjamin Cutler, didn't you? That makes him almost a relative."

Anne was silent a moment, then burst out laughing. "You're too much, Gram! You really are!"

That evening, Sally called to say that the family interested in the house wanted to stop by the next afternoon. "Mr. Cutler said he spoke to you," said Sally with crisp efficiency. "He also wants to speak to Winnie, so be sure she's not napping."

If Sally knew anything about Ben's intentions, she did not let on. It was one of her strengths that she had no interest in the personal except as it intersected with the professional—a fact which might account for her three marriages, each useful for obtaining something—sex, children, money—and rendered obsolete once the requisite item had been obtained. "If my instincts are right," continued Sally, "this guy may be willing to pay top dollar for the house. At this time of year, with no island in your kitchen and the state of your bathrooms, that's saying something. So do me a favor," she warned, "don't screw this up!"

CHAPTER THIRTY-SEVEN

THE NEXT DAY, ANNE WAS HOME BY THREE P.M. and watching *General Hospital* with Winnie. As Sally had instructed, she had put the good lace tablecloth on the dining room table and set out pound cake and what was left of the Courvoisier, which Elihu consumed in great quantities with his golfing buddies. "The types that like houses like yours go in for that sort of thing," Sally had explained. "They have refined taste—or at least pretensions to it."

At four P.M., Anne saw Sally's BMW pull up in the driveway followed by a Volvo station wagon from which Ben, Jonathan,

Pauline, and Kirsten emerged. She had suspected that Kirsten would be there, but the sight of her, this time dressed casually in jeans and a white cable-knit sweater—an outfit that emphasized her unpretentious natural beauty—still had a jarring effect. She felt a fresh pang at the idea that Ben and Kirsten might raise a family together in this house.

Amid the bustle of introductions, the awkwardness of Winnie seeing Ben again was reduced by Pauline's effusive chatter.

"Isn't this the most exciting coincidence!" she exclaimed to Anne. "You knew Bennie way back when, and you work at Jonathan's school, and now we're thinking of buying your house. It's a small world, I always say. Is this your grandmother? I see the resemblance. What a fabulous house! I thought the driveway would go on forever. Like that house in that Hitchcock movie. What was that movie, Bennie?"

"*Rebecca,*" said Ben with amusement.

"Yes, *Rebecca!*" exclaimed Pauline. "It was haunted by the man's first wife, wasn't it? This house doesn't look haunted, thank God."

"We've tried our best to keep the ghosts at bay," said Winnie drily.

"I think the house looks more like Mr. Darcy's house in *Pride and Prejudice,* though admittedly on a much smaller scale," said Kirsten in her intelligent, lightly accented voice. "As I recall, it was his house that made Elizabeth Bennet fall in love with him—she thought it reflected his character." She turned to Winnie. "I'm sure this house reflects yours."

"Well, it should—I lived here long enough," declared Winnie, sitting very straight in her wheelchair.

"I'm sorry," murmured Kirsten, realizing that her observation might be painful.

"No need to be." Winnie shrugged. "It's just a house. People who get too attached to things are fools. Besides, this one's been too empty for too long; it's about time someone else got some use out of it." Having dismissed the subject in her usual common-sense manner, she turned her attention to Jonathan, who was standing off to the side, reading a book. "What's that you're reading, young man?" she called out in a peremptory tone.

Jonathan held up the book: it was *Slaughterhouse Five* by Kurt Vonnegut.

"Vonnegut," said Winnie. "That's a name from the past. He has a certain shallow whimsy, I suppose, but you'd do better with Ken Kesey or even Tom Wolfe. Not that they'd be my first choice."

Jonathan appeared interested: "What *would* be your first choice?"

"Well," Winnie ruminated, "if you're after the absurd, I'd suggest Kafka. After that, maybe Conrad."

"*Heart of Darkness.*" Jonathan nodded. "I heard that's really bleak."

"Yes," said Winnie. "Conrad is bleak but that's no reason to avoid him. You must have a bit of the bleak to steel yourself for when life gets, well, bleak. After Conrad, something lighter. Wodehouse, perhaps."

"I read one of the Jeeves books," said Jonathan. "It was funny."

My, my," exclaimed Winnie, "a well-read young person. You don't see that much nowadays."

"Yes." said Pauline, who had caught the end of the conversation. "All Jonathan ever does is read."

"And what's wrong with that?" demanded Winnie. "Much better he should read for the first half of his life and then live for the next half. That's the proper sequence to know what you're doing. Nowadays, they start off by living and never get around to reading—it explains the mess we're all in. I predict great things for this boy."

"Really?" said Pauline, who appeared ready to be convinced.

"Yes. And he'll be right at home in our library."

"You have a library!" exclaimed Jonathan. "A library is awesome!"

"It *is* awesome," acknowledged Winnie, "and I'm glad to see you realize it. We've had people traipsing through this house who see the library and say, 'Oh so many books. What do you do with them?' 'We read them, you fools,' I want to say. But I hold my tongue. You see I was well brought up."

Jonathan laughed and closed his book, having finally found someone whom he thought was more interesting. Ben, meanwhile, had sauntered over to where Anne was standing off to the side. "Did that fellow who wanted to kill you the other day ever come back to apologize?" he asked casually.

"As a matter of fact, he did," said Anne, relieved to address a neutral topic. "He came in with his wife yesterday morning to say he was sorry he got so worked up. He even told me I should thank the gentleman who calmed him down."

Ben nodded. "I knew he would see things differently once he had a chance to think about it. A little distance always puts things in perspective."

"Ben told me what happened." Kirsten joined the conversation. "It sounds like you have a dangerous job."

Anne agreed that it had its perils, given the fierceness with which Westchester parents became invested in their children's futures.

"That seems to be very American," asserted Kirsten, "In Denmark, you'd never see parents behaving that way. We take a more philosophical view."

"Then again, you don't aspire to much," observed Ben. "Your people are content to remain where they are for generations."

"That's true," agreed Kirsten, "but aspiration isn't always desirable. There are times when it's better to accept one's place."

"It's a very class-bound society," Ben explained to Anne. "Very much a herd mentality."

"And you don't think competing over which silly college your children will attend reflects a herd mentality?" Kirsten laughed.

"I suppose it depends on which herd you want to graze with," mused Ben.

The conversation was interrupted by Sally, who announced loudly, "Time for the tour," and proceeded to lead the group through the house, concentrating attention on the wainscoting and the views from the windows, and moving as quickly as possible past the bathrooms and the island-less kitchen. Anne remained behind with Winnie, who was still talking to Jonathan.

Suddenly, Ben, who had started on the tour, reappeared and stood quietly nearby.

"Why don't you show Jonathan the library, Anne," Winnie directed, interrupting her exposition on the deficiencies of Vonnegut and the merits of Kafka. "Find him a copy of 'A Hunger Artist.' It should be on the second shelf, next to *The Kinsey Report*. What a fuss they made about that book when it came out"—she began ruminating irritably—"there was nothing there that any intelligent woman didn't already know, but a man writes it down and everyone acts as though it's a revelation. Yes, the men have the advantage there.

They make the money and write the books, and the women, poor things, stay home and mope."

"That's a rather old-fashioned view," Ben responded with surprising vehemence. "I see plenty of women making money and writing books. And if you're implying that men feel less than women, I'd have to dis-agree there too. Men mope as much as women do. Perhaps more."

"Well, I think you're wrong!" asserted Win-nie. "It may be an old-fashioned view, as you say, but old-fashioned views generally have something to them. I have nothing against men, mind you; I've spent many enjoyable hours in their company. But the truth is, they can't sustain emotion; it's not in their nature. Aren't I right, Anne?"

Anne seemed flustered to be drawn into such a topic, but she spoke after a moment's pause. "From my experience with high school students, both sexes are extremely sensitive. Boys are more stoic—they're taught to be—but I wouldn't say they feel less than girls; they just don't express their feelings in the same way." She delivered this with embarrassment, without looking at Ben, whose eyes she could feel were on her.

"You say men don't express feelings, and women do," said Winnie, "but it's the tree falling in the forest sort of thing: if no one hears, who in God's name cares? But how did we get onto this topic? It's quite irrelevant. Now, if you don't mind, dear," she addressed Anne brusquely, "please take the young man to the library and find him the Kafka while I speak to his uncle. Give us twenty minutes; that should be all we need."

At the end of the afternoon, after the pound cake had been eaten and the Courvoisier finished off (by Pauline), Sally shepherded everyone outside, where she could be heard expounding on "the authentic English heath" in the backyard.

Anne finally turned to Winnie. "Well?" she said. "What did you tell Ben Cutler?"

Winnie sat a little straighter in her wheelchair: "I told him that I would accept his invitation to stay in the house until I've regained my mobility," she pronounced with a certain formality. "In return for his generosity, I will serve as reading adviser to his nephew and companion to his sister. I am also capable of giving instructions regarding meals, and, if necessary, can direct the housekeeping as well. He offered to pay me a stipend, which I declined. I am not Jane Eyre, just an impecunious gentlewoman with ties to the estate. The arrangement promises to work very nicely; I am quite pleased with it, all things considered. Now if you don't mind, dear, I'm a tad weary. I'd like to take a nap."

CHAPTER THIRTY-EIGHT

As MARCY HAD PREDICTED, HARRY FURMAN DID call and ask Anne out. "to dinner at the Four Seasons," Anne reported to her friend. "Rather pricey for a first date with someone you didn't really get along with, don't you think?"

"Don't take the choice of restaurant too seriously," explained Marcy. "Rich and his partners only know two restaurants in Manhattan: Tavern on the Green and the Four Seasons. It's where they take all their clients. Rich took me to dinner at the Four Seasons on my birthday even though he'd been there for lunch the same day. I would have liked something a little more original, but I didn't eat much anyway."

"Personally, I'm looking forward to the Four Seasons," said Anne. "I haven't been there since I was young and we were still rich."

"It hasn't changed much," noted Marcy, "though now they give you your dressing on the side, if you ask. But hold on—are you saying that you're actually going to go out with Harry Furman? I thought you said he was a creep."

"I did," Anne admitted. "But I decided to accept anyway because I need a lawyer's advice." Carlotta was indeed refusing to vacate the Murray Hill apartment and had changed the locks. Her presence had come to resemble the bamboo that Elihu had planted in the backyard of the Westchester home to make it as he put it, "more like a colonial plantation," and which no army of men with scythes had been able to eradicate. It was Anne's hope that the analogy would not go so far—or that, at least in Carlotta's case, a good lawyer would prove more effective than a scythe.

"You could always ask Rich for help. But of course, Rich is never around," Marcy conceded sadly.

"I'm sure that Harry Furman wouldn't be around either if he were married to me," Anne consoled her. "But do you think it's wrong for me to go out with him just to get legal advice?"

"Since he probably wants to take advantage of you in some other way and since he'll probably charge the meal to the firm, I wouldn't worry about it," concluded Marcy. "Besides, you never know; you might discover that he's more attractive than you thought. There was an article in *Elle* that said women will often change their mind about a man when they go out to dinner with him—especially if it's a nice restaurant."

"Maybe," said Anne, "but I wouldn't count on it."

When the evening of the date arrived, Harry Furman met her at the Four Seasons, as arranged. He smelled of expensive cologne, his fingernails glistened, and his hair seemed an unnaturally vivid chestnut brown. Anne wondered if he had encountered her father in the course of his styling regime. Elihu was a regular at Elizabeth Arden and Georgette Klinger, places once devoted exclusively to women, until men had been liberated to be just as vain.

"You look ravishing," said Harry to Anne, without appearing to look at her. He had been told that this was an effective opening line.

It occurred to Anne, as Harry stood brushed and moussed before her, that he probably was not interested in her at all. He had simply been programmed to date as much as possible until some woman hooked herself onto him, sucked off a portion of his assets, and discarded him, so that another woman could do the same. She supposed the process had some ecological value that might be worth studying.

When viewed from this perspective, Harry was not the exploitative male that she had originally thought, but rather a kind of roving innocent, fated to be continually picked up and dropped by savvy, predatory women. It was a new take that rendered him less absolutely distasteful, if more profoundly pathetic.

They were ushered into the restaurant and settled into Harry's usual spot. As Marcy had surmised, Harry Furman was a regular at the Four Seasons. Indeed, when he wasn't there, he was usually at the gym, burning off the calories acquired from being there.

"Well?" said Harry, once the napkins had been spread on their laps by obsequious waiters. He looked at her hopefully. He was a man who had a hard time with transitions, and whoever had given him his opening line had not gotten around to prompting him on what to say after "you look ravishing."

"Well," said Anne, deciding to get right to the point, "do you happen to know anything about real estate law?"

Her question had a surprisingly animating effect. Harry breathed a sigh of relief. The law was not only his bread and butter, it was the air he breathed. In point of fact, it was the only thing that really interested him.

"Real estate law isn't my specialty," he began modestly, "but"—his tone grew more confident and boastful—"I pride myself in being something of a Renaissance man when it comes to legal matters. You'd be amazed at the kinds of things that cross my desk. I've had clients ask me to draw up euthanasia agreements for their pets and contract killings for their wives." Since he possessed two cats and two ex-wives, the idea that clients would want to kill their pets out of affection and their wives out of hatred did not strike him as terribly incongruous.

"Not that I ever agreed to either," he hurried to assure her. "But let's put it this way, I know the law—and if I don't have the answer for you here and now, I can certainly get it. Did you know that I was a lifeline on *Who Wants to Be a Millionaire?*"

Anne expressed admiration for this surprising fact, which allowed for a detour into the question he had been summoned to answer on national television on behalf of his secretary. It had involved the origin of chicory, learned when he was handling a case involving export law for the Jamaica Trade Association.

"The woman won seventy-five thousand dollars because of me," said Furman, "and quit her job. I haven't found a good secretary since." He ruminated for a moment on this. He had married her successor and she had soaked him for half his net worth.

"I know a lot," continued Harry proudly, not taking into account that he apparently didn't know how not to be a sucker. "I'm actually a lot better with facts than with people," he confessed, engaging in what Anne took to be something vaguely akin to insight.

She saw this as her cue to return to the initial subject. "Real estate law," she prompted.

"Shoot!" Harry settled back in his chair, his arms on the armrests, as though he were still a contestant on *Who Wants to Be a Millionaire?*

"This is the situation," explained Anne. "I rent an apartment in Murray Hill that I've been subletting for the past few months to someone who appears unwilling to vacate the premises now that I want to move back. I went over the other day and she'd changed the locks."

"Is your name on the lease?" asked Harry promptly.

"It is."

"Then there's no problem."

"But the locks?"

"Iron bars do not a tenant make," pronounced Harry pithily. "Let me handle it." He made a sweeping gesture with his hand that also served to prompt the waiter to pour the wine.

"I have to tell you, though," said Anne sheepishly, "I don't have the money to pay you for your help. Our family is pretty much wiped out in the way of financial assets. I've been using my savings to pay off the debts. It's not a pretty picture, and if I lose my apartment, I don't know what I'll do."

Though it might have been a stretch to call Harry Furman compassionate, he certainly wasn't cruel. As he saw it, the chance to expound on his involvement with *Who Wants to Be a Millionaire?* was payment enough. Anne even figured that if she wanted to, she probably could have gotten him to agree to come to Career Day at this moment.

"Honey, this sort of thing is a mere bag of shells to me," boasted Harry. "A damsel in distress deserves a little help from an expert. Give me the address, the landlord's name, and the name of the individual currently in residence, and I'll have it worked out for you in a jiffy. I do this sort of thing in my sleep."

Anne felt a welling of gratitude that did not, however, resemble attraction, since she was not inspired by Harry's halfhearted attempt to get her to go back to his Park Avenue duplex after dinner. All in all, he seemed relieved at her refusal. The evening had been quite pleasant, and he could now retire to his apartment, put on his pajamas, and watch *Saturday Night Live* without anyone to distract him.

CHAPTER THIRTY-NINE

POETRY DAY AT FENIMORE WAS HELD ON OCTO-
ber 31 and billed as a special Halloween
event, a prelude to trick-or-treating that
night. It was one of the paradoxes of high-
school kids that they oscillated wildly between adult and childish pastimes. Even if
they were drawn to tawdry, illicit activities
like drug taking and promiscuous sex, they
still enjoyed simple, innocent ones like wearing cheesy costumes and collecting candy
from their neighbors.

For Poetry Day, students had been instructed to dress up as their favorite poet,
though the notion that they had a favorite

poet involved a certain poetic license in itself. As in the past, many of the less inhibited boys wore tights and came as
Shakespeare—this year, one even wore a
codpiece made from a plastic container.
Among the girls, there were at least a dozen
Sylvia Plaths in shirtwaists and headbands.
(*The Bell Jar* had been assigned in eleventh-
grade English and the Gwyneth Paltrow
movie *Sylvia* had been shown by the substi-
tute during the week when the regular
teacher was sick, conveniently timed so as
to coincide with the end of the Plath unit.) A
few Emily Dickinsons were represented by
starched pinafores and white pancake
makeup. There were also the rock enthusiasts who insisted that the Beatles were
great poets and made a racket in the hall
with their electric guitars, until the instru-
ments were confiscated by Mr. Tortoni, the
assistant principal.

The lazier or more inhibited students favored a more minimalist presentation. They
simply held a sheet of paper with the first
lines of a poem by their chosen poet scrib-
bled on it.

Both the honors and the AP English
classes had been assigned Peter Jacob-

son's poems, and as Anne had predicted, one student even decided to dress up as Peter. He came wearing a black turtleneck and holding a sheet of notebook paper with the first lines of Peter's poem, "The Poet Stutters at Death." Holding the paper aloft, he waved his pen and furrowed his brow as though trying to think of the lines to follow: "I read as she lies writhing in the bed; / She shakes her head; / And it's like death has passed a verdict on the lines I read." Anne privately thought it might be better, with lines like this, to crumple up the paper and start again.

Peter visited the creative writing class in the morning, when he held what the teacher grandly termed "a master workshop." Dana Mosser, a gifted creative writer who wanted to go to Wesleyan, happened to be in this class. Her poems so impressed Peter that he quickly agreed to write a supporting letter to offset her poor math SAT.

He also found something to like in the work of the other students in the class, even those who had taken the course only because it was supposed to be an easy A and fit into their schedules. These types seemed torn between liking poetry and disdaining it.

"It's all bullshit," said one student, "but it's fun. 'Cause you can't be wrong." Not being wrong was apparently a nice change of pace.

"All you have to do to write poetry is find two things that have nothing to do with each other and say they do," said another student. "My heart is like a dripping faucet—that's one I came up with the other day."

"Not bad," said Peter.

He was particularly taken with a very long poem by a student who had spent half his high school career in detention. It was titled "I Hate It":

When my mom comes in and straightens
　　my room. I hate it.
When they give me lots of pennies for
　　change. I hate it.
When they make me run the track in
　　gym. I hate it.
When they want me to turn my home-
　　work in. I hate it.
When I drink so much I have to pee. I
　　hate it.
When moron girls call me a dweeb. I
　　hate it . . .

"You should consider sending that to one of the poetry journals," Peter counseled.

Afterward, he told Anne that she was right about the sixteen-year-old imagination—it was fresh and original. Ultimately, he said, he liked what the high-school students wrote more than what he'd seen in his MFA program.

After lunch, there was an assembly devoted to the puppet production of *Much Ado About Nothing*. It was, to Anne's surprise, a great success. Many students, who normally would have violently resisted watching a Shakespeare play, seemed to find it more palatable when performed by puppets, and she overheard one boy leaving the assembly observe that "the Beatrice puppet was really hot." Even Peter said that he thought the performance had a macabre charm.

After the puppet show, Peter was taken to address the AP English class. The students in this class, who had just wrapped up three weeks on modern poetry, seemed to feel that they could now get the inside track on this whole poetry racket.

"Who are the ten greatest poets of all time?" demanded a spokesman for the class.

Anne thought Peter would see this as a simplistic exercise, but instead, he seemed pleased to wield the scepter of judgment and launched enthusiastically into the countdown:

"One: Shakespeare." ("Shakespeare rules!" yelled the boy with the plastic codpiece, as though he were being personally honored.)

"Two: Milton. He wrote *Paradise Lost.* The greatest action-adventure poem in English. The hero is Satan—but it's still a very spiritual poem." (The students took down this anomaly in their notebooks.)

"Three: John Donne. He makes sex seem really spiritual, and God seem really sexy." (The students nodded, as though this made sense to them.)

"Four: William Wordsworth. Big on nature, but there's more going on than just flowers and trees.

"Five: Walt Whitman—great American poet, sort of started the gay pride movement.

"Six: Emily Dickinson. A nutcase, but brilliant.

"Seven: William Butler Yeats. An Irish poet—I'm partial to that, since I'm Irish on my mother's side. He's got some neat mystical stuff going.

"Eight: Robert Frost. You read his poem 'Stopping by Woods on a Snowy Evening' in third grade. He wrote lots more that are just as good.

"Nine: Gwendolyn Brooks—a woman of color who didn't preach about it.

"Ten: Don Riggs. You probably never heard of him. He lives in Philadelphia and writes for small literary journals and online magazines. Look him up on the Internet. He's a genius."

"Don't you belong on the list, Mr. Jacobson?" shouted one admiring student.

"No," said Peter. "To be honest, I'm not very good." Anne felt almost inclined to like Peter's poetry in the face of such refreshing candor.

"What about T. S. Eliot?" asked another student. They had just read "The Love Song of J. Alfred Prufrock" in AP English.

"Overrated," declared Peter.

"Wallace Stevens?" They had also read "The Idea of Order at Key West."

"I don't understand him," Peter pronounced frankly. The class shifted pleasantly at being reinforced in their own view.

"Don't you think Sylvia Plath belongs in the top ten?" asked one girl belligerently.

She headed up the Multicultural Club and the Gay-Straight Alliance.

"No," said Peter. "She's like me. One subject, beats it to death. She got famous from killing herself. It's a possible recipe for fame—but of course you can never be sure it'll work."

Despite a few students like the Plath advocate who were disappointed that Peter hadn't put their favorites in the top ten (A. E. Housman! Kurt Cobain! The guy who wrote the limericks!), most thought he was really cool.

"I hope you haven't ruined T. S. Eliot and Wallace Stevens for them," murmured Anne as the class was leaving.

"I hope I have," said Peter.

"You seem to be in a very good mood, for you," observed Anne. Peter's involvement with the ailing Rachel had definitely raised his spirits, transferring his emotional focus from someone dead to someone merely convalescing. He and Rachel were slowly working their way through *The Norton Anthology of Poetry*. By the time Rachel was fully recovered, Anne surmised, she would be well versed in poetry (at least in the poetry Peter liked) and would have greatly improved her vocabulary.

*   *   *

As the final event of Poetry Day, Anne had arranged for Peter to give an evening reading that would be open to the community. She planned to use the occasion to thank him formally for his bequest to the school arts program with the hope of inspiring others to do the same. "Most people just don't think of making that kind of contribution," she explained to Vince, "so we have to model for them."

"Good point," agreed Vince. "But my guess is that this guy had more in mind than helping the school." He gave Anne an insinuating look. Vince tended to suspect, based on his own example, that men did most things for moderately impure motives. "Is this Peter Jacobson your latest conquest?" he asked knowingly.

Anne knew she was supposed to laugh and explain that Peter was devoted to her cousin. But a feeling of sadness made it impossible for her to speak. What did that mean: "your latest conquest"? What conquest would ever mean anything to her again? The one conquest that mattered had been made—and lost—long ago.

CHAPTER FORTY

THERE WAS AN ENORMOUS TURNOUT FOR PETER Jacobson's reading that evening, as many people had predictably confused the Pitzer Prize with the Pulitzer Prize, or possibly with the Pritzker Prize, a major architectural award. As Anne looked out over the sea of faces, she saw Ben and Kirsten in the audience, further casualties, she suspected, of the Pitzer-Pulitzer confusion.

The final settlement on the house was about to be completed, and she knew that the Cutlers expected to move in by the middle of November. She had not yet dislodged Carlotta from her New York apartment, but

Harry Furman had assured her that he would solve the problem soon—not to worry. Meanwhile, Ben had begun planning the Scarsdale renovation. An architect and a contractor had been by and spoken briefly with Winnie. And someone had already begun repaving the driveway. "Benjamin said he would hate to have us liable for an accident if someone blew out a tire or worse in one of those potholes," Winnie explained. "Very considerate of him, if I may say so." Winnie had assumed the line that Ben was more of a benefactor than a usurper and had refused to dwell on past history. Anne found this surprising, if not downright odd, but also rather comforting. It made the whole transaction much easier.

After Vince introduced Peter (stumbling predictably over the titles of the more arcane poetry journals in which his poems had appeared), Anne presented him with a certificate in acknowledgment for his generous bequest. As she was about to leave the stage, Peter clasped her hand and kept her beside him as he spoke feelingly into the microphone:

"Everyone really ought to thank this woman here," he declared, gripping her hand tightly, even as she tried to extract it from his grasp so she could sit down. "She is the person responsible for my being here today. Anne Ehrlich, as anyone who has ever met her knows, is a woman of unparalleled intelligence, taste, and compassion. She is devoted to enriching and supporting the lives of students, and a model of dedication and service to her community. We all owe her an enormous debt of gratitude."

There was loud applause, and Anne felt like ducking under a chair. She was unaccustomed to being in the spotlight, and as her eyes grazed the audience, she saw that Ben Cutler was looking at her, his face particularly somber. She imagined that Peter's effusive tribute had sounded an ironic note in his ears.

Once the poetry reading began, she relaxed and prepared herself for a long evening. From her experience, poets commonly forgot that poetry is a distinctive taste and that most people liked to encounter it, if at all, in very small doses. Lengthy dronings of even the most brilliant verse were liable to make even the most enlightened audience restless, irritable, and unwilling to attend a poetry reading again.

Surprisingly, however, Peter turned out to be an exception in this regard. He had the sense to keep his reading short and to provide charming if rather morbid asides and anecdotes that helped the poems go down more easily. "This one was written at the deathbed of a loved one," he said by way of introducing a poem entitled "Frosted Death": "We had just shared a bowl of Frosted Flakes, and I was struck by how the sweetness of that cereal, with its childhood associations, was linked with the sense of being immortal. As you can see, this poem conflates that youthful lack of worry with a mature awareness of mortality." This was just the sort of thing that the Westchester community could handle.

He read about a dozen poems, including one about eating snow, one about getting a bloody nose in grade school, one about watching a nurse try to find a vein for an IV in his dying girlfriend's wasted arm, and one comparing the smell of hospitals with the smell of gummy bears. The alternation between the humorous and the macabre kept the audience alert, both amused and moved. His last poem, "Burying the Dead: Falling in Love Again," which Anne assumed to be about Rachel, produced a wave of tearful delight. Everyone likes happy endings, and the female members of the audience were particularly pleased that such a handsome young man, and so talented (a Pulitzer Prize winner, after all), was on the road to recovery.

After the reading, Anne saw Ben and Kirsten approach and prepared to greet them, even as painful thoughts crowded her head. She wondered, for example, when they planned to get married and whether they would have the wedding at the house. Winnie had always said how much she wanted to have Anne marry under a tent in the backyard, the way her mother had. "That was a beautiful wedding," Winnie liked to reminisce, "even if she did marry a fool."

Anne wished that she didn't think of such things. But with her grandmother remaining in the house, she would have to get used to seeing Ben and Kirsten together. It might be better for her to rehearse the probable scenarios in advance rather than have them sprung on her without preparation.

"Your boyfriend is quite the bard," said Ben, breaking her reverie and nodding toward Peter, who was standing nearby, being gushed over by several female members of the audience. Their admiration seemed to boil down to his writing poetry while being so handsome.

Anne looked at Ben, surprised. He had made the understandable mistake of thinking that Peter was her boyfriend, but what struck her was the sourness of his tone. She looked at him quizzically, and was about to correct the error, when Kirsten declared energetically, "Well, I personally liked his poetry. I thought it was very heartfelt."

This remark appeared to provoke Ben. "Very heartfelt!" he exclaimed with irritation. "Now, there's a recommendation. When are people going to realize that you can feel deeply and still write crap?"

"I think the poems had the strengths and weaknesses of youth," insisted Kirsten. "I wouldn't call them crap."

"Did I call them crap?" asked Ben, his tone growing, if anything, more sarcastic, as he looked at Anne with an air of mock innocence. "I was speaking in general terms. I didn't say the guy's poems were crap! Maybe I think they're crap, but I didn't say so." There was an edge to his voice that Anne realized she had heard only once before, long ago. He was angry—angry when the situation didn't warrant it. She felt a sudden wave of pleasure. Could it be that he was jealous of Peter Jacobson? It couldn't possibly be—and yet his manner seemed to suggest as much.

Before she had a chance to fully assess his reaction, a group of Fenimore parents engulfed her with pressing questions: "Will the admissions office think Shari isn't serious about Syracuse if she visits for only one night instead of two?"; "Should Jacob take the SATs again to try to improve his 2370 score?"; and "Should Dawn list tennis ahead of debate on her college application?" It was amazing how these questions, whose answers were either blatantly obvious or entirely inconsequential, took on weight and urgency for these otherwise intelligent people. But one of the by-products of the college admissions process was that it impaired parental judgment. Like a seasonal disorder or a bout of PMS, the insanity would pass eventually, though not before Shari was ensconced at Syracuse and Jacob launched at Penn.

As she fielded these questions, Anne soon lost sight of Ben and Kirsten. Everyone was herded into the cafeteria by the Home and School Committee, where a nice spread had been laid out. Mrs. Wanamaker's brownies were much praised and, in the end, were possibly as big a hit as Peter's poetry, though they could hardly claim the imprimatur of the Pitzer Prize.

CHAPTER FORTY-ONE

SOON AFTER SHE ARRIVED AT WORK THE NEXT
morning, Anne received a call from Harry
Furman. "The problem with your apartment
is solved," he announced triumphantly. "You
can move back in on Monday."

"Really?" said Anne. She had never
doubted that the law was on her side, but
she had expected there would be more of a
tussle with Carlotta. She had even been prepared to pay her off, within reason. But apparently this was not going to be necessary.
Harry, it seemed, was as good a lawyer as
he had boasted he was.

"Oh yes, the place is almost ready. We'll

leave the keys with the super for you to pick up on Monday. As you know, Carlotta changed the locks, so you'll need them."

Anne paused. There was something in the manner of this communication that struck her as odd. He had referred to Carlotta by her first name. But that wasn't it. Everyone who met Carlotta referred to her as Carlotta. No—the oddity lay in the use of "we.": "We'll leave the keys with the super for you to pick up.'"

Anne tried to sound nonchalant. "I suppose Carlotta made quite a fuss," she said. "She was pretty set on staying in the apartment."

"Well, yes," said Harry slowly, "she did at first. But then things worked out."

"How fortunate," said Anne, "that they did."

"Yes," said Harry, clearing his throat. "Carlotta and I rather hit it off. She's a very attractive lady and, well, she seemed to see something in me. What, I can't imagine."

Anne thought that she could: a duplex on Park Avenue at Seventy-ninth Street.

"So it was simply a matter of transferring her things to my place," explained Harry. "I would have contacted you sooner, but I wanted to make sure everything was cleared out and the place was in good condition.

Carlotta has quite a few things, especially in the clothing department. Fortunately, I have walk-in closets, and we plan to turn the third guest room into a boudoir, as Carlotta puts it. We're also renovating the bathrooms. She says she couldn't possibly live without a bidet."

Anne felt extremely grateful to Harry. He had not only liberated her apartment but also, upon consideration, her father. Not that Elihu would have any sense that he had been trapped. Indeed, since he had no money, it was a matter of semantics as to whether Carlotta had trapped him or he had trapped her. Still, there was no saying what sort of assets she might have wrung out of him in the long run.

As it happened, Anne had made a recent discovery that shed additional light on Carlotta Dupre. It all began a week ago when Fenster had announced that the key to his *Tale of Two Cities* test had been stolen. Vince had then asked Mr. Tortoni, the assistant principal, to get to the bottom of the theft, and Tortoni had commandeered one of his famous "locker sweeps," in which a small army of handpicked staff fanned out into the halls and insisted that students open their lockers on the spot. As a result of this operation, not only was the missing test key discovered in the locker of Sylvius Alexrod (son of Arnold Alexrod, the Corian king), but Sylvius's locker also yielded the keys to a dozen other teachers' tests, along with an extensive stash of hard-core pornography. (Sylvius, apparently, in the entrepreneurial spirit of his father, had been running a media empire from his locker.) Sifting through the material with Vince after school, Anne had had her eye caught by a DVD that pictured a revealingly clad young woman, identified as "international supermodel, Candy Delight." As Anne looked closely at the alleged supermodel in the hot pink jersey, she realized that Candy Delight looked amazingly like Carlotta Dupre.

CHAPTER FORTY-TWO

THE PASSING OF THE SCARSDALE HOUSE INTO the hands of the Cutlers happened with surprising ease. Anne had timed her departure to coincide with their moving in, and as she packed her things in her old bedroom, which she had occupied for the past several months, she could see trucks coming in and out of the freshly repaved circular driveway in a steady procession. They carried the Cutlers' worldly possessions—which were quite literally of the world: Turkish rugs, Danish cabinets, Russian samovars. Along with this cornucopia of exotic objects were boxes of books. That, Anne thought, was one thing that hadn't changed about Ben Cutler. An image of his old Queens apartment with its piles of books lining the walls flashed into her head. She pushed the image away; she had no wish to revisit the memories of that time.

Carrying her suitcases out to the front door, she practically collided with Ben, who was bringing another box of books into the house. Without saying anything, he put down the box, took the suitcases from her hands, and carried them to the car. She followed him out, not sure how she felt. He was helping her—the suitcases were heavy—but the quick, sudden movement with which he had taken them from her had seemed almost hostile. She remembered the anger in his voice when he had spoken about Peter Jacobson and wondered if he was still angry—or—she hardly dared think it—jealous. She watched him as he swung the suitcases into the trunk and found her gaze fastened, against her will, on the curve of his back. She had once encircled that back with her arms, and the recollection engulfed her, despite herself.

"I see you paved the driveway," she said

lamely, after he had stowed the suitcases and turned around. Her mind was in turmoil, and the smooth surface beneath her feet was all she could think of to talk about.

He ignored the comment. "Feel free to stop by whenever you please," he said in a clipped tone. "I know how devoted you are to your grandmother."

Was there irony in his voice? She didn't know. She had the impression that he was about to say more, but Pauline now called loudly from one of the downstairs windows. "Bennie—where do you want to put these books? Don't you think we should give them away since you already read them?"

Ben gave a short laugh. "She can't understand that books don't get used up. I've tried to explain that they aren't like clothes or furniture—that we keep them because we might want to read them again."

"And because they remind us of how we felt when we read them," added Anne softly.

He nodded and was silent a moment. "Well, I'd better get going before my philistine sister gets rid of all my books." He paused a moment longer. "Don't worry about your grandmother." His voice had an undertone of gentleness. "Pauline may not be good with books, but she's excellent with people. She'll take good care of her."

Then, he turned, and she watched his back as he walked to the house, leaving her alone.

CHAPTER FORTY-THREE

ANNE HAD NOT BEEN BACK TO HER MURRAY HILL apartment in months, so when she finally lugged her suitcases up the three flights and opened the door, she almost turned around and walked out—she thought she had come to the wrong place. The apartment was immaculate. A cleaning service had obviously been in, which had washed and ironed the curtains and bedspread and had eliminated all babka crumbs from the corners of the kitchen, all crushed caviar from the rugs, and all champagne from the ceiling. These were casualties that Anne knew had occurred during Carlotta's residence, having visited once or twice to pick up a few items during that period.

A new coat of paint had also been applied to the walls, and some of the appliances had actually been replaced. Anne could only put this astonishing transformation down to Harry Furman's intervention. Certainly, it could not be ascribed to Carlotta, a woman who had never for a moment thought of anyone's comforts but her own.

Indeed, her suspicions regarding Carlotta's past occupation had been confirmed after she had slipped the tape of *Supermodels Burn Up the Sheets* into her handbag when Vince wasn't looking. After Winnie had gone to bed, she popped it in the VCR and was confronted with the unmistakable person of Carlotta Dupre, "operating," so to speak, under the name Candy Delight. One could hardly say she was burning up the sheets—she seemed to be rather bored— nonetheless there was a good deal of activity with multiple partners that did not look simulated, in the parlance of the industry. Clearly, Carlotta had done things for cash that were not on the intellectual level of *The Widening Gyre*.

But Anne assumed that the subject of

Carlotta Dupre had been thankfully put to rest until one Sunday, soon after she had moved back to her apartment. She was drinking her morning coffee when the downstairs buzzer rang.

"It's Carlotta," said the voice over the intercom.

Anne couldn't imagine what Carlotta would want to say to her, but she buzzed her in. Perhaps she had left a thong behind the bookcase.

To her surprise, Carlotta and Harry both appeared at the door. Harry was carrying a bottle of champagne and Carlotta, a bouquet of roses. "These are for you," she said.

Anne couldn't help noting that there was a difference in Carlotta's demeanor. Physically, she looked the same. Indeed, if anything, she was more glamorously attired—in a suede miniskirt with fringe and a lemon yellow silk blouse. "Versace," she commented in an aside to Anne, "this year's line."

"We came to thank you," she continued. She was holding Harry's hand and smiling happily. Harry also looked extremely pleased.

Anne took in the couple. It suddenly

struck her that this might be a felicitous match after all. Carlotta's apparent happiness seemed to derive from ridding herself, finally, of all money worries. It was no longer a matter of adult videos, runway remnant sales, sublet apartments, or assistant editorships at small unremunerative poetry journals. She was now the queen of her own domain, beholden to no one—soon to be on the board of the Met and the New York Public Library.

It occurred to Anne that Carlotta had merely suffered a kind of money deprivation in the way diabetics suffer insulin deprivation. Provide the needed substance and the patient revives—becomes animate, lively, even pleasant to be around. Now that Carlotta had money via Harry—who had loads of it and no compunction about sharing it, so long as his partner showed him a modicum of gratitude and affection—she no longer had any reason to be nasty.

"We wanted the apartment to look as good as possible," she said. "It was my idea to have it painted. I was going to do the walls in teal, but I didn't want to take the liberty. I know you go for a more classic look. So I went with white, like you had before."

"That was nice of you," said Anne, referring both to the painting of the apartment and the fact that Carlotta had restrained herself from painting it teal.

"It's just so wonderful that I met Harry," continued Carlotta, "and I feel I owe it to you. He told me about having dinner with you, and how you told him you were really poor, which was news to me." She gave Harry a knowing look.

"Carlotta wants to apologize," said Harry. "She feels that she hasn't behaved very well to your family."

"Yes," said Carlotta. "I bared my chest to Harry." Harry nodded and looked down admiringly at Carlotta's extensive cleavage. "Including some work I did when I had no money. As it turned out, I didn't have to tell him; he recognized me. He, sort of, admired my work." She gave a tender glance toward her fiancé, who patted her hand. (When Harry had gone to check out Anne's apartment that first time and Carlotta had opened the door, he had been thrilled to be confronted with Candy Delight, whose "work," as he later confessed, he had long followed with appreciation.) "Not that he would ever want me doing anything in that line again—

except privately," she explained, squeezing Harry's hand.

"I probably owe your father an apology too," continued Carlotta. "I was sort of leading him on. It's so hard when you don't have resources. But now that I'm with Harry I can see how morally bankrupt I was."

"'Morally bankrupt' is too strong," insisted Harry.

"Well, misguided then," Carlotta amended.

"But we both feel as though we owe you something," said Harry. "When I told Carlotta about your situation—how you had no money and you were helping your grandmother, she felt really guilty. She's got a heart of gold, you know—when she can afford it. We feel we want to make it up to you somehow."

"No need," said Anne hurriedly.

"But we want to do something to express our gratitude, so we thought we'd like to have you be the maid of honor at our wedding," continued Carlotta. "Neither of us has much family, except my dad in France, and Harry's ex-wives. It's just going to be a small ceremony, but we feel really strongly about wanting you to be part of it."

Anne drew a breath. What she really wanted was for these people to live happily ever after and never see her again.

"I'd be honored," she said.

"Great!" exclaimed Harry. "Now, let's get a move on, Candy; you've got a fitting at Bendel's this afternoon."

He was infatuated, but he hadn't neglected to draw up a prenup. After all, he'd been a lifeline on *Who Wants to Be a Millionaire?* He wasn't stupid.

CHAPTER FORTY-FOUR

DURING THE WEEK OF HER HOSPITALIZATION, Rachel's relationship with Peter Jacobson progressed rapidly. Together, they had waded through most of the *Norton Anthology* and devoted a large chunk of time to Wordsworth's *Prelude,* which Peter maintained was one of the great poems of all time, to which Rachel, though she tended to doze during some passages, agreed. Her taste in poetry coincided uncannily with his, which made it inevitable that they fall in love.

When she was finally released from the hospital, the question arose as to where she would go. Rachel, inspired by Frost's "Mending Wall," had mended her relationship with her mother and therefore had the option of moving back to New Jersey, at least until she decided what she wanted to do next (the acting dream had officially died, and she was thinking about taking some elementary ed courses). But Peter begged her to move in with him. She had been reluctant at first— "it's such a big step and I wouldn't want to get in the way of his writing"—but he had convinced her that if she didn't move in, he would certainly write nothing. "I agreed for the sake of his art," she announced with an air of regal self-sacrifice. "He says I'm his muse."

Winnie had responded that being a muse was a role not to be taken lightly, and that she should be sure that she ate well and got plenty of rest so as to be up to it. When Rachel noted that they did not have much money to live on, Winnie was dismissive. "You're young, you'll figure out something. The important thing is to follow your heart." Anne had stood by and listened to this advice with a pang. How she wished it had been given to her thirteen years ago.

Meanwhile, the Cutlers had moved in and Winnie had dealt with the upheaval with surprising equanimity.

"Are you all right?" Anne asked, when she called her grandmother soon after the move.

"I'm fine," Winnie said airily. "It's hectic, but I have to say it's a pleasure to finally redecorate, especially Elihu's side of the house. Your father thought he was Rudyard Kipling—all that leather and dark wood, not to mention the bamboo in the yard. I'm happy to say we're ridding the place of all traces of Colonialism—except the bamboo; it's there for good. A very tenacious sort of plant. Kirsten and I decided that we rather admire it for that."

"So you and Kirsten are getting along?"

"Oh yes," said Winnie. "We both agree that pale yellow will be best for the second-floor halls. Not that I don't have my hands full, what with talking about Kafka with Jonathan and directing Pauline in the kitchen. She did do extremely well with the veal chops last night. Benjamin said they were the best he'd ever had—which is saying something."

"It most certainly is," said Anne.

"Now, Anne, there's no need to be sarcastic. Just because I'm getting along so well without you. You know I miss you. But these people aren't bad. Benjamin is very busy with his guides, but he comes in to chat every now and then. He's quite the gentleman, I must say. If I had known . . ." She trailed off.

"If you had known what?" snapped Anne.

"If I had known that the house would end up in such good hands, I would have sold it sooner," Winnie said quickly.

"If you'd sold it sooner, then you wouldn't have sold it to them," said Anne a bit sourly. "It was all in the timing."

"Yes, yes," said Winnie distractedly. "You know what I mean. But I have to get off the phone. We're preparing for Thanksgiving, and I'm overseeing the dinner. Pauline is sous-chef, and Kirsten will set the table and take care of the desserts. It will take quite a bit of planning."

"But you'll be out of the house by Thanksgiving," said Anne. "I thought the doctor said you could start putting weight on the ankle."

"He said I could start," corrected Winnie. "That doesn't mean I can hop up three flights of stairs to that shoebox of an apartment of yours."

"Gram!" protested Anne. "You know that

would only be temporary. We'll start looking for an elevator building as soon as you move into the city."

"I know," said Winnie in a gentler tone, "but there's no reason to rush things at my age. Especially since the Cutlers are happy to have me. I'd even flatter myself by saying I make a contribution to the household."

"I'm sure you do," said Anne, "but still—"

"The subject is closed. I'll leave when I'm ready. Or when they throw me out. Meanwhile, I expect you here for Thanksgiving."

"I don't know," said Anne doubtfully.

"What do you mean, you don't know? You have to come. We always celebrate Thanksgiving together Besides, it's tiresome always talking about you. We might as well have you here in person."

"Who's always talking about me?"

"Well, I am," said Winnie. "And Kirsten is very interested."

"Is that so?" said Anne, feeling confused.

"Of course," said Winnie. "You're one of our favorite topics of conversation."

CHAPTER FORTY-FIVE

THANKSGIVING AT THE EHRLICHS' WESTCHESTER home had once been a major festive occasion. In the days when Anne's mother was healthy, people—some of them quite famous—had vied for invitations. Even when she was dying, there had been a wonderful last Thanksgiving, as Winnie told it. All the Mazurs were present—now deceased or scattered—as well as a generous sampling of New York intellectuals and people from the arts whom the Mazurs had been adept at collecting. Anne's mother, though weak almost to the point of being unable to stand, had somehow rallied and made the sweet potatoes with marshmallows. Winnie had gone all out with three kinds of stuffing. Elihu had bought the best champagne, and everyone had gotten pleasantly drunk and, despite their intellectual pretensions, recessed to the library after dinner to watch football. Anne could not remember this occasion—she had been only three at the time—but she imagined that she did. That had been Thanksgiving as it was supposed to be.

Her actual experience of the holiday tended to be less pleasant, since it usually involved the grudging participation of her father, her sister, and a motley assortment of their friends, brought along to ease the strain of family contact.

This year, however, promised to be unpleasant in a different way. Anne would have preferred the more familiar awkwardness of celebrating with Elihu and Allegra, but Allegra had conveniently flown off to a poetry conference in Hawaii. (Why the conference couldn't be held in, say, Yonkers was anyone's guess, but Allegra wasn't going to let the expense of such a trip get in her way. She was as adept at getting grants to far-off places as other women are at finding bargains in luxury department stores.)

Elihu was also otherwise engaged. He had promised to celebrate Thanksgiving with members of his club (which club wasn't clear—perhaps it was a composite festivity involving all of them). "I've given my word, and my word is bond," he announced, never explaining *why* he had given his word.

Anne wondered if her father was nursing a broken heart over the loss of Carlotta, but concluded that this was unlikely. If his blood was on the order of expensive cologne, his heart was like the pedal on a high-end exercise bike: It performed its function extremely well but did not harbor any of the mysterious attributes that that organ was supposed to possess.

Even though Elihu had no gift for true feeling, he was able to accrue companionship (friendship would be too strong a word). His companions were men like himself, thoroughly disconnected from their emotional lives, who enjoyed spending time together because no demands were placed on them. They ate expensive food, drank expensive liquor, took potshots at their allegedly philistine peers, and modeled their latest bespoke shirts and jackets for one another. There appeared to be a legion of such men living in

New York City, and Elihu seemed to know all of them.

Anne had little choice but to accept the invitation Winnie had proffered—and that Pauline made a point of seconding in an e-mail. Winnie had also determined that Rachel should come. And since Rachel was now living with Peter Jacobson, Peter should too.

"Of course, we must have him," Winnie had said. "Kirsten is very keen on his work. And the young man is devoted to Rachel, which speaks volumes in his favor."

Anne found her grandmother's assumption that it was her Thanksgiving, though the house was no longer hers, a bit presumptuous—but let it go. Winnie seemed happy.

As for herself, she had her work, her health, and her New York apartment back. What more could she want?

CHAPTER FORTY-SIX

ON THANKSGIVING DAY, ANNE PUT ON THE sleeveless red dress with the scooped neck that she had bought at Saks several years ago. It had been purchased for a New Year's Eve party, but she hadn't worn it because she thought she would freeze to death.

"You're supposed to wear a cute little cover-up that you take off at the opportune moment," Marcy had advised her.

"But I don't own a cute little cover-up," noted Anne, "and if I wear a shlubby little sweater, it'll look stupid."

"Then, just wear the dress and be cold," counseled Marcy, who believed that a sexy dress was half what was needed to get to the altar (she cited *Cosmo*), and Anne ought to wear it even if she caught pneumonia. It was the sort of sacrifice one made for love. It was because Anne had refused this advice, Marcy declared, that she was still single.

But Thanksgiving Day was balmy, and Anne found herself putting the dress on, taking it off, and putting it on again. In the end, she concluded that it would be wrong to let such an expensive garment go to waste and decided to wear it.

When she rang the doorbell of the Scarsdale house, Pauline greeted her with her usual effusiveness: "That dress—my God, you're a vision! Not that anything wouldn't look great on you—with your figure! Kirsten, come look—it's Anne. Doesn't she look stunning?"

Kirsten, who was wearing an understated silk suit, looked at Anne a moment and said simply, "You look great—and I'm so glad you came. This was your home, and I hope you'll always feel welcome."

"We can't tell you how we love it here," gushed Pauline. "It's like we're in one of those *Masterpiece Theater* programs: *Downstairs, Upstairs*. And your grandmother is such a classy lady. She's even rubbing off on me. She told me to stop wearing so much eye shadow and to get rid of all my designer logos. I still like my pumps with the double C's, but to everything else, I said good riddance and gave them away to Goodwill."

Anne secretly pitied the homeless who would now be obliged to wear T-shirts and handbags emblazoned with Chanel and Louis Vuitton logos.

"Let me show you some of what we've done," continued Pauline, dragging Anne through rooms that had been replastered and painted for the first time in decades. The changes were startling, not just in making things brighter and more shipshape, but in revealing the underlying beauty of the house. Though it was no longer hers, she could still feel pride at seeing her childhood home brought back to life.

One side of the house was in a state of disarray, still in the throes of extensive renovation. "This will be Bennie's office area," explained Pauline. "It's hard to see how things will look, but Winnie and Kirsten say that it's going to be fabulous. Not that it wasn't fabulous before," she hurried to assure Anne.

They had approached the kitchen and

Pauline now became flustered. "We used to order from Boston Market for Thanksgiving, but your grandmother said we had to do everything from scratch this year. Not that I'm complaining. Winnie told me what to do and I did it. My goodness"—she glanced at her watch—"it's been half an hour since I looked at the turkey! I wonder if the button popped!" She ran off to see.

Left on her own, Anne wandered toward the dining room, turning into the back hall, where she practically bumped into Ben coming out of the library.

He stopped, embarrassed, and his eyes scanned her person, registering the dress but saying nothing. Anne felt a wave of excitement pass through her as they stood silently looking at each other for a few seconds. He finally spoke. "I want to apologize for my outburst the other day at the poetry reading. I was less than gracious. I had no idea that the young man was seeing your cousin."

Anne looked at him curiously. "Are you saying this would have modified your judgment?"

Ben looked confused for a moment. "I think it would," he finally said brusquely. "My response, in any case, was not entirely just. The poetry isn't so bad."

"Yes," Anne added, "after all, it did win the Pitzer Prize." They both laughed, tacitly acknowledging they had the same opinion on the subject. She felt suddenly lighthearted: "I've been meaning to tell you how much I appreciate what you've done for my grandmother. I haven't seen her so happy in years."

Ben nodded, taking this up. "She's a real addition to the household. She actually gets Jonathan to talk. And she has an improving effect on Pauline—calms her down somehow—not to mention teaching her to cook." He paused. "Kirsten likes her too."

The reference to Kirsten brought her up short once again. She had felt an exhilaration she had no business feeling. Ben was trying to be friendly, to "mend walls"—but there was no ignoring that he was engaged to be married. It was absolutely necessary, she told herself, that she keep any feelings that she still harbored for him under control.

"My grandmother likes Kirsten too," Anne muttered, lowering her eyes for a moment.

"Well, it's nice to have her approval at

last." Ben spoke with an edge to his voice, so that she looked up, surprised. His eyes flickered and he seemed about to speak again, but Pauline's voice was heard from the kitchen, announcing excitedly that the button had popped and everyone should come to the table.

CHAPTER FORTY-SEVEN

MOST OF THE DINNER WAS SPENT WITH PAULINE describing the places in the world the family had lived.

"Did you know that we spent six months in India? Beautiful country, but the women in those *shmattes* in the hot weather—I felt for them. Then it was a year in Denmark. You talk about the frying pan into the fire. That's where Bennie bought me my first fur coat. I didn't say no. Who thinks about animal rights when you're freezing your *tuchis* off?"

"Copenhagen isn't cold," protested Kirsten. "It has the Gulf Stream."

"Gulf Stream, shmulf stream, I was chilly."

"But I thought you loved Copenhagen."

"I did, but it was cold. And everyone looked like you. It didn't help my self-esteem."

"But you were such a big hit!"

"I guess I was. If everyone is tall and blond, the short Jewish girl stands out."

"Pauline, everyone loved you! My father thought you were a riot."

"I know, I know. Your dad was a doll." Pauline patted Kirsten's hand. "Everyone was very nice. And of course Bennie met you, which made it worthwhile."

"How did you two meet, anyway?" asked Rachel, curious in the manner of someone in love about other people's romances.

"Kirsten was with one of those tour groups," explained Pauline, "and Bennie was looking around for material for the guides. Someone must have told him to contact her, since Kirsten is famous in Copenhagen."

Kirsten waved her hand modestly.

"It's true," insisted Pauline. "Everyone knows you. Wherever we went, they said: 'You should talk to Kirsten Knudsen.' So, one day Bennie comes home, and he looks like the cat who ate the canary. I knew it must be a woman. And about time. There'd been someone when I was off in California having

Jonathan—but since then, nothing much. No girl was good enough. That is, until Kirsten came along."

Anne kept her eyes on her plate.

"I can identify with that," Peter jumped in. "I walked into this house and saw Rachel, a vision of pulchritude—'beauty,'" he clarified quickly, as Rachel furrowed her brow, "and it was like the proverbial cupid's arrow: I was smitten on the spot. I suppose it was the same for you." He looked to Ben for confirmation.

"Pauline—what did you think of the food in Copenhagen? Kirsten tells me it's very fresh." It was Winnie, interrupting and taking the conversation in a different direction.

"I suppose," said Pauline doubtfully, "if you like that sort of thing. Plenty of fish. Not that I don't like a good lox or whitefish spread now and then. But their lox had no taste. I always told Jonathan: 'Put a little salt on it and you'll like it better.' But I was dying for a bagel all the time we were there."

"We have bagels," protested Kirsten.

"No offense, but those mealy rolls were not bagels," said Pauline. "And the other bread was worse. You know those little packages of party rye?—that's what they liked to eat. I kept on thinking: OK, this is the hors d'oeuvres, let's get to the main course. But we never did."

Kirsten looked slightly hurt, but Peter intervened again with more questions about travel. "Did you get to Ireland by any chance? I've been wanting to go. I have a few relatives there, on my mother's side. They keep telling me to visit."

"We did go to Ireland," answered Pauline. "We spent a few months in Dublin in the late nineties. Very warm people. If it wasn't for the drinking, you'd think they were Jewish."

"Pauline!" reprimanded Ben.

"I'm just saying there were a lot of bars," said Pauline.

"Pubs," corrected Kirsten.

"Whatever."

"Jonathan," said Winnie, "since you've been to Dublin, you should read Joyce's *Dubliners*."

"I read 'The Dead,'" said Jonathan. "It was really deep."

"Yes, it's a profound story," mused Winnie. "It shows how you can't control someone else's thoughts, even if you love them." She spoke with uncharacteristic emotion, then caught herself. "Tell us more about the places you've lived," she requested of Pauline.

"Well . . . we spent six months in North Africa. That was an education!"

Ben nodded. "It's a compelling part of the world. There was a point I thought I'd like to settle there—like Rick in Casablanca." He shot Anne a glance.

"Fortunately, I was around to get him moving," noted Pauline. "He couldn't very well park himself in Africa when he had Jonathan and me to take care of. At least he can thank me for that."

"I thank you for a lot," said Ben, smiling but speaking seriously. "I thank you for being the most generous, open-hearted person I know. For showing me how it's possible to get outside yourself and feel for other people." Anne realized he was paying genuine tribute to his sister, who had done things for him that were less concrete but no less important than what he had done for her. It was a glimpse into a more vulnerable side of his nature, and it touched her to see it.

"Well, you couldn't help but feel for some of the people we met," said Pauline, showing that she had no interest in dwelling on her own qualities or hearing herself praised. "We saw a lot of poverty, you know—wherever we went there were people in need. It made us appreciate what we had."

"Yes." Ben laughed. "Pauline was always giving my clothes to the poor before I had a chance to wear them. I recall one particularly nice cashmere sweater that she gave to some teenager in Northern Ireland because she said he looked cold."

"He did look cold," insisted Pauline.

"One of the reasons I decided to settle in Westchester," continued Ben, "was to hold on to my sweaters."

Pauline nodded. "It's true. I haven't seen much poverty here."

"Not in Scarsdale," Winnie agreed. "But there's a good deal of moral poverty."

"I wouldn't know what that is."

"No, you wouldn't, dear," Winnie said gently, and Anne understood that her grandmother had finally taken the measure of this family and appreciated the qualities she had failed to notice years ago. It pleased Anne to see this, but it also saddened her that the appreciation had come too late.

"So what's next?" Peter addressed Ben with curiosity. "You seem to have published guides for all the more accessible destinations. Are you going to penetrate into the Amazon and Antarctica now?"

"We have Alaska, not Antarctica," noted Ben, "and we do have a guide to the Brazilian rain forest, though it's not a big seller. But what I really want is to update and expand the more popular guides. That's why I moved here."

"A base of operations, so to speak?"

"Exactly. In the past, I've done the legwork myself, visiting all the churches and museums and hiring occasional temps to do the supplementary research and writing. But now I plan to have a regular staff and field the work out."

"It's about time he settled down and started a family," piped in Pauline.

"I'll be looking for some cultured, intelligent people who like to travel and want to get paid for writing about it," continued Ben, ignoring Pauline's remark.

"That sounds like me," said Peter. "I'm a starving poet with a taste for foreign climes."

"Bennie will hire you then," said Pauline promptly.

Ben laughed. "If my sister says so, I will of course. But seriously, if you're interested, we'll talk. I need an update for the guide on the English Lake District. Do you have an interest, by any chance, in the Romantic poets?"

"They're my lifeblood!" exclaimed Peter. "I used to think I was Keats reincarnated; then when I failed to die at twenty-six as expected, it was Shelley. I waited for the death by water, which didn't come, so now I've switched my sights and I'm trying for Wordsworth. He lived the longest and had the best relationship." He looked fondly at Rachel. "Rachel likes the Romantics too," he added.

"Hire them both," declared Pauline.

Ben smiled. "Maybe we *can* arrange a gig for the two of you—romantic sojourns in the Lake Country written by a young man in love. You could add a trip to Dublin during the Joyce festival to update the section on Bloomsday. After that, I wouldn't mind using you here for some writing—maybe even some poetry for the guides. It would be a nice marketing element: 'Cutler's Guides to Culture with Original Poetry by Peter Jacobson, Winner of the Pitzer Prize.'" Anne was amused that Ben's revised view of Peter's poetry now went so far as a willingness to publish it. He may have read her thoughts, because he turned quickly to Kirsten. "What do you think, Kirsten?"

Kirsten said she thought this was an excellent idea. "And if you go to England," she added, "you could take a detour to Copenhagen. It's not that cold and the food is very good, no matter what Pauline says."

Everyone laughed.

"Kirsten gets homesick," said Ben.

"You're going to have to roll me out of here like a barrel!" Pauline announced suddenly. "This stuffing is too delish! I can't believe I made it. Of course, it's Winnie's recipe and she told me what to do."

Winnie said there were many more recipes, just as good, that she would teach her.

"If you teach me how to cook, I'll blow up like a balloon!" exclaimed Pauline.

"My dear," said Winnie, "it's all a matter of ingredients and proper portions. I'll teach you how to cook and eat so that you don't blow up like a balloon. In fact, I promise you'll lose weight."

"Now that would be a miracle!" said Pauline. Then, turning to Anne: "But your grandmother does work miracles. She's helped us all so much."

"She's the genie in the house," said Kirsten seriously.

"No, my dears," said Winnie, "I'm just an old woman who's finally learned something. God knows, it took me long enough."

CHAPTER FORTY-EIGHT

IN THE DAYS AFTER THANKSGIVING ANNE FOUND herself in a state of nervous excitement. Though she had initially denied it, she now began to think there might be signs that Ben still had feelings for her. She remembered his apparent jealousy when he thought she was with Peter, then his sudden change of tone when he discovered she was not. And there was the way he looked at her at Thanksgiving—that penetrating gaze she remembered from before. On top of all this was his remark about Kirsten: "She gets homesick."

If these signs meant anything, wasn't it imperative that she let him know how deeply she regretted giving him up thirteen years ago? She had been malleable and passive once; she was determined not to be so again. Sitting at her desk on the Monday after Thanksgiving, during a lull in student appointments, she picked up the phone and recklessly dialed the Scarsdale number.

When Pauline answered, Anne began speaking quickly. "I just wanted to see if you have any last-minute questions about the early admissions process." As she spoke, she remembered that Ben had dropped off Jonathan's Columbia application the week before. "I realize that you've already turned in the application," she backtracked, "but sometimes people think of things later, and some parents get confused by the financial-aid forms. Not"—she amended hastily—"that you need to worry about that." She knew she was barely making sense, but Pauline was mercifully oblivious.

"Thanks a bunch, honey, but it's not my area," responded Pauline airily. "Bennie takes care of all the school-related stuff. He's the brain, you know."

"Well, can I talk to the brain?" asked

Anne, amused, despite her confusion, at this characterization of Ben Cutler's intellect.

"Oh, but he's out," proffered Pauline. "He and Kirsten are spending a few days in the mountains. Not the Catskills, where we went when we were kids; it's one of those classy spots where there's nothing to do. But it's a darling place—I saw the brochure. There's a big front porch where you can snuggle, and cozy little bedrooms with feather beds—not that I expect they'll be sleeping much," she insinuated in her cheerfully vulgar way.

Anne held the phone away from her ear for a moment and caught her breath.

"Are you still there, dear?" called out Pauline.

"Yes, I'm here," said Anne, her voice tight. The image of Ben and Kirsten snuggling together at a romantic bed-and-breakfast wiped everything else from her mind.

"It's so good for a couple to get away," Pauline rattled on. "Maybe if Jonathan's father and I had done that . . . But then, he never held down a job, so taking time off wasn't really the problem." She sighed at the recollection, then returned to the subject. "But Ben and Kirsten deserve a nice vacation. They work so hard and they're so in love. I'm sure they'll take their honeymoon in Copenhagen, where Kirsten's family will be on top of them, so they might as well take advantage now, if you know what I mean."

Anne felt a wave of anger at Pauline for destroying her hopes, but she quickly regained perspective. If anything, she was grateful for this guileless chatter. It would have been far worse had she gotten Ben on the phone, and he had had to set her straight. By the time she hung up, she had resolved never to let wishful thinking override her good judgment again.

She had always resisted Marcy's advice about finding a husband because she assumed that you didn't look for love; it just happened. But now, for the first time, she saw things differently. She had told Winnie that a wonderful life was not a privilege of birth; you had to go out and make it. Well, what was she waiting for?

She took out a pencil and a yellow pad and proceeded to write:

Single female, 34, seeks male soul mate.

There. That was a beginning. But what next? Obviously, if she was going to advertise for a soul mate, she had to describe his qualities. She looked at her watch. It was getting late. You didn't describe the qualities of a soul mate off the top of your head; it was something that took time and thought to get right.

Anne put the pad into her drawer, locked it along with the student transcripts in her desk, and gathered her things to go home. Ben Cutler was behind her, she knew that now. But somewhere out there was the person who was right for her. She would consult Marcy, and together they would figure out the qualities he should have. Once this was done, he was bound to recognize himself and make an appearance.

It would be a short step, she told herself, from having her soul mate on paper to having him in the flesh.

CHAPTER FORTY-NINE

As MID-DECEMBER APPROACHED, ANNE BEGAN to get calls from her contacts at various schools informing her of their verdicts. She learned, for example, that Felicia Desiderio had been admitted to Georgetown. "We were impressed by her sincerity and industriousness," said the admissions officer; "her essay lent credence to her many supporting letters." And that Dana Mosser had gotten into Wesleyan. "That letter from the Pulitzer Prize winner, what's-his-name, really clinched it," said the admissions officer, a not very culturally savvy young man. "We look for that sort of extra piece to the puzzle. Her math scores sucked, but the famous author put her over the top, not to mention your point that she'd be making big bucks writing for *The New Yorker* someday and that the school would benefit by huge alumni donations. Just kidding . . ." Anne saw no point in correcting the reference to the Pulitzer as he shifted gears. "We did not, I'm afraid, accept the other candidate, Jodi Fields, who, despite her involvement in numerous extracurricular activities, did not seem quite up to Wesleyan standards. There was the letter from her social worker about her struggle with ADD, but it wasn't fully documented and we didn't quite know what to make of it. I'm sure Ms. Fields will do very well elsewhere."

A not surprising disappointment was Jonathan Cutler, who was deferred from Columbia. "There's no reason to give up hope," the admissions officer explained encouragingly. "There were a number of very strong early decision applicants in the humanities this year—one who published a novel that's been optioned for Tom Cruise, another who completed a translation of *Catcher in the Rye* into Chinese. Then you have your conventional editors of the school paper and literary magazine who also have perfect grades in math and science. It's no reflection on your candidate; he seemed a dedicated and interesting young man. But you have to understand that we get bushels of dedicated and interesting, so when someone has a passionate love of literature, a devotion to Habitat for Humanity, and 2400 SATs, we can't very well turn them down in favor of someone who just doesn't show that range."

Anne felt that the whole process was tainted by the necessity for "range"—often a facsimile of range created by the likes of Fink and Fisk—but she understood the reasoning. Jonathan was a narrow student and not as competitive as those with wider, more dramatically impressive credentials.

She called his home, intending to relay the news immediately, but when no one answered, she left a message asking for Pauline or Ben to call her back.

She had expected a phone call, so she jumped when, on looking up an hour later, she saw Ben standing at the door. Her first thought was to ask him how his romantic sojourn in the mountains had been—but instead she looked at him with as clinical an expression as she could muster.

His face was slightly flushed—no doubt

the result of the mountain air. "Your secretary wasn't at her desk, so I took the liberty of walking in," he explained. "I got the message you called. Pauline's out with Kirsten and your grandmother looking for curtains." He spoke hurriedly and there was a note of tension in his voice.

"Curtains are important," said Anne lightly. "Winnie says they're the eyelids of the house."

He nodded and seemed to relax a bit. "Your grandmother has a way of expressing herself. Our lives are much more interesting for knowing her."

Anne thanked him—it was another instance, she thought, of his being polite—and decided to get to the point. "The reason I called," she explained crisply, "was to relay the rather unfortunate news that Jonathan's been deferred from Columbia. I have to say that I'm not entirely surprised. His grades in math and science are lower than they like. This doesn't mean he won't be accepted in the spring—we can follow up with some additional letters, and he can retake some of the SAT IIs. But obviously, you need to have some backup options."

Ben's expression changed. She could tell

that he was disappointed and thrown off by her coolly professional manner.

"Believe me, there are many good schools that would be right for Jonathan," she assured him, her voice softening slightly. "I still feel that someplace smaller and less urban would give him a better sense of belonging."

"I see," said Ben, who didn't appear to be paying much attention.

"I compiled a list of some good liberal arts schools that he could consider. Check the Web sites. You could take a long weekend and visit—it's not too late. And if you settle on one or two, I could make some calls. I have a reputation, you know, so some of the admissions people will listen to me."

"Not at Columbia, apparently."

"There's only so much I can do," said Anne, peeved by what she took to be an accusation.

"Your family used to have leverage there."

It was true that Winnie had once been friends with some members of Columbia's Board of Trustees, but that was another time. "We had money then," Anne responded simply.

"I have money," noted Ben somewhat

sourly. "Maybe I should endow a chair or fund a program."

"I suppose you could," observed Anne, "though the cost of that sort of thing is greater than you may think. Some schools put out a list of funding opportunities—you can do anything from name the medical school to pay for a plaque on a bathroom stall—though even that can run a cool thousand or so. But assuming that you're financially up to it, is that really the way you want Jonathan to get into college? My suggestion is that you consider other schools."

Ben said nothing, but took the list she had drawn up and put it in his pocket. "Thanks for taking the trouble," he said.

"No trouble. It's my job." She paused, realizing that she sounded flip, and added, "I've been meaning to thank you for Thanksgiving."

"Our pleasure," he responded stiffly.

"It means a lot to me to see Winnie so happy."

"Yeah," said Ben, as though suddenly irritated, "I know what your grandmother means to you. Thanks for the leads." He patted his pocket. "I'll speak to Jonathan and Pauline. And maybe I'll consider an endowment." The shadow of a smile crossed his face. "I could underwrite the Cutler Cultural Center at Columbia. If nothing else, I like the alliteration."

CHAPTER FIFTY

MARCY WAS ECSTATIC WHEN SHE HEARD THAT Anne wanted to run a singles ad.

"You could do J-Date—which obviously limits the pool, ethnically speaking. Or Match.com, which opens it maybe a little too wide. Or *The New York Review of Books,* which could mean a lot of pretentious assholes. Or *New York* magazine, which might be a little too hip." She contemplated the limitations of each of these options for a moment and then concluded: "As I see it, we write the ad and send it to all of them. *Cosmo* says it's good to cast a wide net."

She took out a piece of paper. "OK, let's get started. How should we describe you?"

"I thought the idea was to describe the man," protested Anne. "You know, my soul mate."

"Oh no," corrected Marcy. "You need to sell yourself. You have to seem so desirable that all the good men want to date you. Then you sift through and find the soul mate."

"Hmm," said Anne, considering the enormity of such a sifting process, but letting Marcy continue.

"OK," said Marcy. "'Single, high-powered professional woman—'"

"But I'm a high-school guidance counselor," protested Anne.

"So?"

"It's not exactly what people think of as a high-powered professional woman."

"Listen, a high-powered professional woman is in the eye of the beholder. Besides, you have to make out that you're hot stuff or who's going to pay attention?"

"But they'll eventually find out I'm a high-school guidance counselor."

"And they'll see that you're hot stuff. So: 'High-powered professional woman, thirty-one—'"

"I'm thirty-four," corrected Anne.

"Everyone says they're five years younger, at least. I'm letting you get away with thirty-one because I know you're on the conservative side and would probably not mind an older man."

Anne let this pass.

"'Exotic beauty.'"

"Exotic beauty?"

"That's a code phrase for Jewish."

"'Sensuous—'"

"I really don't think—"

"It means that you like sex but aren't promiscuous; code for not having any sexually transmitted diseases."

Anne couldn't quarrel with that.

"'Cerebral.'"

"Cerebral!"

"You have to say cerebral. If you say smart, it doesn't sound sexy. Then: 'Loves good music, fine wine, and romantic dinners in Parisian bistros.'"

"I do?"

"Of course you do. Who doesn't?"

"I don't think you're really communicating who I am."

"The point," said Marcy irritably, "is not to communicate who you are. It's to get men to contact you. Once they get in the door, you can be who you are. It's just like the kids applying to college. Once they're admitted, they can be themselves, but they don't have a snowball's chance if they're not packaged properly. You've said so yourself."

"Well, I'm not applying to college," said Anne huffily. "I'm trying to find my soul mate. I'm not going to run an ad that makes me sound like Mata Hari."

Marcy put up her hands. "Have it your way."

"I will," said Anne resolutely. "I'm going to write an accurate ad that describes what I'm looking for. It may take me some time to compile an accurate list of attributes, but I'm convinced that once I do, my soul mate will recognize himself and answer."

"Go ahead." Marcy shrugged. "But I'm warning you: You can describe your soul mate all you want, but you're going to end up with a lot of overweight fifty-year-olds going through messy divorces who want to take carriage rides in Central Park. That's the standard fare, and if you don't go with exotic, sensuous, and cerebral, that's all you're going to get."

CHAPTER FIFTY-ONE

EVENTUALLY, ALL THE EARLY NOTIFICATION LET-
ters had been received and everyone knew
the fate of everyone else. Besides the positive verdicts from Georgetown and Wesleyan that Anne had learned from her
contacts, there was one early acceptance to
Yale (Ilene Gupta), one to Harvard (Aaron
Finkelstein), and one to MIT (Skyler
Landow). There were also two to the University of Pennsylvania (Hilary Steinberg was
deferred, allowing her to apply to Duke), and
one, respectively, to Stanford (Chelsea
Beemer, who'd given the coach the thumbs-
up a month earlier), Smith (Aurora Mendel-

sohn, who would eventually learn to roar, acquire a Mohawk, and become a tough-as-nails labor negotiator); Brandeis (Albert Odoms, where he would be a regular at Shabbat dinners); Lehigh (Tim Dougherty—"diligent and nice" had obviously paid off); Cornell (Lyle Peterson who, his voluminous research aside, had opted for the institution where his father was on the faculty of the medical school); Williams (*not* Trevor Hopgood); and Flemington (a white student, who had been sold on the novelty of the minority experience). Trevor had heard favorably from Drexel, his first choice, and Felicia had already worked out their visiting schedule for every other weekend, except when she had papers due. Toby Tucker was admitted to F&M with a scholarship (as the admissions officer had confided, under deep cover, that he would), and Paul Wasser, to Molson, Anne having effectively "negotiated" on his behalf.

It was an impressive record by any standard, especially for a smaller public school like Fenimore. Vince said it was the best year ever, "a real home run."

But there were also disappointments. Along with Jonathan Cutler and Jodi Fields, there was Sandra Newman, deferred from Georgetown, and Kyra Pearlstein rejected from Bowdoin (Kyra's case, it must be said, was hardly dire, given the number of backup applications she had ready to go out). There were also about two dozen other students who had hoped for an early acceptance but were not greeted by the animated mascot or flashing coat of arms when they logged on to the desired college Web site. As a result, Chanukah and Christmas were gloomy affairs in many homes, and even the Hermès handbag and the new video iPod could not stanch the tears.

When school finally resumed after New Year's, the first convulsions of misery had subsided and been replaced by the more subtle pain that comes of suffering the triumphalism of successful peers and the mournful looks of disappointed parents. This period could be the hardest—the one most likely to leave the teenager open to high-risk behavior, not to mention a greater than usual tendency to oversleep first period and tell Fenster to go f- himself.

Anne had hit on staging what she called "Consolation Workshops" for students who had been deferred or rejected from their first-choice schools. The idea had come to her as a practical remedy to ease the pain of their disappointment, which, she knew, could be particularly acute when parents shared in the disappointment and were continually rubbing salt in the wound.

The workshops turned out to be a great success. It was actually quite uplifting to sit in on these sessions and hear students express outrage on one another's behalf.

"Tara, you are so awesome, I think Yale was, like, retarded to defer you!"

"Stanford should kiss your ass!"

"I don't think Princeton was right for you anyway. You're way too cool to go to that jock, tight-ass, Abercrombie school. Not to mention that it's in New Jersey."

During one of these sessions, Jonathan Cutler wandered in, looked around curiously, but showed no inclination to take part.

"Are you feeling a little down?" asked Anne.

"Not really," said Jonathan. "I wasn't that gung ho about Columbia. But my uncle was, and he's a pretty good guy. I thought maybe I could pick up some tips on how to make him feel better."

"I don't think you need to stay on his account," Anne counseled, touched by his concern, but seeing in it a typical example of what psychologists call "parentification." "I'm sure he'll get over his disappointment on his own."

At one point during the workshops, a reporter from *The New York Times* showed up, alerted to the story by Vince, always on the lookout for a good PR opportunity. The reporter was so taken with the proceedings that she put herself forward as a case study: She had suffered the pain of being rejected from Brown, and now look at what she was—a hot-shot *Times* reporter! She proceeded to interview Sandra Newman and Jodi Fields, for whom being in the *Times* more than made up for not getting in early to their first-choice schools. They especially liked the photo session with the *Times* photographer, who snapped about a hundred pictures of them in front of their lockers in their Smith Brothers and Juicy cut-off T-shirts. "We'll probably use only one," said the photographer, "but we like to take a lot, just in case." Sandra and Jodi knew that he just liked taking pictures of their exposed torsos.

It was also during this period that news

arrived that Karl Kingsley, Fenimore's AP chemistry teacher, had won a National Teacher Award. The ceremony would be held the following month in Washington, D.C., where the Secretary of Education would bestow the honor.

"Who's the Secretary of Education, anyway?" asked Vince. Anne didn't know but happened to pass Felicia Desiderio in the hall, who did.

Euphoric, Vince sent a quick fax to the *Newsforum* for the next issue. This meant another large plaque for his office, not to mention a slew of stories in the national and regional press. Kinglsey, meanwhile, showed himself to be truly deserving by worrying about missing the unit on oxidation during his time in Washington.

CHAPTER FIFTY-TWO

ANNE HAD DROPPED BY THE SCARSDALE HOUSE several times after she had spoken to Ben about Jonathan's deferral from Columbia. Things seemed always to be in a state of confusion and hectic activity. Workmen were busy tearing down and putting up walls, and a steady stream of temporary employees were coming and going, doing research and typing for the guides. Anne rarely encountered Ben during these visits. On the few occasions when she did, he would mumble a few words, then duck upstairs to where he had set up his office until the renovation was completed.

On one occasion, she came across Kirsten reprimanding a sheepish-looking temp who had failed to proofread a description of New Year's Eve celebrations in Reykjavik.

"For goodness' sakes, this paragraph on the bonfires is absolutely crucial to any trip to Iceland, and it's a mess," fumed Kirsten. "There are five typos and two dangling modifiers! Don't you even know your own language? Your job is to proofread, not file your nails and talk on the phone with your boyfriend. I'm sick to death of your shoddy American work habits!" She had looked up at the end of this tirade and, seeing Anne, had turned red and hurried away.

"They're on deadline for the Iceland guide," explained Winnie when Anne told her what had happened. Her grandmother had assumed the haughty air of knowing everything that was going on and of being an invaluable resource to everyone. Many of the temps had, in fact, become dependent on her wide-ranging knowledge, using her in lieu of a dictionary and an atlas. "Yesterday, I had to define 'sectarian,' 'dissolute,' and 'peregrination,'" she said proudly, "and I had to give one poor child a geography lesson; she thought Majorca was in India."

Sometimes Anne found Winnie sitting in a chair that had been arranged for her in the kitchen, supervising the preparation of the evening meal.

"Your grandmother is teaching me all her recipes," explained Pauline happily, "and I really have lost weight." She smoothed her hips, which to Anne did not look appreciably smaller.

In addition to all this, Winnie had been helping Jonathan research colleges that would suit his interests. "Vassar is a possibility," she told Anne, "though it's hard for me to think of the place with men. My friend Phyllis went there. She studied art history and then married Bernie Zucker. I always wondered about their art history department after that.

"But there are so many options," she continued blithely in her new role as college counselor. "At the moment, I think we're leaning toward St. John's, the Great Books college in Maryland. Did you know that they read the Greeks during the freshman year? A knowledge of Aristotle, I always say, is indispensable to an educated person."

Anne didn't recall Winnie's always saying this, but she did think St. John's would be a good choice for Jonathan. She had included

it on the list she had given Ben, but had assumed he wanted his nephew to go to a
more high-profile school.

"But what does Ben think?" she asked now.

"What do you mean?" responded Winnie
with surprise. "What does Benjamin have to
do with it? It's the boy's life, not his."

CHAPTER FIFTY-THREE

IT WAS FEBRUARY, THE VAST SIBERIA OF THE school year, when the weather was raw and school had moved into a numbing routine. In February some of the seniors had given up on all semblance of work. They slept in class or spent class time passing notes about the whereabouts of the beer party that weekend. Their parents, now resigned to whatever outcome was in store, had gone into hibernation; some had actually flown off to St. Thomas or St. Croix for this purpose (thereby leaving their liquor cabinets unattended). Even Eleanor Greenbaum ceased to show up with her tube socks.

Yet it was also during this period that the juniors and their parents began to gear up for the college application process. Some had already embarked on the prerequisite college tour—that whirlwind of campus visits at which carefully selected guides, all of whom looked like they had been plucked out of Calvin Klein or Abercrombie ads, said the same thing: "X is an awesome college and everything is way better than high school." For the students, the stress of keeping the colleges straight (they all seemed pretty much the same, especially if it was raining) was compounded by the presence of their parents asking continual, annoying questions: "Is there Lactaid in the cafeteria?" "What kind of campus security do you have?" "How many doctors are on duty at the health service?" Having one's mother ask such a question was enough to make a kid want to hide under the nicely upholstered chair in the recently refurbished recruitment hall.

By March, juniors were frantically pursuing school activities that they had never been interested in before. A posse of cheerleaders suddenly turned up at the Environmental Club, announcing a pressing desire to save the ozone—though why they had waited until March of their junior year to save it was not clear. Poems written in the third grade were suddenly being submitted to the literary magazine, and the volleyball team doubled in size—everybody assumed that volleyball was easy (having played it at the beach when they were ten), and thereby a shortcut to a varsity letter. Teachers were plied with gifts of Godiva chocolate, and complaints about Fenster spiked into the double digits as grade-grubbing grew rampant.

Anne knew that spring was in the air when she received the following four e-mails in quick succession one morning:

> Hi! This is to inform you that we have decided to move to Mamaroneck for Steven's senior year. Steven has exhausted all the AP course offerings at Fenimore, and is eager to take the AP geography course offered in Mamaroneck to further boost his GPA.
> With apologies in advance for any inconvenience,
> Dr. Jessica Collins and Dr. William Faber
> (parents of Steven Collins-Faber)
>
> To: Ms. Ehrlich, Head of Guidance
> cc: Vince Flockhart, Principal; Sandy Stevens, Softball Coach; Flora Feldstein, Di-

rector, Fenimore Community Service Center
It has come to our attention that our daughter Cara's softball practice during spring term will conflict with her volunteer service at the battered women's shelter. Would the school kindly arrange to have the battered women eat an hour later so that Cara will not have to miss softball?
Thank you for your cooperation,
Jerry and Sally Saperstein

Dear Ms. Ehrlich,
I know that Kathleen's smuggling of vodka in ginger ale bottles during the track meet in upstate New York last week was an infringement of school policy. However, I feel that the one-week suspension and enforced community service at the battered women's shelter are excessive. I will be obliged to initiate legal action against Mr. Babinsky, the track coach, as well as unmask other offenders (i.e., the entire track team) should the school insist on enforcing this unreasonable penalty.
Best regards,
Myron S. Cornfield, J.D. (Kathleen's dad)

Hi again,
We have decided not to move to Mamaroneck after all (re: above e-mail). Upon con-

sideration, we realize that Jeffrey might not excel in AP geography, due to his color blindness and consequent map-reading disability. Please excuse any inconvenience if you have already forwarded his transcripts, scores, and other paperwork. We will call this afternoon to discuss our decision further.

With apologies, after the fact, for any inconvenience,

Drs. Collins and Faber

The rest of the day would now have to be spent discussing with Jerry and Sally Saperstein the distance between the battered woman's shelter and the softball field, listening to Drs. Collins and Faber explain why Jeffrey could distinguish between purple and red but not purple and green, and convincing Myron S. Cornfield, J.D., that it might not be a good idea either to implicate the track team if he wanted Kathleen to have any friends, or to sue Mr. Babinsky, the track coach, if he wanted Kathleen to be recruited by any of the top schools (where Babinsky, she hinted, had friends).

If such parental demands and complaints weren't enough, Anne also had to deal with the perpetual smaller crises of high-school

life: lost homework assignments, humilia-
tions in gym class, personality conflicts with
teachers, and broken hearts. The last of
these was by no means the least important
in Anne's view. Almost every day found
some sixteen-year-old in the throes of de-
spair, using up Kleenex in her office and
needing to be reassured that her heart
would mend and some new and improved
candidate would soon appear on the hori-
zon. Anne was expert at giving these as-
surances, though nothing in her own
experience had borne them out.

CHAPTER FIFTY-FOUR

ONE FRIDAY EVENING IN MARCH, ANNE WAS SITting in her apartment, trying to relax. She felt exhausted after her week at work, though nothing unusual had happened. Besides the standard appointments and paperwork, there had been the conventional run of traumatic events: a student with a bad haircut who hid in the bathroom for three periods; another, who broke out in hives during a pop quiz; a third, who brought sexual harassment charges against another student but dropped them when he asked her out on a date—and so on.

Now, as she tried to unwind, she took out the yellow pad with the draft of the singles ad she had begun three months earlier. She had told herself that deciding on the qualities of a soul mate was not a trivial task, and it was important not to rush it. The problem was that she had so little to show for her efforts. She glanced down at the page, which despite a good deal of crossing out and adding on, now consisted of a mere nineteen words:

Single female, 34, seeks male soul mate. Must have a sense of humor, like children, books, conversation, and travel.

Three months of labor and the result was what any single woman, thirty-four, seeking a soul mate, could have come up with in three minutes. It was, quite frankly, pathetic.

But just as she was about to crumple the paper and throw it away in disgust, a revelation burst upon her. She looked again at what she had written, and saw what she should have seen all along: Bare bones as it was, this was not an ad for a generic man at all. It was an ad for Ben Cutler. He was lurking behind each prosaic word. She had only one soul mate, and she had lost him.

She didn't know how long she had been brooding over this sorry fact when the phone rang. Her pulse quickened as she recognized Ben's voice; her first thought was that some mystical force had intervened—that the ad had somehow been channeled to him and he was responding.

But all thoughts of her own situation fled as she caught the gravity in his voice. "You need to come over," he said simply. "It's your grandmother."

When she arrived at the house, he told her that Winnie had resisted going to the hospital and that the doctor, an old friend of the family, had been in to see her. He had said that it was another stroke, a final one, and it was best to let her be.

Anne went upstairs and sat down at the side of the bed. Her grandmother's eyes were closed; her face, calm. After the last stroke, there had been the predictable distortion of features that had gradually subsided. But now there was no distortion. Winnie's face was serene. She was wearing a white embroidered nightgown; her mass of gray hair, neatly spread behind her head on the pillow; her hands, with their long, patrician fingers, folded on her chest.

"Gram, it's me," said Anne, taking her grandmother's hand.

Winnie did not open her eyes, but smiled slightly.

"OK, you're smiling; that's good. You'll pull through this one, the way you did the others. So many people need you now. You have to get better."

Winnie moved her head very slightly from side to side.

"But they do," Anne insisted. "Pauline is just learning to cook. And Jonathan is just learning to talk. And Kirsten says you're the only oasis of sanity—I'm quoting directly here."

Anne saw her grandmother mouth a word. She leaned closer:

"Benjamin."

"He needs you too," she said simply. "And I do, Gram. I need you most."

Winnie moved her head slightly again.

"I do. You're all I have."

At this, Winnie smiled slightly again and squeezed her granddaughter's hand with surprising force. Then, she breathed a long sigh—a sigh that somehow sounded like an expression of great relief—and Anne knew she was gone.

CHAPTER FIFTY-FIVE

IT WAS NOT A LARGE FUNERAL, WINNIE HAVING outlived all of her contemporaries.

Elihu was there, of course—his natural complacency enhanced by having pocketed a fresh three million from the sale of the house. With this money, he could pay off his old debts and begin to acquire new ones. It was the one activity at which he excelled.

Beside her father stood Allegra, attired in a simple but perfectly fitting black dress and a small hat with a veil. She looked so much the part of the elegant mourner that she might have been in a photo shoot for a funeral, rather than the real thing.

Rachel and Peter were also present. Rachel, largely recovered from her Lyme disease, was leaning on Peter and sobbing continually through the ceremony. It seemed that neither Frost nor Wordsworth had succeeded in consoling her.

Anne stood with Marcy and Rich Fineman. Rich had never met Winnie, but seemed pleased to be present, as if enjoying the novelty of being outside the office in the role of Marcy's husband. Marcy also seemed pleased, and while she held Anne's hand throughout the service, she also occasionally touched Rich's arm, as if confirming the fact that he was there.

Harry and Carlotta had also come, though neither knew Winnie. Their sense of goodwill toward anyone within the circle that had brought them together inclined them to make an appearance. Carlotta spoke cheerfully to Elihu, who appeared to bear no grudge—perhaps he had forgotten that he had once been predisposed in that direction. Elihu's memory, especially when it came to errors in his own actions, was unusually porous.

Vince, Gus, Cindy, and Daphne were also present, a sign of their respect for Anne.

Daphne was wearing a black dashiki and appeared to be meditating during the ceremony. She later told Anne that she had communed with Winnie's newly liberated spirit.

Eleanor Greenbaum was there too, which might have been surprising if one were not familiar with her habits. Just as she had started researching the college application process when her children were still in grade school, she attended area funerals as a form of preliminary research for her own—though precisely what good this knowledge would do her was unclear.

Anne looked around with trepidation for the Hopgoods and discovered, thankfully, that they were not there. Ditto Curtis Fink. A frequenter of bar mitzvahs, which he saw as great networking opportunities ("The kid is thirteen, but you plant the seed so that three years later, bam, they're primed to hire you"), he was known to make appearances at funerals too, since the children of the deceased would now be possessed of greater disposable income with which to ensure the future prospects of their children ("And wouldn't Bubbie and Zadie have wanted that?"). But there were no prospects here for Fink and Fisk, and Curtis must have realized that he couldn't hit on Anne at a funeral.

Prominent among the mourners were Ben, Kirsten, Pauline, and Jonathan. Anne noted that Elihu behaved exceedingly well toward the Cutlers. Ben had apparently risen in his estimation through paying such a good price for the house—though in typical fashion, he had let on that Ben had gotten a bargain: "An old friend of the family. Didn't want to be so vulgar as haggle."

Elihu also responded with surprising politeness to Pauline, overlooking her Queens accent and even tolerating her hug. Normally, Elihu stiffened at any display of affection, fearful that his suit would be creased or his hair messed, but Pauline's profusion of gold jewelry and designer clothes apparently made her effusiveness more palatable. Allegra too was gracious. It had occurred to her that the Cutlers were wealthy enough to be a resource for *The Widening Gyre*, which could always use new infusions of capital (the business of poetry, if not the art, was expensive).

Anne was in a daze during the ceremony.

She wanted it to be over as quickly as possible, though she knew there would be the additional hours spent at the shiva that Ben had told her would be held at the house. How could she protest? It had been Winnie's home to the end, and the place most associated with her life. That it was no longer technically hers had ceased to seem meaningful.

The ceremony was short. The rabbi said a few prayers, Elihu pontificated on "this noble woman of inestimable taste," and then, to Anne's surprise, Ben stood up and cleared his throat. He spoke briefly and with formality, but there was an undercurrent of emotion that Anne felt resonating behind the simplicity of his words.

"My family has, until recently, been a kind of nomadic family. We didn't know what a settled home was. But Winnie gave us such a home, both literally, by selling us her house, and more profoundly, by teaching us how to live in it. She was a woman of substance: knowledgeable, opinionated, but not, in the end, dogmatic. She was capable of changing her mind—something that much younger people are not able to do. For many reasons"—he shot a glance at Anne—"the relationship we developed with her was extraordinary. We'll miss her, but she has imprinted herself on our lives forever."

CHAPTER FIFTY-SIX

AFTER THE FUNERAL, WHEN EVERYONE HAD RE-
turned to the house, there was the usual
muted festivity that accompanies a shiva.
Rachel had been temporarily lifted from her
misery and was conversing with Peter and
Ben about the Lake District, where she and
Peter would be going next month for a combined honeymoon and research expedition.
Eleanor Greenbaum was talking to Daphne
about the ten pairs of boxers she had
bought for Jeremy at Target, while Daphne
was nodding her head and appeared to be
communing with spirits from another world
(the best way to engage with Eleanor

Greenbaum). Vince, Gus, and Cindy were talking about whether the announcements over the PA system were too loud and whether they should buy rocking chairs for the main office waiting room, since parental blood pressure ran high there too. Elihu and Allegra were discussing the changes that had been made to the house, with Elihu noting that the Cutlers had used antique sconces in the hall.

"They didn't spare expense," he added with approval. Elihu had taken the tack that the house, though he no longer lived in it, was still somehow about him.

Harry and Rich were talking business, while Carlotta and Pauline were trading recipes. Carlotta had embraced the domestic role with a vengeance and appeared to be trying to master it with more diligence that she had brought to her previous occupations.

Anne was sitting with Marcy. "These ruggalah look delicious," said Marcy, who, though she didn't eat, had a keen visual sense of food quality.

"Winnie taught Pauline to make them," noted Anne. "It's nice to know that her recipes will live on. They certainly wouldn't through me."

"Other things about her live on through you," noted Marcy.

"That's true," said Anne. "But I'm going to miss her terribly."

"Of course you are. But I somehow feel confident that you'll find companionship." Marcy's eyes had been scanning the room and perhaps picked up information that Anne missed. She had noted, for example, that Kirsten was standing off to the side.

"I'm going to bring some of these ruggalah over to Rich," she announced now. "He's talked enough shop. I'm going to ask him to concentrate on me for a while." Marcy's marriage had allegedly been energized lately by an article in O. "It said that the problem with most women is that they nag and complain, but they don't ask," Marcy explained. "Instead of saying, 'I never see you,' you need to say, 'It makes me happy to see more of you.' It's amazing how framing things that way can help."

When Marcy had left to tell Rich that it would make her happy if he concentrated on her now, Kirsten sat down beside Anne. "I want to extend my deepest sympathy," she said quietly. "I liked your grandmother more than I can say. I loved her, in fact. She was an enormous help to me."

"Really?" said Anne, wondering how Winnie had helped Kirsten.

"I'm going back to Denmark, you know."

Anne felt suddenly light-headed.

"I know what you're thinking. It's not because of you. Or at least not just because of you. I always sensed there was someone else, and when I met you, I knew right away that it was you. That outburst at Peter's poetry reading confirmed it. But I've been homesick ever since I got here. Ben and I had a fling—I think that's the right word for it—but it was never quite real."

Anne felt a wave of joy pass over her. "Does Ben know?" she asked, her voice almost a whisper.

"We haven't discussed it directly, but he knows, I think. We've both dragged things out over the past few months—he didn't want to hurt me and I wasn't ready to leave. But now I am. I wouldn't ever want to have children in this country, and he could never settle in Denmark. And now that you've appeared on the scene, I know that, in his heart, he thinks about that."

"You do?" said Anne, feeling dizzy.

"I do. It's the way he looks at you." Kirsten and Anne glanced across the room where Ben was speaking, his face at an angle, so that it seemed to be intentionally averted from them. "And the way he doesn't look at you," she added. "And I see the way you don't look at him. It's fortunate that I'm not a jealous person. Your grandmother and I were alike that way. We take the world as it is, and we draw conclusions."

"I'm glad she had you as a friend at the end," said Anne softly.

"I am too," said Kirsten, patting Anne's hand. "And now that I've said what I had to say—what Winnie would have wanted me to say—I'm free to go. Have a good life—and if you're ever in Copenhagen, look me up. It's a wonderful city and the food, whatever Pauline may say against it, is very good."

CHAPTER FIFTY-SEVEN

A FEW DAYS AFTER THE FUNERAL, ANNE ARranged to drop by the Scarsdale house to go through the last of Winnie's things. Most everything of value had been sold long ago, but there were clothes and minor articles that would have to be disposed of, and items of no real worth but much sentimental value, that she would want to keep.

When she knocked, Ben opened the door. "You'll want to go through her things alone," he said quickly. "Let me know before you leave." He disappeared before she had a chance to respond, and she went into Winnie's room by herself. Everything had been left in the most meticulous order. Her grand-mother's few dresses hung neatly in the closet alongside the crisply ironed blouses. The underwear was carefully folded in the drawers—even at eighty-seven, Winnie had insisted on a little satin and lace. There were a few Hermès scarves and one nice Coach handbag. The jewelry was mostly good cos-tume jewelry: bakelite earrings and Venetian glass beads. There were a few gold pins, one with Winnie's initials that Anne knew she would wear discreetly at the top of a blouse or the side of a sweater, and there were two gold and diamond bracelets, the only two left from the ten or so that her grandfather had given Winnie over the years in a touching lack of imagination.

At the bottom of the jewelry box, there was an envelope marked *Anne*. Anne picked it up gingerly, opened it, and felt her throat tighten at seeing the familiar handwriting—bold and vigorous until the end. The letter was dated three weeks before her grand-mother's final stroke.

She sat down at the little vanity, where Winnie had always done her hair and put on her makeup, and read the letter slowly:

Dearest Anne,

If you are reading this, I have finally made it to the other side. It's been long enough, you know, so no need to cry about it. You know that I am not inclined to fairy-tale thinking, but I will indulge myself in the possibility that I am now romping hand and hand with your grandfather and your mother. It's hogwash, but it's a pleasant fantasy, and at my age (and given that by now, I'm dead), I should be allowed to indulge it. Meanwhile, I am pleased to say that everything promises to work out well in the realm of the living. Perhaps Kirsten has already told you her intentions. Trust me, my dear, I did not interfere; I merely listened and supported, and in my unassuming fashion, pointed the way. She is an excellent woman, but she is not in love with Benjamin and he is not in love with her. Which simplified matters enormously. Had things been otherwise, who knows what I might have had to resort to?—something lurid in the style of General Hospital, I assume. But it all worked out nicely, without my interference. You therefore can rectify the error that I encouraged you to make so many years ago.

You have been given what is so rarely given to people: a second chance. Make the most of it and have a wonderful life. I regret not being there to see it—but then, I have seen enough. I love you, my darling, and will for eternity.

Winnie

P.S. Please be sure Kirsten gets one of the bracelets. You see your grandfather bought the right number after all. If she has already left for Copenhagen, send it to the address on the card. Jonathan must have the library. And Pauline should have all my recipes—they are in the little brass box under my desk. As for Benjamin, give him your grandfather's wedding ring. It's in the bottom compartment of my jewelry box. I sold my diamond years ago, which is just as well. He should buy you a much bigger one. In diamonds, remember, don't worry about being vulgar—there is never such a thing as too big.

I think that covers everything. I do wish I could know the end of General

Hospital—but I don't suppose it will ever end. That, at least, is a consolation. WM

Anne began to cry.

CHAPTER FIFTY-EIGHT

WHEN SHE HAD WIPED HER TEARS, ANNE LEFT her grandmother's room and made her way to the library, where she found a young woman at the desk in front of a pile of books. The woman was clearly an employee and looked more competent than the girl she had caught Kirsten yelling at a few weeks earlier.

"May I help you?" the young woman asked, peering over her funky, black-rimmed glasses as Anne paused in the doorway.

"I'm a friend of the family who's been going through some things on the other side of the house. Mr. Cutler said I should find him before I leave."

"Oh, yes," said the girl, "he's upstairs. We're working on deadline for the new edition of the Venice guide."

"Oh?" said Anne, stepping forward and glancing at the book the girl had put down on the desk. It was Ruskin's *Modern Painters*. "You're reading Ruskin?"

"Not reading, exactly," said the girl with a sigh. "It's pretty unreadable. But Mr. Cutler asked me to find something that might work for literary background. He was very definite about it. But I have to say that I can't make head or tail of the sentences; they're so wordy and old-fashioned."

Anne picked up the book. She and Ben had read *Modern Painters* together. *Stones of Venice* had brought them together, Ben said; why not continue with Ruskin? And so they had—reading him at a slow pace, since they tended to be distracted along the way.

"I think I can find something that he might want to include," Anne murmured now as she thumbed through the book. "Why don't I go upstairs and discuss it with him?"

"Go ahead," said the girl, relieved to have the burden of Ruskin taken off her hands. "It's the first door on the left."

Anne climbed the stairs and slipped in the

door, which had been left ajar. The room had been her old bedroom and was one of the few rooms in the house that had not yet been renovated (there were still the marks of the masking tape where the John Travolta poster had been attached to the wall over her bed).

Ben was seated at the desk that had been hers—a small wooden desk of the Stickley variety, a bit low for someone of his size, so that he sat hunched forward. He had his back to her, facing the window, and he had a pile that looked like printed galleys in front of him. But he was not looking at the galleys. He was staring out the window.

He had not heard her enter, and she cleared her throat.

She saw him shudder slightly before turning around: "You surprised me," he said simply. "Are you all right?" He could see she had been crying.

She nodded.

"I thought you would be longer going through your grandmother's things."

"There wasn't much." She held up the shopping bag. "What's left can go to Goodwill. She did a pretty thorough job of sifting before she died."

He didn't say anything.

"I was speaking to your assistant in the library," said Anne, aware that he was looking at her intently. "She said you were working on a new edition of the Venice guide and that you wanted a passage from Ruskin."

He just looked at her.

She held up the book. "I think I may have found something." Without pausing, she read aloud: "'There is set in the deeper places of the heart such affection for the signs of age that the eye is delighted even by injuries which are the work of time; not but there is also real and absolute beauty in the forms and colors so obtained.'"

"Let's see," he said quietly, when she stopped reading.

She brought the book to him and leaned over the desk as he examined it. She could feel his breath on her neck, and it seemed as though no time at all had passed since they had pored over books like this, their heads close together, paying attention to the material they were reading, until, unable to restrain themselves, they put the books aside and veered off in another direction.

They had the book in front of them, and a strand of Anne's hair, normally pinned back,

had fallen from the coil at the nape of her neck. It fell like a curtain so that, bent forward, she could not see his face. They were poised like this for what seemed a very long time. Then, she felt his hand touch the strand of hair, and then reach back and remove one pin and then another, until all her hair had fallen loose around her shoulders, the way she used to wear it. She did not move as he separated the thick strands and bent forward and kissed her neck. Then gently, he took her chin in his hand and turned her face toward him. She realized that she had been holding her breath. "I've been waiting for you," he murmured.

She looked at him. "I've been waiting too," she said simply.

"I didn't know." His voice was hoarse with emotion. "I thought you were just embarrassed to see me again."

"I wasn't embarrassed—I was full of regret. It was painful to see you with Kirsten."

"It was? Why didn't you say something?"

"I tried. I called after Thanksgiving. But Pauline told me you and Kirsten had gone off to a romantic bed-and-breakfast together."

Ben gave a sardonic laugh. "We were checking out a site for the New England guide. And it was anything but romantic: Kirsten said the scenery was much nicer in Denmark, and I said that maybe she should go back to Denmark. We'd been sniping that way for months. Pauline, innocent soul that she is, never noticed."

"Winnie did," mused Anne.

"I'm not surprised. Kirsten said she was the most perceptive person she'd met in this godawful country. They were alike, you know. Both wonderful women. But not really my type."

"What is your type?"

"I don't have a type. It was just you."

Anne nodded. "I don't have a type either. I tried to describe my soul mate—I was actually going to run a singles ad—but it was all about you."

Ben looked at her. It was the look she remembered—and had never expected to see again. "I'd like to read that ad someday." he murmured. "But now, I only want—" He stopped, then very slowly but very deliberately, he brought her face to his.

They had been given a second chance. The injuries of time had laid bare the beauty of their affection, and they had now arrived at that moment when they could appreciate it—not just the beauty that remained after the passage of time but, in Ruskin's words, "the real and absolute beauty so obtained."

CHAPTER FIFTY-NINE

GRADUATION AT FENIMORE WAS ALWAYS A JOY-
ous occasion—it was the great cathartic
event that capped a stress-laden and
chaotic year. By the time of graduation,
everything, for good or ill, had been resolved. The last homework assignments
were long since due, the final exams were
thankfully over, and teachers had given up
and passed those students who had resisted doing any work in the last months. Only
Fenster remained steadfast in his meanness
and threatened to fail Jodi Fields until Vince,
adept at bribery, had promised him an extra,

under-the-table personal day if he'd raise her 59 to a 60 for senior English.

The final college admissions information had come in by late April. Jonathan had been admitted to Columbia after all but had chosen to go to St. John's instead. Ben found that he was even more proud to have his nephew turn down the school he had thought so highly of, and out of a sense of magnanimity had gone ahead and underwritten Cutler's Cultural Center at Columbia, a summer program for students interested in travel writing. Anne warned that with such a program in place, it was only a matter of time before it became a full-fledged academic program and parents started making their kids do unpaid internships in travel agencies in order to get in.

Jodi Fields was going to the College of New Jersey (which had been sympathetic to her ADD), and Sandra Newman had gotten into Georgetown (which had broken with precedent and admitted two from Fenimore after all—though admittedly only after Sandra's father had had several meetings with the head of Alumni Giving). A few students, with their hearts set on NYU's Tisch School of the Arts, had had to settle for

SUNY Purchase, and some of the lesser jocks, despite the personalized, individualized letters from Blitz Athletic Recruiting, had not gotten the full scholarships to the colleges no one heard of and been obliged to settle for SUNY Binghamton. In short, some students had been gratified, some had been disappointed, but in the end, all had finally come to terms with the way things were going to be. The greatest source of stress for parents and children had been uncertainty; once this was removed, everyone relaxed. Graduation was about acceptance—replacing competition with a rite of passage. Every kid was moving on, away from high school into the larger world, where other, more pressing issues would crowd out the much smaller one of where one went to college.

Now, as parents faced the prospect of separating from the progeny whom they had been nagging and yelling at for years, there was the predictable profusion of feeling. Gifts of Mercedes and Caribbean vacations were not unusual among this affluent population. "After all," Mrs. Fields said of Jodi's Mazda convertible, "she earned it." Anne could hardly see how any of these kids had actually earned such gifts. Then again, Anne thought, graduation gifts were not really about the accomplishment of graduating. They were tokens of feeling from parents to their kids, frail baubles used to convey the ineffable sense of love and loss.

Vince opened the ceremony with a few characteristic remarks. "This is a great day, folks," he barked exultantly (when Vince spoke to large groups, one often felt he would have liked a megaphone). "We slid into home plate. We scored a touchdown. Let's show our support for this gold medal team and send these gladiators into the arena of their college years with a big round of applause."

No one seemed to mind this profligate mixing of metaphors. For Vince, the more athletic allusions he could cram into his re-marks, the more festive the occasion. Much appreciated was his gift for keeping things short. He knew that everyone was hot under those caps and gowns and wanted to get on to the graduation parties as quickly as possi-ble (he had an acute memory of how he had felt when he was graduating from high school).

Following Vince came the valedictory address. The selection of valedictorian and salutatorian had been uncontroversial this year. This was in contrast to several years back when there had been a vicious battle over the salutatory spot. The thing had come down to a fraction of a point based on an AP English grade—Fenster, who had taught the course that year, had strung both candidates along with vicious glee, finally awarding the higher grade to the kid he disliked least.

This year, however, Ilene Gupta and Aaron Finkelstein had been unchallenged in their respective slots. Ilene, the school's Olympian hard worker, had been so far ahead that even Aaron, winner of the prestigious Westinghouse science prize with a space reserved for him in a Columbia's genetics lab when he finished Harvard, was a full one-twentieth of a point behind. In the old days, this sort of gap might have been considered negligible, but in the present climate, it was huge.

Ilene, despite her stellar record, was notoriously shy. She slunk to the podium and mumbled her speech rapidly so that no one could catch a word. Not that anyone minded. They were glad to have the ordeal pass so quickly and painlessly, and applauded with enthusiasm as Ilene slouched gratefully from the podium. She was followed by the president of the senior class, a popular jock, who shouted out a few disconnected phrases: "best class ever," "remember the prom," "Jodi Fields is bodacious," and "good luck at F&M, Toby Tucker"—phrases that were received with roars of approval from the student body.

After this died down, Vince stepped forward to read out the names of the graduating seniors. It was his favorite moment in the school year: shaking the kids' hands and presenting the oversized envelopes containing the diplomas, the tangible evidence that he had done his job and shepherded this group to a place where they were no longer his responsibility.

Now, with the ceremony almost over, the president of the senior class stepped forward again. It was time to make the yearbook presentation, the closing event of the graduation program. It had been decided some years ago that the The Fenimore Fanfare would be distributed following graduation instead of a week prior, as had previously been done. The change had been precipitated when Anne had discovered Ms. Gonzales-Stein, a young and well-endowed member of the language department, in tears in the faculty ladies room. It seemed that the boys in her fifth-period remedial Spanish II class had been trading anatomical drawings of her in one another's yearbooks. Ms. Gonzales-Stein had somehow gotten wind of the portrayal (perhaps had even glimpsed it, when signing one of the yearbooks with her trademark "Felicidad" and smiley face). The portrayal had included a representation, creatively enhanced, of her ample bosom and even more ample posterior, about which Gonzales-Stein was particularly sensitive. After this incident, Anne had convinced Vince that distributing the yearbooks after the graduation ceremony would curtail the period in which they would circulate, thereby cutting down on the likelihood of such distressing incidents. It would also add another festive note to the graduation ceremony.

It had now become conventional for the president of the senior class to present the first copy of the yearbook to the principal, who accepted it, with great pomp and ceremony, as a symbol that the class had navigated the arduous journey from one end of high school to the other. The presentation ceremony also included the announcement of the yearbook dedication, the paramount honor that the students could bestow on a faculty or staff member.

"As members of the senior class we want to present this first copy of our yearbook to our principal as a token of our respect for our school, its teachers, and its staff," said the president of the class, taking a sententious tone (the ability to oscillate between obstreperous conviviality and sententiousness was one of the prerequisites for being elected class president). "This year, our class has dedicated *The Fanfare* to a very special person: Fenimore's head of guidance, Anne Ehrlich. As everyone knows, Ms. Ehrlich is awesome at guidance! She's been there for us during this whole college thing—good luck at F&M, Toby Tucker!" The obstreperous side of the president erupted but was quickly reigned in. "We could trust Ms. Ehrlich to tell us the truth, even when we didn't want to hear it. She always had our best interests in mind, and she wasn't afraid of our parents. Let's face it, we wouldn't have made it this far without her. Way to go, Toby Tucker! Jodi Fields is bodacious!"

The ceremony would have normally ended here, but Vince stepped forward to speak again. This was unusual, since he tended to avoid public speaking wherever possible. Now, however, he cleared his throat and declared his intention of "saying a few words about this special lady here.

"I know that people expect you to say certain things on occasions like this, so no one really thinks it means much. But in this case, it does. I don't know if I could do my job as principal without the help of Anne Ehrlich. Her competence, judgment, and kindness have been invaluable to me. I cherish her as a colleague and I love her as a friend. Thank you, Anne, for being there for Fenimore, our Blue Ribbon School."

It was an uncharacteristically eloquent speech. Anne felt her eyes well up with tears. She stepped forward as Vince and the class president kissed her on the cheek (to hoots and catcalls). Then everyone exploded in celebration: Hats were thrown in the air, balloons were popped, a few of the more imaginative jocks showed they were naked under their gowns, and several of the more sensitive girls burst into tears as they contemplated the end of their high-school years—despite having spent a good portion of that time in the nurse's office suffering from stress-related illnesses and romantic complaints.

Graduation marked the symbolic end of childhood as these kids moved out from under the wing of parents and teachers. Now they would at least have to pretend that they were embarking on responsible adulthood. Not that many saw things in such momentous terms. They would grow up slowly, at their own rate, making their own mistakes and gaining ground in their own time. The real rite of passage, Anne thought, was for their parents. They were the ones who really deserved the graduation gifts. Like artists who had worked on a canvas over a long period of time, they now had to release their work into the world, not knowing if it was important or original, or even, God knows, finished. The hysteria over college was an expression of the anxiety of child-rearing, an imperfect art if there ever was one. Now they would have to stop their continual meddling and nagging, and let go.

Anne looked around her and was struck, as she often was when she looked at the kids in the school, by how beautiful they were. Their beauty was dazzlingly present in their strong bodies and open faces. It was the wondrous adjunct of their youth. Being young made them capable of shrugging off the sorrows and disappointments that would later stall and weary them. It was important to trust them, she thought, to believe that they could, despite their ignorance and inexperience, ultimately turn out OK.

The graduates and their parents were moving on, but for Anne and the other teachers at the school, graduation was only a temporary pause in a recurring cycle. In the fall, a new crop of freshmen would flood the halls of Fenimore, their parents hovering in the wings, preparing for the siege to come. The cycle would begin again. But for now, Anne had the summer stretching out in front of her.

"So I hear you and Ben are going to the Lake Country for your honeymoon," said Marcy as they surveyed the spread that Home and School had laid out in the cafeteria after the graduation ceremony.

"Yes, it's the one place where he never felt

444

he spent enough time. Rachel and Peter are there, working on the update for the *Sojourns with the Romantic Poets*, so we'll probably see them. But there's no work involved for us. It's pure pleasure," said Anne, coloring slightly. It seemed to her that the passion she had felt for Ben long ago was as strong now as it had once been. It said something for having lost the love of your life at twenty-one; if you had the good luck to get him back thirteen years later, you could feel twenty-one again.

"I admit that Ben did turn out to be as good as you thought he was," said Marcy. "You two are a perfect match. It just took a little time for you to see it."

"I knew it all along."

"Only you let your grandmother talk you out of it."

"That's true. Winnie had great influence on me. But it wasn't her fault. She did what she thought was best at the time, and I shared some of her prejudices and was afraid to act on my own. But you know, I don't regret the past. I like to think that it's best that things worked out as they did."

"I suppose," ruminated Marcy. "If you'd married him earlier, he might never have gotten rich and your grandmother might never have gotten to like his family so much. And you wouldn't be able to keep the house and have that great wedding in the backyard. By the way, what are you going to do with the Murray Hill apartment?"

"We decided to hold on to it. We thought that we might want to spend some evenings in the city, and it's nice to have a place to escape to."

"A house in Westchester and a pied-à-terre in the city." Marcy nodded. "Very impressive. *New York* magazine says a pied-à-terre is the new status accessory."

"Maybe it will replace the Harvard decal."

"I don't know," mused Marcy, "although Yale would be good too."

Anne looked at her friend. It suddenly struck her that Marcy was actually eating her turkey sandwich—and drinking a glass of milk.

"Marcy!" she said. "Marcy—you're not—?"

"Yes," said Marcy sheepishly. "I'm pregnant. And Rich is ecstatic. He says it's what he's always wanted but was afraid to tell me. One day he just said: 'You know, I'd really like you to have my children.' When he put it that way, how could I refuse?"

"You couldn't," Anne agreed.

"So, as you can imagine, I've been busy," said Marcy, breathlessly. "I'm taking the enhanced mothering seminar at the Y and the prenatal exercise program at the Health and Racquet Club—*Parenting* magazine says it can improve your child's chances of becoming an Olympic athlete or at least making the travel soccer team by twenty percent. I'm sitting in on the 'tips for preparing for preschool' at the library—I know it's early, but I want to be ready for the hard questions. And of course, I'm playing Vivaldi and doing French immersion for the baby in utero."

"Of course," said Anne, amused that it had already begun. Perhaps, soon, she would be joining the ranks of nuttiness herself.

But for now, she would revel in being in love and childless—which is to say, carefree and sane.